Country Secrets

Country Secrets

The Mackenney Family Saga Book One

by Caz May

First Published 2020
ISBN 978-0-6484998-9-3

Published by Caz May

To my amazing, beautiful and supportive Nanna.
I'll always have fond memories of the farm and the days
spent there.

Table of Contents

Also by Caz May

Always Only You Series

Bk 1-Roommates Don't Kiss & Tell

Bk 2-Friends Don't Say Goodbye

Bk 3-Feelings Don't Play Fair

A Holiday Romance Duet

Bk 1-Take Flight

Please be aware this story contains some content including domestic abuse and rape which may be triggering for some readers.

(1) Savannah

The highway had seemed endless, driving away to who knows where with no clear direction in my head.

I just needed to get away, make my escape.

Glancing around my surroundings, it's clear that I'm a long way from 'home' now, if you could even call what I was escaping from 'home.'
For three tumultuous years, he'd made my life a living hell, constantly beating me to the point of bruises. Even now I'm sporting a black eye, bruises and scratches all over my body.
Feelings of utter worthlessness plague me still and nothing had been harder than walking out the door, knowing that this time no matter what, I'm not going back.

It wasn't just the abuse that caused the pain, but my own stupid body, rejecting the one thing I want so desperately. The words always in my mind, doctors saying it like it's a disease, 'Unexplained Infertility'.
Like what does that even mean?
It's a disease with no cure, the pain I had to endure, over and over again, rejection of the worse kind.
Until Dante showed up in my life, rejection was something that I'd felt many times over and the prospect of 'Unexplained Infertility' was rejection by my own body, as well as it feeling like a curse, some unexplained mystery that medicine couldn't solve.
Doctors love to think they always have the answers, but in my case no, even when I was waving a positive pregnancy test in their faces, my period late, they waved me off, not believing the proof right in front of

their eyes. But despite all that here I am three months later, no bumps in sight, except for the road ahead.

My mind is still a blur from my last doctors' appointment, having finally reached the point of doing IUI. Part of me wanted it to have worked, so at least walking away I had something or someone to show for the hell of the last three years, but if I'm being honest with myself, I don't want his baby growing inside of me.

Shaking my head I have to focus on blocking out the memories, the bad experiences as the only way forward now is to rid my mind of him and continue my escape.

I'm not feeling confident, not sure if I'm ever going to make it somewhere that I can put the past behind me, but I've taken the first step in running and I have to try.

Putting the past behind me isn't going to be easy though, even in my crazed *'get the fuck out of there'* state I know that.

I only have a hundred dollars, which won't even last a week. It isn't even enough for a tank of petrol.

Fuck petrol?

I'd not even thought to check the tank when I skipped out. The gauge for the petrol tank is dangerously low now, teetering on empty and I'm in the middle of fucking nowhere with a phone that has practically ceased to function, not even one signal bar, nothing, absolutely nothing.

I'm officially 'Up shit creek without a paddle'.

~~

Sleeping in the back seat of a car, wasn't comfortable at the best of times. Since leaving I'd spent my nights in the back of the car and it had caused my neck to crick.

Being in the middle of nowhere, with practically no petrol and no working phone is making me apprehensive. Even locking the doors of the car hasn't helped curb my feelings.

For all I know an axe murderer is on the loose and is going to take me to my doom. Dread fills me and my panic is rising.

I've barely slept a wink when I wake up in the most excruciating pain of my life. Never in my twenty-five years of life have I experienced such pain.

Clutching my stomach, fearing the worst I know in my gut, in that moment, that the IUI had worked.

My brain had been fuzzy since making my escape and I hadn't even thought to bring sanitary items, nor thought about my period coming at all. It isn't that I was even thinking about the IUI having worked either, it was more a rush of craziness, a I just need to leave and I'll just throw some clothes in a suitcase before he wakes up kinda scenario.

The pain is overwhelming, it's certainly doesn't feel like my period coming at all. The cramps are intense, all across my abdomen and down into my pelvis, stabbing pain like knives repeatedly being pushed into my flesh.

The urge to vomit is rising in my throat.

Frantically clawing at the door locks to open them, the cool night air comes as a welcome relief.

I wretch, cough and sputter, leaving projectile vomit spatter down the side of my car. It really couldn't get any worse, except I have a desperate urge to pee that makes me shoot out the car like a rocket.

Scanning the surroundings, for somewhere to relieve myself, I seek out a small bush and duck behind it, dropping my track pants to my ankles. Squatting to pee, even in the dark I can see my knickers are soaked with blood. Blood is dripping down my thighs.

This is so not good.

Yanking my track pants back up I stumble back to the car.

Fuck this pain is...

Instinctively I grab my stomach as more pain grips me when I reach the car. Unlocking the boot I rummage through my minimal luggage, only to find white underwear and another pair of track pants. Without thinking about where I am I slip off the blood-soaked ones, shoving them into the boot, after using them to wipe away the blood already on my body.

I hope that putting on two pairs of white knickers and the black track-pants should help curb the bleeding for the moment, enough at least for me to try to get some rest.

Sliding back into the car, I sprawl out across the backseat, and allow my eyes to close, trying to breathe through the pain. A glance at my watch tells me its three am.

Daylight would soon arrive around five am, so I can only hope some rest would come before.

(2) Hunter

Grabbing my tatty brown Akubra from the hallway stand always makes me feel like I'm ready to get out there amongst the paddocks of the farm. The incessant crazy barking starts the minute the front door closes behind me.

Ruffling the furry head of the cattle dog at my feet makes the barking increase, "Sounds like you're ready to go, Blitz, hey?" I question my cattle dog, who is eager to head out droving, a lot more than I am on this dismal looking night.

Droving is a part of running the farm, but a love, hate part of it. Moving my cattle around is important but the drought hasn't made life easy, as my paddocks are bone dry and my feed supply is dangerously low.

Blitz would stay out droving all day and night, always in his element running amongst the cattle. But sometimes I'd rather not have to do it, not having to brave the elements just to move my cattle from outlying paddocks to other paddocks for feeding purposes.

The clouds seem threatening as I venture down the verandah towards the ute as if they are going to let down their fury at any moment.

I feel like diving under the covers of my bed, instead of heading out to curl up in my swag when I hear the booming thunderclap around the farm. It's like a deafening shock to the ears.

Blitz cowers, the sound of thunder making him no longer the tough dog on the farm.

He becomes a big sooky when a storm is looming.

His ears prick up though hearing the creak of the passenger door of my old beaten down ute. He knows that means he's riding shotgun inside the comfort of the ute, stretched across the passenger seat.

Throwing my swag in the back tray is no easy feat. It weighs all of about ten kilos, which shouldn't be a struggle, but the fact that it is makes me admit to myself that I'm maybe not in the best shape.

Maybe it's time to get out the weights again.

Jumping in the driver's side I reach over to shut the passenger door, giving Blitz a pat on the head. He nuzzles my hand, barking again when the engine of the ute roars to life, the key in the ignition finally turning over.

The storm approaching still has me a little tentative about leaving tonight, but I have no time to waste, needing to get the cattle moved quickly.

The main road is the best to head down to the back paddock, quicker than bounding through the middle paddocks and in the storm if there is a possibility of rain it's also the safest option if I don't want to get bogged.

Lurching out the front gate, I begin to drive into the darkness, trying to focus on the road and block out the looming thunder.

Turning the radio on, cranking the volume to sing along to my favourite song 'Body like a back road' is a good distraction.

Not even half an hour down the road, close to the far paddock turn off is when I first see the car.

It still has its headlights on, but no interior lights are on and there appears to be no driver or anyone inside the car at all, that I can see.
Not having time to stop, I drive on, but my interest is piqued.
No one ever drives this far out of town without a reason.

Thankfully the storm has subsided by the time I reach the top paddock and no significant rain has battered down.
Stopping the ute in a clear part of the paddock, I grab my swag out of the back, unrolling it next to the tailgate.
Blitz has jumped out of the ute and run off to relieve himself before he settles down with me for the night.
Nothing beats lying in the swag staring up at the stars. Droving could be lonely at times, even with Blitz by my side.
Out in the paddocks though on a clear night loneliness felt worlds away, despite no other humans being around.
My mind drifts towards my parents, sensing my Dad looking down on me. Missing him really broke me sometimes, especially when droving. He'd always been by my side, teaching me the ropes. Dad falling ill had taken its toll on Mum. She really wasn't suited to the farm life to begin with, but loved Dad more than life itself.
Now she was a shell of a woman, holed up in the rest home in town, her MS making things even harder.
Blitz has returned, manoeuvring himself and shifting next to me, turning his body around and digging a space to make it more comfy.
"Settle Blitz," I say soothingly, as he lies back next to me.
Stroking his fur, his eyes look up at me searchingly and I mutter into the darkness, "I know buddy. I should go visit her."
He always has a way of knowing what I'm thinking or feeling, sensing whether I'm happy or sad. Tonight I feel uneasy, and closing my eyes to slip into sleep my mind wanders to the car on the side of the road.

Caz May

Something is eating at me about it. I should have stopped to see if there was anyone inside.

Guilt is a feeling that I hate experiencing. It eats away at you, multiplying itself over and over. I really don't need anymore guilt in my life.

Part of the reason I'd stuck around to run the farm was the guilt I felt when Dad got ill, knowing I was the oldest and my younger brother Quentin was never going to cut it living on the land.

He'd always preferred to spend his time inside, whereas I'd have spent every waking minute outside, in my element.

Maybe that is why I don't mind the droving so much, being outside on the farm, taking care of the cattle is where I belong. On the farm is where I belong.

Yeah, I do get lonely, and can't escape the country town gossip of all the old biddies wondering when I'm going to settle down but little did they know that I'm more than ready for that life. Instead I'm still heartbroken that who'd I wanted to make a life with couldn't handle it.

She'd wanted me to give up the farm, sell it and make a life in town. She never wanted to even try to be with me on the farm, as though my life meant nothing to her. And nothing, not even losing Dad, had broken my heart more than her vindictiveness towards the life I wanted to live.

I truly thought she'd loved me, as much as I loved her.

I shake my head trying to get rid of the image of her in my mind. Maybe I should have known that someone as breathtakingly beautiful as her wasn't meant for me and maybe I should have thought about the past that maybe meant she wasn't for me either. But I didn't.

I'd still fallen in love with her and some nights I still think of her lying in bed with me, her long blonde hair cascading over her pillow, her body pressed against me. I miss that more than anything, having a woman I love lying in my arms.

Taking a deep sigh, I roll over in the swag, Blitz protesting with a growl.

"Sorry buddy. I'm a little restless tonight," I sooth him.

I let myself slip into sleep, trying to block out the thoughts of my ex and the guilt of not stopping to check out the car by the side of the road. Sleep is crucial as I need to move the cattle at the crack of dawn on the horizon.

But I have a feeling it's going to be one of those nights, when sleep doesn't come easy.

(3) Savannah

No sooner than what feels like a minute after I closed my eyes, the pain rushing through my body again is like a thousand knives stabbing me.

It's torturous.

The cramping is becoming more intense, especially curled up in the back seat of the car.

I need to get out and find help or I'm surely going to die out here alone in the middle of nowhere.

Dawn is beginning to peer over the horizon now, spreading a glow around and enough light is present now that I can see where I'm going.

Grabbing my phone, wallet and car keys I stumble down the road with the crotch of my pants weighing me down.

I don't even want to know the reason, knowing it's bad. Images flash in my mind of being found out here with blood soaked clothes, half eaten by dingos.

My surroundings have me confused, as it's a never ending sea of trees and paddocks.

I can't shake the feeling that I'm heading away from the town I'd driven through earlier, but I need help now and that town is at least thirty kilometres away.

I'll die alone, in the middle of nowhere if I try to get back there.

The morning sun is warm, hitting my face and giving me the strength to push on.

Walking numbs the pain a little, the stretching of my legs and my body not feeling so constricting, making it easier to keep going.

I know I must be heading east as the sun is rising in the direction I'm heading in. Stopping a moment I lean against a fence, sighing and wiping my face with my sleeve.

It has been unseasonably warm for autumn, and out here the morning sun feels warmer than when I was surrounded by city buildings.

Turning around to vomit from the pain, I see that beyond the fence is a farmhouse, a rundown possibly un-lived in farmhouse.

Seeing this farmhouse even though no one may live there seems like a light at the end of the tunnel.

Scanning the fence line for a way in seems futile in the low morning light, and I soon realise the only way to get there is to climb over the fence.

It's not high, but barb wire is poking out in all directions. Sighing and trying not to think about anything other than getting to that farmhouse I put one leg over the fence and then the other, catching my pant leg on a stray wire.

Pain like a knife slicing my flesh rips through my leg and I fall flat on my face into the red dirt.

It's gritty in my mouth, making me gag and spit.

I need to get to that farmhouse.

I can feel my leg is bleeding, can feel the gush of my blood filling my pant leg and I grab it to try to curb the blood.

Trying to stand up is excruciating and it seems the only way forward is to crawl.

Edging along the dirt like a snail causes the pain to rush through my body. I want to scream out help, but fear opening my mouth and getting another mouth full of dirt.

Caz May

Reaching the farmhouse seems like a mirage, as I hoist my body onto the verandah.

It stretches around the whole house and is weathered and tired looking, reminding me of what I must look like.

The whole house is definitely rundown, looking like it hasn't been painted or taken care of for years.

My heart is pounding in my chest and I'm cursing myself for thinking anyone lives in this shithole of a house.

Of course no one lives here, look at the place Savannah.

Crawling along the verandah is even more painful than the dirt and I'm leaving a trail of blood behind me. I should probably consider myself lucky that the sight of blood doesn't bother me or I'd be a goner for sure. The front door is in sight now and using it to support myself I stand up and beat my fists against the metal screen door, finding my voice screaming, "Hello, is anyone home?"

No answer comes.

Maybe no one lives here.

The door handle feels loose in my grip, so loose that the lock clicks to open when I depress the handle. The wooden main door behind the screen door slips open when I turn the handle as well.

Grabbing the walls for support I stumble into the house, calling out, "Help, please someone help."

But again no answer comes.

The inside of the house appears to be lived in. All I can see from the hallway is the dining table in the large kitchen and the dirty coffee cups and plates that are piled in the sink; just looking at them makes me cringe.

A rush of pain overcomes me, causing me to clutch my stomach.

I need to lie down.

I stumble down the narrow hallway, peering into the rooms as I pass them, a study, a bathroom and a large bedroom, followed by a smaller one with a single unmade bed in the middle.

A bed has never looked so inviting.

Falling into it, I claw at the unmade sheets pulling them to my body in comfort.

My eyes are closing, my thoughts wandering back to noticing men's clothing hanging in the open wardrobe in the other room.

Hmmm, a man's house.

A thought of panic comes to mind, but my eyes are closing and i'm thankful to slip away for a while.

(4) Hunter

The sun is just making an appearance when I force myself to rise from the comfort of my swag.

Blitz licks my face with his usual sloppy doggy smooch.

I've become used to his morning greeting, although it's different in the swag as I'm at his level and he doesn't have to stand with his paws on my bed to reach me.

"Ok buddy, I'm getting up," I muse softly, stretching my arms above my head in a further effort to wake my body up.

He gives me an excited bark, watching and cocking his head towards me as I pull on my boots.

It's a warm morning and I debate whether or not to even wear a shirt, but think it's best as the morning sun can be fiercely hot.

Pulling the dark blue t-shirt on over my head I sigh a moment, stretching my legs out, cursing myself for wearing jeans to sleep in.

Blitz starts barking eagerly, ready to start the day and get into droving.

Ruffling his furry head quietens him, "You're eager today Blitz. Something up?" I ask him, even though I know he can't answer with anything but a bark.

My mind is definitely elsewhere today, wandering to thoughts of the car by the road as I roll up my swag before throwing it in the back of the ute. Blitz follows behind, jumping enthusiastically in the tray.

"You ready buddy? Let's get this over with."

I'm really not in the mood to move any cattle today, as I have a feeling they are going to be stubborn about moving to the middle paddocks but I need to get them out of the top paddocks to regenerate their feed source.

My savings aren't enough to be buying in feed.

Sliding into the drivers seat, I turn the reluctant ignition over and the engine sputters to life.

Nothing is more comforting that the rumble of the Utes engine. Knowing the ute is running is a special kind of freedom.

I crank the window open and it squeaks down reluctantly. I can't help but think about getting out the WD-40 to fix the squeak, wishing there was some miraculous cure to fix broken hearts too.

Crunching the ute into gear I drive off into the paddock. It isn't long before the cattle come into view and Blitz begins to bark at them.

It's always such a marvel listening to him and watching the cattle follow suit, seeing the unspoken connection between animals, even though they're different species.

Hand out the window, slowly edging the ute forward, I speak calm orders to Blitz to direct the cattle to the gate between the paddocks.

He jumps from the ute tray and shoots between the cattle when I pull up to the gate.

It too screeches as I open it.

I really do need to get out the WD-40.

Blitz is keeping the cattle still, so I can drive the ute through the open gate.

He's like a lighting bolt, jumping straight back into the tray as soon as I pass through the gate.

He barks towards the cattle and then follows my lead through the gate. Once the last cow has passed through the gate, I jump out and run to close it.

Back at the ute I ruffle Blitz's fur, "Jump in the front buddy. It's getting hot out already."

He barks in response, jumping through the drivers door and settling on the passenger seat for the bumpy drive back to the house.

Glancing at the clock on the dash tells me it's seven am. The sun is up and it's certain to be a warm day.

Blitz sits up, looking around panting as we drive through the paddocks. I'm more than relieved to see the farmhouse come into view.

I really should paint it though, it's certainly looking rundown.

Pulling up to house, I cut the engine and step out. Blitz follows, sniffing the ground and pawing at the dirt.

Puzzled by his odd behaviour I follow him, gazing at the dirt and finding a trail of blood that leads up onto the house verandah.

Blitz has reached the front door, barking crazily to be let in. He knows he isn't normally allowed inside the house except at night to sleep, so I'm a little fearful as to why he is desperate to get inside.

Depressing the handle slowly I open the screen door. The main wooden door isn't closed which is not how I left it the day before.

Ready to strike any potential intruder I grab my golf umbrella from the hallway stand and follow Blitz and the trail of blood down the hallway.

It stops at the spare bedroom, on the bed, collected around a figure on the bed.

I drop the umbrella in shock. On the bed is a woman, lying on the now blood soaked sheets.

Blitz is by her side, immediately sniffing her and letting out a whimper.

"It's ok buddy. I think she's alive." I kneel next to the bed and shake her slightly. "Miss, are you ok?"

She doesn't respond, her body seeming lifeless, but I can see the rise and fall of her chest and can feel her breath on my cheek.

Evidently she's unconscious, but thankfully still breathing.

Extracting my mobile from my pocket, I hesitantly dial '000', asking for an Ambulance.

It clicks through immediately.

"Ambulance, this is Kat."

"Kat, it's Hunter."

"Hunter, whats wrong? Are you hurt?"

"No, no, not me. I...just..returned." I pause, my heart thumping in my chest. The thought crosses my mind that she's from the car on the side of the road.

"Take your time," Kat reassures me.

"From droving...and there's an unconscious woman on my spare bed in a pool of blood."

"Is she breathing, Hunt?"

"Yeah she's breathing."

"Great, any evidence of trauma?"

"Her leg has a nasty cut but I don't think all the blood is from there."

"Ok, Hunt. We'll dispatch the guys now."

"Thanks Kat. Whats their ETA?"

"Prolly thirty minutes I'd say. Just talk to her. Let her know you're there."

"Ok Kat. Thanks. I'll catch you at the pub on Saturday yeah?"

"Yeah no worries. Just doing my job."

Blitz is still by the mystery woman's side, whimpering and nudging her chin.

It melts my heart at how caring he's being. He never seemed to like Addison, she was always slapping him away in disdain and seemed scared of him, if that was even possible.

Stupid bitch that she was, beautiful but nasty.

"It's ok buddy. The ambulance is coming." His head turns to me, his ears pricked up, as though he's asking what I mean.

"They'll help her Blitz."

Kneeling down beside the bed, next to Blitz I stroke a hand up her arm, feeling a rush of emotion course through me.

Oddly I feel a pang of attraction for her, wanting to kiss her but curse myself for thinking such things about an unconscious woman.

I can't deny that she's beautiful, her dark chestnut hair pulled tightly into a ballerina bun, highlighting her features.

My eyes are drawn to her lips and I brush my finger across them. I quickly draw it back, sure that she made a sound and flinched at my touch.

Her eyes are still firmly closed and I find myself wondering what colour they would be. I have no doubt that they'd be striking whatever colour, set off by her dark hair.

The wailing of the sirens is becoming closer to the farm. I race outside, to open the gates and usher them in. Blitz is still glued to her bedside, his whimpering not subsiding for a second.

Once the ambulance has stopped, they greet me with a firm handshake.

"Hey man," Mark greets me, "where's this mystery woman?"

"In the spare room," I respond, knowing that to Mark that probably sounded sexual. He often proved to have a dirty mind, joking about his sexual escapades at the pub.

It seemed an odd profession for him to work in at times, but he always kept his personal life seperate from his work life.

Entering the house, he calls back to me, "Trust you to only have an unconscious woman in one of your beds, Hunt."

I playfully punch him in the arm. He knew I'd not really been with anyone since Addison left and he'd been a good friend as well, trying to set me up with other woman on our nights out at the pub, but even though i'd gotten over Addison I hadn't found anyone I wanted to move on with. Despite his professional nature he's always down to earth.

"Fuck man. What'd you do to her?" he says looking at her still lifeless body on the bed.

He gently pushes Blitz aside, and begins checking her pulse and other vitals.

I feel extremely anxious, watching as they slip an oxygen mask over her mouth and nose.

"Hunt, relax man. You don't even know her," Mark says to me as my breathing becomes laboured in panic.

I feel like I do know her. At least I want to know her and that's a scary thought.

"Do you know anything that happened to her?" Mark asks.

"Nothing, I just found her like this when I got home from droving this morning," I state, trying to remain calm.

"Any idea how long she's been out?"

"No, I'm guessing that maybe that car down the road is hers, but look I don't know anything man."

I step out of the room, as the other ambulance officer wheels in the stretcher.

Bracing her neck and covering her badly cut leg they lift her onto the stretcher. Slowly they wheel her out of the house to the ambulance. Blitz has followed, jumping in the back of the ambulance.

"Blitz, come on buddy. You can't go with her."

His head droops.

"BLITZ!" I yell at him, knowing that raising my voice always causes him to correct his behaviour.

He jumps out and wags his tail when Mark pats him on the head.

"Good work Blitz, we'll take it from here," he coos to him, shutting the ambulance doors behind him, before jumping in the drivers seat and turning the sirens on.

Blitz and I watch as they tear through the gate. Walking over to shut the gate, the flood of emotion hits me again. Shutting the gate behind them I notice the piece of fabric hanging from a loose wire and the wire is stained with blood.

That must have been how she cut her leg.

I feel even more guilty now, than I had about not going back to the car.

I should have helped her.

(5) Savannah

My eyes flutter open, scanning the surroundings. Panic rises in my throat, my chest when I realise I'm in a hospital bed. An IV is connected to my left arm, red liquid flowing from it's bag into me.
My heart begins to pound harder in my chest, feeling intense pain in my leg, an ache that runs up my calf to my thigh.
Pulling back the blankets, seeing the bandage on my leg, from my knee to my ankle, I feel the colour drain from my face. Questions plague my mind

How did that happen?
How did I end up here?
Where is here?

Breathing deeply to try and calm myself, I again scan the room I'm in. It's a private room with a door, small windows and cupboards along the wall, as well as a nightstand by the bed. A jug of water and cup are the only items on it.
Straining to reach it I pour myself a glass, gulping it down. It feels so good sliding down my parched throat. Eagerly I pour another glass, gulping that down as well. I have never felt so unbelievably thirsty.
I feel like picking up the jug and pouring all of the remaining water down my throat. But I know that would end up with me getting water all down the front of myself. I shiver at the thought of it, sensing the room is rather cold. Reaching over by the bed I press the nurse call button and wait.

Not even a minute passes, before the door cracks open. The person walking into the room is clearly not a nurse or a doctor.

Quickly I focus my eyes on scanning him, snapping them shut so he won't know I'm awake.

His presence in the room is intense, stirring something inside me, deep in my belly. It's almost an instant attraction.

He crosses the room to my bedside and hesitates a little stepping up next to me. I feel him place the bouquet of flowers he'd been holding on the bed beside me. The smell of jasmine and rose floating into my nostrils is divine and blocks out the hospital smell for a moment.

"Hi," he says gruffly, as though he wants to say more but the words are caught in his throat.

His hand brushes my cheek, it's coarse but his touch is sensitive and it sends shivers through my body, sending the feeling in my belly a flutter again.

A simple gesture like that has never stirred a feeling like that in me before.

I want to open my eyes so desperately.

One quick look at him has caused such an ache in me, but I don't know this man. I can't help but think if he is the reason I'm here.

If he has something to do with the cut on my leg?

And the reason I have an IV attached to me filling my body with blood?

Shaking my head I try to remember what has happened over the last couple of days, since I'd made my escape.

Intentionally I'd blocked a lot out, so the only thing I can remember is running out of petrol and waking up in the back of my car in unbearable pain.

Instinctively I clutch my stomach, knowing that it's over. My baby is gone.

The pain, the blood, the cut, it all comes rushing back in my mind but I can't remember anything after that, certainly not how I got to be in a hospital bed. Surely from all the pain and the blood loss I should have been dead.

I can't help but wonder if the man standing by the bed still has something to do with the fact I 'm not dead.

It definitely seems as though he knows me, even though I have no idea who he is. The ache in me wants to know him. But to know him I need to look at him again.

Forcing my eyes open I slowly take him in, my eyes scanning his body first, then his face.

The man standing by the bedside could have been described with many words.

Ones that shoot to my mind immediately are delicious and handsome.

His jawline is chiselled, dotted with dark brown stubble and his eyes are a striking iridescent shade of blue that are so dreamy I could get lost in them. He's wearing a flannelette shirt, unbuttoned a little too low, sleeves rolled up to his elbows and tucked into his dark denim jeans, that are worn at the knees and held up by a tan belt with a bronze buckle.

His outfit choice shows off his muscular physique and I wonder what his chest looked like underneath his shirt.

I curse myself for thinking such thoughts about someone I don't even know.

Staring at him is cut short, when he realises I'm now awake.

He looks down at me, again brushing my cheek with his hand.

"Hi, good to see you awake," he says softly.

His voice rings in my head, sexy and gruff. The opening of his mouth with his words makes me scan his face closer. I deviously want to run my hands through his mass of curly hair to mess it up and I can't help but smile slightly. The corners of his mouth rise up in a sexy as grin, showing perfect dimples and teeth. Just looking at his lips makes my insides stir again with the strange fluttery feeling.

Again I curse myself and my body's reaction to this scrumptious man in front of me.

A soft murmur escapes my lips and hearing it he looks straight into my eyes when he speaks softly and calmly, "Its ok you're safe. Don't speak."

No words escape my lips. I feel like I've forgotten how to form words, one look at him and I'm speechless, but it's more than that and I'm petrified. I have no idea where I am, or what has happened in the last few days. Speaking and getting involved with him, some mysterious gorgeous stranger, with his world would only make it harder to continue my escape.

I need to get out of this hospital bed.

Reaching down I tear at the edges of the tape of the IV. Ripping it out won't be nearly as painful as what I've experienced, by someone I'd loved.

It's strange to think of my husband in past tense. I'd once loved him, but the pain he'd inflicted on me ate away at that love.

The mysterious new man puts a hand over mine, shaking his head. I stop tugging at the IV, feeling defeated and sighing heavily when the door cracks open again. The nurse finally walks in and from the look on her face it's my guess was I'm not going to get out of here anytime soon.

(6) Addison

Coming back to Ridgehope hadn't been part of my plan. After breaking his heart I'd escaped to the city, wanting to get away from the small town gossip about why we broke up.

Rumours were abundant, including that I was pregnant with someone else's baby. If only they knew the truth, they'd know how much those words hurt.

Escaping to the city though hadn't exactly worked out as planned either. The pain of the past was just too much.

Physically I probably fitted in there better, but I was a country girl at heart.

I'd only been back a month and was settling into working at the hospital. It was a little more fast paced than being a General Practitioner as I was before and focusing on obstetrics had been a welcome change.

Ridgehope Memorial is a small hospital, but we always had a number of patients and serviced a wide farming community.

One patient in particular that came on ward in the last few days has piqued my attention.

Brought in by ambulance, bleeding and unconscious I was assigned as her doctor, by the annoying new doctor that has swanned in like he owns the place.

At first I was confused, but when a routine ultrasound was done on her it all made sense. What didn't make sense though was the person who was by her bedside when I walked into the private room.

My heart leaps in my chest, pounding fiercely as I take him in, watching her on the bed.

I knew it was inevitable to see him at some point, but in these circumstances I'm taken aback.

"Hunter?" I ask, even though I know it's him. His head is down looking at the woman on the bed, "Is that you?" I continue.

His incredible dreamy blue eyes look up at me, and he scowls.

"Addison, what are you doing here?" he asks, with an odd tone in his voice.

I think his question is rather ridiculous, considering I'm wearing scrubs, but I answer, "I work here Hunter."

He shakes his head at me, not believing my words.

"I thought you moved to Adelaide," he states, even though it's technically a question.

"I did, but I missed it here. I came back a month ago."

He stands up, pushing back the chair back he was sitting in hastily. His hands ball into fists like he's angry.

"And you didn't think to contact me and tell me?"

"I wanted to but..." I pause, unsure of what excuse I could even say. I'd wanted to contact him, but I knew that he probably wouldn't have wanted to talk to me anyway. The pain of my rejection was no doubt still raw in his heart.

"Oh come on, Addison. It's always been about you. What you want, what you need," he says, cutting through me with the words that have a vindictive tone, that is so unlike him.

He's almost at the door to leave, but I can't let him go, yet, without saying something.

"Please Hunter, let me explain," I beg.

"No, I don't want to hear it Addison, I didn't then and I don't now," he says with the same vindictive tone, shaking his head.

Sighing deeply, I touch his arm and nod to the woman on the bed, "Um, Hunter, do you know her?"

He shakes his head again. It isn't like him to not have anything to say.

"No, I don't. I found her passed out in the farmhouse," he says with a hint of pain in voice.

To say I'm taken aback is an understatement. I really thought he knew her, from the way he was looking at her and soothing her with his words.

"Oh well, um, I can't disclose her details to you then," I state, feeling like a bitch even though it's my job.

His reply doesn't come, instead he turns his eyes away from me and goes straight out the door without another word.

On the bed by the mystery woman is a bunch of flowers. Something about the whole situation doesn't sit right with me. I can't help but wonder if Hunter had done something to her?

But I knew he couldn't have, he'd never do anything to hurt someone intentionally.

I need to tell this woman about what had happened, but I don't want to wake her, as she'd slipped into sleep again when I was talking to Hunter. Busying myself with checking her IV and putting the flowers in a vase on her bedside I wait a few minutes, hearing her murmuring as though she's about to wake up again.

Her eyes flutter open just as I'm about to leave.

"Hi, how are you feeling?" I ask calmly.

She grunts back, not saying anything coherent.

"Thats ok, you don't have to say anything."

I pull the seat up by her bedside, taking a deep breath to speak my next words.

"Miss did you know you were pregnant?"

She shakes her head, and I can see tears stinging her eyes. It's clear she's possibly hiding something and I'm intrigued. When she doesn't offer a reply I continue speaking, delivering the bad news.

"Unfortunately you had a miscarriage," I say matter of factly, trying to leave out the emotion in my voice.

The tears on her face begin streaming down her cheeks then.

I feel heartbroken for her.

Telling people this kind of news never gets easier. It's the worst part of my job. Again she grunts, as though she's trying to speak, to tell me something.

"You also had a deep gash on your leg that needed ten stitches and...."

She reaches down and touches the bandage as I speak, "You also have multiple other cuts and bruises."

She's sobbing uncontrollably now. Part of me wishes I could hug her but it isn't professional to do so.

"Let me change your dressing and I'll get some pain relief for you," I state when she lets out a deep sob.

Standing up to collect supplies she grabs my scrubs, pulling me back.

She doesn't speak but asks with a hand gesture for something to write on. I know this private room well, and there is note paper in the bedside drawer. Grabbing it out I hand it to her with a pen.

Quickly she writes in scrawly handwriting.

'Who is he?'

"Hunter Mackenney. He's a local farmer." I say in reply. The words sound strange in my head.

She sighs deeply, smiling as though she's thinking dirty things about Hunter in her head.

I completely understand that sigh as another woman to know Hunter Mackenney. He has that effect on every woman he meets.

She begins writing again, pausing, tapping the pen on the paper as though she's unsure of the words she wants to write.

'When can I leave?'

"We are keeping you in for a least a few days until your bruises and things heal. You're lucky to be alive."

'I should be dead'

What am I supposed to say to that?

No one should wish such a thing and it makes me wonder what has really brought her to Ridgehope.The only thing I can think to do in response is to shake my head.

"Don't say that." I laugh lightheartedly before continuing, "Plus Hunter seemed pretty interested in you."

A smile spreads across her face. She is as affected by Hunter as I am, but sadly for her Hunter isn't hers. Seeing him again has definitely sparked the feelings inside me again. The feelings I'd tried to bury deep within my heart are still burning and I'm going to do everything in my power to get Hunter Mackenney back.

We belong together.

(7) Hunter

Rushing out of the hospital to reach my ute feels like an endless maze.
I needed to get out of there fast as the air in the hospital private room
became stifling as soon as Addison entered.

I can't deny that she's still breathtaking and definitely still looked mighty
good in her scrubs, but my body didn't have the same reaction to her it
once did.

The same can't be said for my heart though.

There's still an ache for her there for sure, but it's more an ache for a
woman in general and a longing to be with someone again.

Loneliness is eating away at my heart, but if Addison thinks I'm going to
take her back she is sadly mistaken.

She'd always had bit of a 'my shit don't stink' attitude, just because she
had a degree, had gotten out of Ridgehope for a while to 'make
something of herself'.

She'd left me heartbroken and her vindictive nature was infuriating.

I'd never understood why she'd wanted me to give up the farm my family
had worked so hard for.

It was my life, and I wanted her in my life as well but it was never about
what I wanted.

It was always about Addison.

Driving back out to farm I drive past the car, still on the side of the road.
It seems strange that it's still there. I wonder if maybe my brother
Quentin doesn't know about it, as the local cops were usually onto things
like that fairly quickly.

The woman from the hospital hasn't left my mind and I'd spent most of my time in the hospital with her, just talking to her about my life and telling her jokes that made her laugh.

She hasn't spoken a word, seeming so damaged and it makes me long to know her story. Desperately I want to know why she is covered in bruises and scratches, other than the one on her leg.

Part of me feels guilty that my badly maintained fence has caused the large gash on her leg.

My lack of farm maintenance has caused her to experience more pain and I want to make it better.

Taking her pain away is the least I could do. It always pained me that I couldn't take Dad's pain away when he got ill.

I've always loved taking care of others, even when I was younger I'd looked after the lambs, hand raising them when their mothers couldn't.

It was possible my need to take care of people was part of the reason Addison and I didn't work out. She had that need as well, which was what led her into medicine. But I resented her taking care of me, as I'd always had an independent streak too, liking the solitary life and my own company.

Still I craved the touch of a woman, to feel close to someone and to share my life with someone who wanted the same things I do. It hurt more than anything that Addison hadn't wanted to share her life with me.

Arriving back at the farmhouse I'm greeted by an eager Blitz. He'd gobbled all his food down and is pawing at his bowl for a refill.

Laughing at his silliness I let him follow me inside the house.

Seeing the blood still on the floorboards makes my heart sink. She really had gone through an ordeal.

I really want to know what happened to her, as I want to make it better and take her pain away. Addison doesn't seem like she's going to give me that information easily, and the only way is to be vindictive like she is. It's against my better judgement and so out of character for me, but I have to do anything possible to find out about the mystery woman.

Blitz is following me around, literally a lost puppy dog. He tries to bite the mop when I pull it out of the cupboard. He thinks it's a monster that must be attacked when in use.

His crazy behaviour always makes me smile, but angers me at the same time, especially when I just need to get something done, like mopping up the blood I can't bear to look at any longer.

My Mum had taught me well when it came to household chores.

I can hear her voice in my head *'Cold water for anything to do with blood'*.

Following the voice I let the cold water rush into the bucket with the disinfectant. Slowly I mop the floorboards, her blood disappearing from the floor and turning the water in my bucket red.

My heart feels truly wretched for her, for what she's experienced.

If I'd not been out droving I'd have been here to help her.

The guilt of my absence strikes my heart, her beautiful face appearing in my mind.

Trying to shake her image from my mind I busy myself, cleaning the sheets, soaking them in cold water. Thankfully I'd had a waterproof mattress protector on the bed, so the blood had not reached the mattress.

Tidying up made me feel content. The farmhouse isn't in the greatest condition but when it's clean and tidy it feels like home.

My thoughts are filled with her, her laugh and her blue green eyes that sparkle when she sees me coming into the room.

I have questions in my mind, wondering where she's from? And why she can't go home?

Not knowing her name, or anything about her just makes me curious.

She's astoundingly beautiful, in a different way to Addison, which makes my curiosity towards her unnerving.

I'd always gone for the pretty blonde types, the women so different to my own dark haired appearance. But her dark chestnut, almost black hair and beguiling blue-green eyes had captivated me the moment I lay eyes on her.

When she woke up in the hospital, her eyes trying not to focus on me tugged at my heart and stirred something inside my body that I haven't felt for a long time.

It's lust, but feels deeper than that, a more emotional connection, not just physical.

I can tell by the way she looks at me that she feels something to.

Normally I'm not someone who's bitter but I have a devious plan ticking over in my mind to find out more about my beautiful mystery woman.

(8) *Addison*

Every day, every god damned day he came in and sat by her bedside.
I didn't even want to venture in to check her charts, or change the
dressing on her leg. Her bruises and the gash on her leg were healing well
and her bleeding from her miscarriage had lessened, to the point of
barely anything now.
I still knew nothing about her past, her reason for turning up in
Ridgehope and she hadn't uttered a single word since she'd been there.
She still preferred to write everything down, so I'd tried to get some
information out of her when Hunter hadn't been around which was near
impossible, as he seemed to be spending every waking minute at the
hospital.
I can't help but wonder who is running the farm in his absence. It's
unsettling me, more than it probably should be but I'm curious as to why
he's taken a sudden interest in her. It's going to make getting him back a
hundred times harder.
Peering through the window of the room he's seated beside her again.
He's talking and she's giggling at his words, obviously enjoying his
presence. His hand is resting on hers, and he caresses her cheek with the
other.
They look so happy together, like they're a couple and anyone would
think that he did know her intimately. Just the thought of them being
together makes my heart constrict in my chest.
If he does though he would have kissed her in that moment but he
doesn't, instead he stands up, placing his Akubra back on his head and
turns to head out the door.

It's as though he senses me being there and is trying to go out of his way to avoid me. If I'm being honest with myself, I know he's trying to avoid me and it hurts like hell. I really just want to talk to him, to explain my reason for leaving.

I turn the door handle just as he does, bumping straight into his muscular physique.

God, I've missed his amazing body.

He pushes at my chest to steady us both, his hands a little too high on my body, causing my nipples to react to the touch.

"Hi Addison," he says in his sexy voice.

At least it sounds sexy to me, my heart now pounding in my chest.

"Hi Hunter. I was just coming to check on her," I say, trying to not sound breathless from his touch.

"Yeah, cool. Is she going to be released any time soon?" he asks casually.

I shake my head in response, before replying when a look of shock crosses his face, "Not as yet. She's definitely better, but we don't know anything about her so the chief is reluctant to release her."

"Oh, so you know nothing about her? She won't speak to me."

"She's not speaking at all Hunter," I say sternly.

"So can she speak?" he asks, worry in his tone.

"We honestly don't know, but she is communicating by writing things down."

He glares at me, like he's trying to break down my defence. He wants to know something about her and professionally I'm not supposed to tell him, but my heart wants him back and I need to play nice to win him over.

"Oh so what has she written then?" he asks.

"Her name is Savannah Galison," I say shrugging.

He whispers her name under his breath, looking back at her in the bed.

A smile spreads across her face at the acknowledgement.

My stomach lurches. I shouldn't have told him. He wants her. He doesn't want me anymore.

I'd blown my chance with him, when I didn't want to live life on the farm with him, when I didn't accept his proposal a year ago.

I curse myself, *Stupid Addison, stupid.*

It doesn't feel like a year ago though. It feels like yesterday, and even though I've had a few casual relationships since, gone on a few dates, not one had compared to Hunter.

He's the total package in a man, amazingly handsome, genuine and an all round good guy, but stupid selfish me hadn't thought about anyone but myself.

Being away from life in Ridgehope had made me realise how much I missed the place and how much I missed Hunter, more than anything.

I still love him desperately and I need to think about how to get him back.

My shift is nearly over and it honestly can't come any sooner. I need to confess to Hunter. Confess something I should have said a year ago.

(9) Savannah

He's been in, my gorgeous mystery man, sitting beside me, every day for over a week now. Seeing him walk through the door each day has my heart leaping in my chest. I don't even know who he is, other than a brief mention from the doctor of his name. After recent experiences I want to keep my heart guarded though.

I always have had a knack of falling for people I shouldn't. Falling for Dante had gotten me into this mess. Part of me always knew I'd end up in hospital because of him, but I'd loved him and it blinded me.

I should have never married him in hindsight.

He was always so sweet, waiting for me to be ready to take our relationship further. He never pressured me until he put the ring on my finger and I was legally bound to him.

It was as though a switch triggered and he took me for himself, the first bruises appearing mere hours after our first night together.

I should have known then that he wasn't the man I'd spent the last four years with. The man who inflicted so much pain on me that first night together was not my Dante but some evil man, who hurt me over and over again for the next few years.

Why I'd wanted to start a family with him amidst all that pain is now beyond me. I honestly don't know how I could have been so naive.

Yes, I thought that maybe starting a family would make things better, but the thought had often crossed my mind of what he might do to our child. He had shown his violent nature more than once and the bruises he left on me could have killed a child. It's certainly too painful to think about.

Escaping him had been the most difficult thing i've ever done. In some ways I feel safe in this new place, but part of me also feels I'm not far enough away from Adelaide; that I should have been more careful at getting away and tried to hide my identity more along the way.

In a way it's comforting that these new people don't know my real name. It's scary to admit to myself that I want to tell my mystery man my identity though. He's getting under my skin and I'm truly scared. Scared at what trusting new people will mean and scared that if I open up, staying in one place for too long that Dante will find me.

My eyes are tightly closed, but sleep won't come. It's partly because I know he's just entered the room, as I heard the creak of the door hinges and partly because I'm so uncomfortable after being cooped up in the hospital for around two weeks.

At first the bed was a welcome relief to my tired aching body, after sleeping in the back of my car, but now it feels as hard a plank of wood and no better than sleeping in the back of the car.

I've barely gotten out of it, except to visit the bathroom.

And that had been stifling as well, as I was not allowed to go to the bathroom, even to just pee unaccompanied.

The doctors were afraid I was going to make a runner straight out the door. But it hadn't even really crossed my mind if I was being completely honest.

Being in the hospital made me feel safe, especially when the mystery man was nearby.

If Dante found me, I don't think he'd stand much of a chance of getting to me or hurting me.

He was of a similar build to Dante, but he had a presence that made him seem intimidating but also sweet and genuine.

Each day he'd been in I'd laughed, at his jokes and listened intently to his stories of his life on his farm. His past was traumatic too from the brief things he'd told me and my heart felt pained for him.

There is also something odd between him and the obstetrician. He hasn't directly mentioned her, but has said something about an ex that fits her description.

Honestly I don't like her at all. She has a sweet caring side when it comes to medicine and is dutiful changing my dressing, and inspecting my bruises, but whenever he's in, she gives me cold stares, as if to say, 'Don't touch him, don't think about him.'

What makes her think he is hers?

Opening my eyes I focus on him in the room again. He mentions not being able to stay long, as the farm is calling but he needed to see me. His words make butterflies flit in my stomach.

He wants to see me.

He wants to see me just as much as I want to see him.

Seeing him is the only thing making the days in hospital bearable. He stands up to leave, putting his hat back on his head. It makes him look incredibly handsome.

I let out a muffled giggle at the thought of seeing him with just that hat on and I curse myself for the naughty thoughts flashing through my mind.

Stop it Savannah, you don't know the guy.

It feels strange to be using my alias in my head, but I've been making a conscious effort to become Savannah. All part of leaving my old life behind.

As he leaves the snotty obstetrician enters, bumping straight into him. Their conversation is muted, and I never was good at lip reading. The only thing that makes any sense, as he turns towards me for a moment is that she'd told him my name. He looks straight at me, whispering it but I hear it loud and clear as though he's whispering into my ear.

A smile spreads across my face and my insides are doing flip flops.

If him just saying my name is effecting me so much I have to be even more careful or things are not going to end well.

He's different to Dante for sure. I know that in my heart, but scars from what I've endured run deep.

Much to my disappointment as soon as the obstetrician comes in and their awkward conversation ends he leaves and I'm in the room with her again. She checks my dressing, deciding not to put a new one on as the wound is almost healed and the stitches are nearly ready to come out. The whole time she gives me the cold stares and it makes me feel sick.

It seems as though she's jealous of the time he's spending with me.

She barely says a word to me, except for a warning as she finishes filling in my chart. Her warning comes out more as a threat, that has me worried considering she's my doctor. Her warning seems very vindictive and downright scary, sending a chill through me,'Stay away from him, or you'll be back in this hospital bed again.'

The tone makes me shiver, like she's walked over my grave, or actually is sending me to my grave.

I hope it's not some kind of curse she's trying to put me under, that is the last thing I need.

But who is she to tell me to stay away from him?

I'm not going to do nothing of the sort.

I want to find out more about him and she's not going to stop me.

Dozing was the only sleep I was really getting. Every noise in the hospital tumbled in my head. No end date seemed to be in sight, of when I would get out of the place.

I had nowhere to go anyway so it shouldn't have really mattered, but it does.

I need to keep running. Running is freedom from my horrible reality.

I need to keep running from Dante, as even being on the other side of the country won't truly be far enough away from him.

Startling me from my thoughts is a loud tap on the door.

Of course I don't say anything to let them know to come in, but the handle turns and a police officer enters. He's a burly, older man, his badge showing his rank of Sergeant.

This alerts my mind that they are taking my appearance into town as something criminal and it makes me feel a little worried.

Is Dante here? Do they know who I really am?

Stopping by the bed, the Sergeant begins asking me questions. My head can't come up with any coherent thoughts. I haven't spoken to anyone else yet and I'm not planning on starting to talk now.

The less anyone knows about me the better and especially the police, as I can only think of how my appearance in an outback town might appear on the news and Dante would find out where I am.

It was all too much to think about.

I shake my head in response to the Sergeants questions before bursting into tears.

He reaches out to touch my arm in comfort but instead his touch causes me to shrink back into the bed and pull the covers up over my body.

I feel completely exposed and vulnerable.

He is about to leave, when my not so friendly obstetrician and so called doctor pops her head around the door jam.

"How's it going in here?" she speaks casually, not directly to the Sergeant or me.

"Not good Addison. She's not saying anything."

She beckons for him to follow her outside the room and she doesn't close the door, behind her, which I'm sure is deliberate, as she doesn't try to hide her conversation with the Sergeant.

I hear her tell him my name, which she doesn't know isn't my real name, but no one in this town is going to know my real name.

It would only make getting away again harder.

She also mentions the details of my accident, mentioning my miscarriage in a clinical manner, like it doesn't even matter.

I hear her mention the farmer's name and for the first time the details emerge that I was found at his house.

Some of the connection between us now makes sense.

I really want to keep running, but a part of me is beginning to want to stay for him, the mysterious farmer whose house I stumbled into when my body told me to stop running.

Maybe it really is time to stop running and find some new hope.

(10) Hunter

Driving back to the farm feels endless, with my head spinning with a thousand thoughts.

Not knowing anything about Savannah is really getting to me.

I don't even know her, but an overwhelming want is beginning to consume me.

I want to know her and help her escape from whatever she is running from.

It reminds me of when I was younger at school and my childhood best friend Jett Yorke rolled back into town for the second time after his parents whisked him and Addison to the city for a while.

Being a little shy country boy, the crazy whirlwind of a city boy he'd become he didn't really notice me at first, but I desperately wanted to befriend him, as I'd always thought he seemed like a great guy growing up.

I've always curious about people, wondering often about what happens behind the closed doors of peoples houses.

He lived in town, as his family came back to take over the general store and honestly we never would have crossed paths again, if we hadn't had to team up for a stupid diorama project in Year eight history.

I still remember how lame our diorama was, although the teacher thought it was a pretty great effort for two boys who seemed to not do any work in class.

From that day we were pretty much inseparable. Hunter and Jett through thick and thin, except when it came to his younger sister.

Despite his disdain towards my feelings for her, he brought out a mischievous side to me, and we definitely got up a lot of no good growing up.

Our favourite pastime was throwing batty old Martha's precious gnomes in the river.

No sooner would a new one appear, that to would be it be smashed and thrown in as well.

It always surprised me that we never got caught, but it was probably partly due to the fact that Martha was practically blind and never saw us.

Jett turned out to be a country boy at heart, managing a farm a few towns over after we finished school.

I'd never really gone to his house much, as it was attached to the general store and he was a little wary of me meeting his family.

I found out part of the reason for his wariness in our second last year of school when I found myself getting reacquainted with his younger sister Addison at a party.

I was almost immediately smitten with her, even though years had gone by since I'd first met her but as she was a number of years younger than us and extremely headstrong, winning her affection was a challenge.

Jett never approved of our relationship, not even really speaking to me when he moved away.

I'd fallen so quickly for Addison, that I was truly heartbroken when she up and left to study and completely disregarded my feelings.

I'd never told anyone that we had as so much as broken up for the three years she'd been away.

She came back, desperate to get me back, whilst completing her studies at the local General practice. And me because I'd not gotten over her I stupidly took her back like nothing had changed, but it had.

She didn't know anything about my father's illness or my mothers breakdown.

Partly because I hadn't told her, but partly because she didn't seem to care about life back home.

Staying around for a while she completely took over my heart again, even more so than before and I really thought she loved me as much as I loved her.

But after she'd been home for a year I proposed to her, only to be shot down by her saying she didn't want to live on the farm.

Fuck Hunter, you pansy, be a man.

I wipe my eyes from the tears stinging them from thinking about life gone wrong.

I want to know more about Savannah, and know that getting close to Addison again is the ticket to that, but if I'm crying like a pansy thinking about how Addison broke my heart, how am I ever going to pretend I want to be with her again?

I'd been slowly driving home, only causing myself misery.

As though a mirage I noticed that the mystery car was still there by the road, about two kilometres from the farm.

It had to be Savannah's car.

It made sense.

I pull up behind it, and take a picture of the registration with my phone, before jumping out of my ute to inspect it to see if there is ID or other information about her.

But there is nothing on the seats except a blanket and some clothes when I peer in the window.

I don't dare touch the door handles or any other part of the car, just in case there are any fingerprint details.

It's best to leave the investigating details to the professionals.

I jump back in the ute, making a mental note to call Quentin when I get back home.

~~

As usual when I arrive home lately, Blitz is even more eager to see me then ever. He paws at my clothes, as though he's sensing I've been at the hospital with Savannah. He'd shown really odd behaviour when it came to her.

He'd never liked Addison and always growled at her, but he showed a genuine love and concern for Savannah and I honestly didn't know what to think.

I hang my hat on the coat stand and strip off my shirt.

It's a perk of living alone.

No sooner had I taken it off Blitz grabs it in his mouth and retreats into the kitchen, dropping it on his bed and nuzzling it.

He really is acting peculiar.

Shrugging I proceed to grab a beer from the fridge, flicking the cap off and pulling back a chair.

Slinking back against the kitchen chair I grab my phone from my pocket and dial Quentin's number.

It's five pm, so I guess he would be finishing up at the station and wouldn't answer, so I'm a little dumbfounded when he answers on the second ring.

"Hey bro."

"Hi Quent. Can I ask a favour?"

"Yeah sure, whats up?"

"Have you heard about the car thats down the road from the farm?"

"Nah, no one's reported it. Whats the favour?"

"I think it might the woman's that's in the hospital. You know that I found in the farmhouse."

"Oh yeah? Sarge tried to speak to her yesterday. She didn't say anything."

"Yeah I've been in to see her everyday. She hasn't said a word to me."

There's silence on the line. Quentin isn't one to be at a loss for words.

I speak again, "Quent, you still there?"

"Yeah Hunter. I was just thinking."

"That's never good."

"I'm guessing you've seen Addison then?"

"Yeah," I sigh, "I don't want to talk about her. So Quent, my favour?"

"Yeah?" he asks, almost sarcastically.

"Could you run a search on the rego of the car?"

"Yeah, no worries bro. I'll send someone out in the next few days to search it as well ok?"

"Thanks Quent. I'll text you a picture of the rego in a bit."

"Ok bro. I'll catch ya on Friday at the pub yeah?"

"Yeah, see ya then."

I hang up and gulp down the rest of the beer.

It pays having a police officer for a brother.

He's always up with happenings around the town, so I'm a little surprised that he didn't know anything about the car.

It makes me even more curious to find out if it's Savannah's and what clues it might uncover about her sudden appearance in town.

Her sudden appearance that is turning my world upside down and making my heart feel something I never thought it would again.

I couldn't possibly be falling for her, could I?

(11) *Addison*

Part of me knows that trying to get Hunter back is futile.
He'd made it pretty clear a year before when I ran off to the city again
that he didn't want me back, nor did he love me anymore.
But the selfish part of me wants him all for myself again.
I hate admitting to myself that I'm a tad possessive.
It was what drove all my boyfriends away, if you could even call anyone in
my past since Hunter a boyfriend, as most guys I'd been with I'd barely
even had a second date with.
It's a family thing, my brother Jett has a possessive streak too and he still
kind of has a grudge against me for getting with his best friend.

But truthfully how could I not have fallen for Hunter?

He's genuinely a good guy, outrageously gorgeous and probably the best
I've ever had in the bedroom, not that I'd ever tell him that.
Jett is bound to be forever furious with me when he finds out that I'm
about to knock on Hunters' door in a desperate attempt to win him back.
He'd called me vindictive and I truly hate that word but thoughts had
crossed my mind of trapping him into taking me back.
Pretending after seducing him to be pregnant.
He would never know the truth until it was too late.

Could I really be so cruel to him? To the man I love?

I stop at the gate to the farm, panic rising in my chest.

It seems crazy, my whole plan tumbling in my head.

I've never really stopped loving Hunter but I still can't feel any love for his home.

Making him fall in love with me again is probably going to be the easy part of my plan in getting him back. I still don't want to live on the farm, but I probably would finally have to give in if I wanted Hunter in my life.

Happily I find that he still doesn't have a lock on the gate. It squeaks open and I proceed to drive my car in, before jumping out again and closing it behind me.

He'd never forgive me if his stupid dog got loose.

Opening and shutting the gate was such an annoying part of farm life. Again jumping back into my idling car I pull up closer to the house.

To my surprise his stupid dog doesn't come bounding towards the car. He'd always hated me.

It wasn't like I'd done anything to the ugly mutt but he still had something against me.

Closing the car door behind me, I lock it out of habit before walking slowly up onto the verandah.

I can't believe I'm really going to do this.

Reaching the front door, I knock as hard as I can muster on the screen door.

The sound of barking and pawing at the door is evident, but there doesn't appear to be any lights on that I can see.

Tapping my foot, I'm about to turn to leave when I hear Hunter's voice trying to calm the dog.

"Down Blitz," he says, opening the wooden main door.

He looks at me with disgust, before asking, "What are you doing here Addison?"

"I wanted to talk."

"What would we need to talk about?" he asks me.

It makes me feel like an intruder.

He hasn't even opened the door and the stupid dog is snarling at me.

"Um...us," I say trying to be calm.

"There is no us Addison," he replies spitefully.

"Please Hunter. Can I just come in?"

He still glares at me.

Maybe I shouldn't have come.

He'd told me before he didn't love me, but I have to try.

I've never gotten over him and if I don't try to get him back I probably never will.

He doesn't say anything but sighs and reaches to the handle pushing the door open to invite me in.

The dog jumps up on me and not in a friendly greeting way either.

It makes me a little tense.

Hunter again tells him down and points towards the kitchen.

The dog thankfully retreats.

I take a deep breath before focusing my attention back on Hunter, following him towards the living room. He'd stopped in the hallway with his hands on his hips.

God, he's so gorgeous.

Me, I'm completely tongue tied.

I'd crazily come here straight from the hospital, still dressed in my scrubs and I'd not even really thought about what I was actually going to say.

The silence between us is strained and the thought crosses my mind of literally throwing myself at him and kissing him, but my mind knows I have to talk to him first.

He's the one to break the silence.

"So why are you here Addison?"

The way he says my name makes me cringe.

But I have to get straight to it, "I came back for you Hunter."

"Why Addison?"

"Because I still love you. I've never stopped loving you."

He shrugs, "Seriously, come on Addison, you never loved me."

He's literally tearing my heart out.

He'd never been so insolent about my feelings before.

"How can you say that Hunter? I..."

My words are frozen on my tongue.

Why does it feel like there was nothing between us?

Like we have no past together?

This isn't the Hunter I love.

"Oh I don't know Addison, maybe because you brushed me off twice, ran away to the city and..."

He stops talking.

I know what he's going to say next. He's going to bring up my rejection of his proposal.

"And because I didn't say yes?"

"Ding ding ding."

"I'm sorry Hunter. But please just let me explain."

"Whats to explain? You didn't want to marry me. What would have changed?"

"Me, Hunter. I've changed."

Again the silence envelopes us. There isn't really anything else I can say, but I haven't really gotten anywhere.

"Maybe you should prove it to me," he says again breaking the silence and shocking me to the core in the process.

Before I can respond to his strange words he's headed down the hallway. Hesitantly I follow.

Knowing the house so well I know he'd gone to the bathroom, so when he calls back, "Just give me a minute," I knew where he'd gone.

I tiptoe further down the hallway until I reach his bedroom. Nothing has changed.

It seems like yesterday I'd been in that very room.

There is only one way to prove to him that I still love him, that we are meant to be together.

I inwardly thank myself for still only having my scrubs on.

I never wore anything but underwear with them and today I'd worn a lacy bra and g-string as I'd not had time to wash my normal everyday underwear.

Pushing my pants down my legs without pulling my shoes off was hard to do quickly.

I knew it was a little weird that I wore high heels to work with my scrubs, but I always found them comfortable.

And now practically being half naked wearing high heels was as sexy as hell.

Naked and wearing high heels had never failed at getting Hunter hot for me before.

He was probably finished in the bathroom so I have to hurriedly pull my top over my head.

Hearing the toilet flush is my signal.

It's now or never.

I lay down on his bed, leaning on my elbows with my butt and legs in the air.

The bathroom door creaks open and he calls out, "Addison are you still here?"

I giggle and call back, "Find me."

I can hear his bare feet on the creaky floorboards. He stops in the door jam, leaning against it.

He looks insanely gorgeous.

"Seriously Addison? This is your plan?"

"Come on Hunter. You never could resist me."

Tentatively he steps further into the bedroom, closer to the bed.

Grabbing his hand sends a shiver straight through my body.

Touching him still wakes the same lust in me.

Fuck, I want him so much.

(12) Hunter

To say I was shocked to find Addison half naked lying butt up on my bed is an understatement.

She'd said she was only here to talk, but as usual she can't help but flaunt herself.

She'd always had a way of getting a reaction from others using her body. Practically every guy in town had fallen victim to her charm and tried to get into her panties, but she shut them all down.

I'd been the only stupid idiot to fall in love with her though. She'd tried to tell me she loved me too, but after all the rejection she'd put me through I thought that pretty unlikely.

Now standing in the door jam of 'my' bedroom looking at her half naked on my bed, I can feel my body betraying me.

Stepping closer to the bed she grabs my hand. Lust shines in her eyes and lust swells in my jeans.

I inwardly curse myself for being a male, but it isn't because it's Addison but the fact I've not been laid for close to six months and the touch of any woman would have given me the same reaction.

Her eyes are on me, lustfully begging me.

My mind wanders to Savannah for a moment and I can't help but feel like I'm cheating on her, as crazy as that seems, considering I've not even kissed her.

My thoughts are cut short though when Addison stands up, forcing her body to crash into mine.

Her words are filled with lust, "Do you still want me Hunter?"

I want to say no, but my body is saying yes.

Even though it's wrong and I've been thinking about a possible devious plan like what is happening for over a week, it's the right time to make Addison think I do want her back.

Getting her back of course is not what I really want, there isn't anything I want less, but she's a pawn in getting information about Savannah and part of me also wants her to feel the heartbreak I did, as this time she'd shown she isn't over me, even though I'm definitely over her.

Looking directly into her eyes I whisper, "I want you Addison," before crashing my lips onto hers. Hungrily she responds to my kiss.
It feels like a whirlwind kissing her again.
It makes my head spin and I want to pull away, to push her away.
But that won't make my plan work.
I have to continue playing along, to make her feel like I do want her, when I clearly don't.
When she's the one to pull away I don't stop her from lifting my t-shirt over my head but have to stop myself from cringing when she runs her hands down my bare chest, her touch feeling wrong.
Her hands stop at my belt buckle and she fumbles to undo it.
It has be done even though it's wrong.
I don't want this but I have to do it.
Pushing her back on the bed causes a giggle to escape from her mouth.
I take her mouth in a kiss again as she continues to help me wiggle out of my jeans.
Again she pulls back from my kiss, and this time she speaks, "Make love to me Hunter," she begs reaching behind her back to undo her bra.
The straps fall down her arms and she's even more exposed to me, naked except for small fragment of lace of her practically non-existent g-string.
In time gone by I would have marvelled at her naked body before me, knowing she was mine but now I don't want her.

I can't deny she's still breathtakingly gorgeous, but I don't love her and despite my body's reaction to her I can't have sex with her.

She'd hurt me in the past but taking advantage of her now isn't the right thing to do.

Shaking my head I stand up by the bed.

The smile she has on her face moments before fades into a frown and I think she's going to cry.

I'm taken aback by the possibility of Addison showing any emotion.

"I can't Addison," I declare.

Sobbing she replies meekly, "Why Hunter? Don't you love me anymore?"

Can I really tell her that I don't love her? Now when she's starting to sob uncontrollably half naked on my bed.

"No, Addison I don't love you anymore."

My words are like a knife, cutting down any defence she has left.

The tears are streaming down her cheeks.

It's her turn to stand up from the bed and she looks at me sadly, the hurt evident in her eyes.

Despite everything I really don't want to hurt her, but I don't know what I could have say to make it better. She lifts a hand close to my cheek like she's going to slap me.

I know I would have deserved it if she did but before her hand makes contact with my cheek, she instead wipes it across her own tear stained cheek and bends down to pick up her clothes before running down the hallway, not even looking back at me.

Blitz starts barking when he hears the screen door slam shut.

It's hard to decipher what has just happened.

If she'd come to my house just six months earlier and forced herself on me, I would have taken the chance, as idiotic as that seems.

But now my world feels completely changed.

I don't really know what has changed but something has and Savannah is part of it for sure.

Blitz is still madly barking. Going out to calm him I listen at the door for the sound a car engine and the scrape of tyres on the gravel but outside it's eerily quiet.

Addison is still here.

It might be a foolish next move, but I rush out of the house in my boxer shorts and pad down the verandah.

She's sitting in her car, her head in her hands, sobbing into the steering wheel.

I've have a plan to pretend to get her back to try and find out more about Savannah, so even though it's probably foolish I tap lightly on her window.

She jumps at the noise, but seeing me shivering in my underwear makes her giggle as she rolls down the window. "What?" she spits at me.

Ok, here goes nothing, Make her think you still want her.

"I'm sorry Addison. I panicked."
"What?"

Is that all she can say now?

"I'm sorry. I just think we should take the possibility of getting back together slow ok?"
She nods. "Ok, I can deal with that."
I lean into the car and press a kiss on her forehead. "Goodnight Addison, Drive safe."

Caz May

She rolls up her window after saying goodnight to me and waves as she drives towards the gate.

I don't stay to watch her drive away down the road, instead retreat quickly inside.

Back in the house Blitz stares me down, giving me a look of disgust.

It makes me laugh that even my own dog is judging me for the choice I'd just made, but it's a choice that had to be made.

Addison doesn't need to know that I honestly don't have any intention of truly getting back with her.

The only thing that's getting to me now is that I'm being vindictive and I feel so guilty.

Guilty. And I hate nothing more than feeling guilty for my actions.

What have I gotten myself into?

(13) *Quentin*

It had been a surprise to hear from Hunter a week earlier.

He'd been so caught up with things on the farm and I really feel like I never really see him.

He'd always been an attentive older brother, always looking out for me, but we had drifted apart a little as we gotten older.

I know it's partly due to the fact that I kind of had a thing for his ex-girlfriend Addison.

Their relationship was so complicated though and even though they broke up I knew he'd never forgive me if I tried pursuing her.

Being part of the police force as well, I had to ensure that I did the right thing by everyone in my life and I had to be on top of what was happening in the town and surrounds.

So when receiving the phone call from my older brother about the abandoned car near the farm I feel like I've failed at my duties.

Granted I hadn't been on patrol out there for weeks. I wasn't sure if anyone had.

Hunter had text me a picture of the car registration. Tapping it into the police database gives me some out of the ordinary results. It's registered to a male with an Adelaide address.

What puzzles me is the name wasn't the same name as the mystery woman's name.

The mystery woman who ended up in Hunter's house.

I'm sure they are connected somehow, but a search on her name produces no results, at all.

There is no record of a Savannah Galison anywhere.

It's against police protocol to divulge any information to members of the public about cases, but I have to call Hunter.

He seems close to the mystery woman and as his brother I have to tell him about what I've found out.

It's close to knock off, so I quickly jot down some notes in the file the Sergeant has started on the mystery woman case and tidy my desk.

Jumping in my Kingswood, I dial Hunter's number. He answers straight away.

"Hey Quent? Did you search the rego?"

"Yeah bro I did."

"And?" he asks me, a hopeful tone in his voice.

"It's not exactly good news Hunter."

He sighs heavily into the receiver.

"What do you mean?"

"Its registered to a male from Adelaide."

"So?"

"With a completely different surname."

"That doesn't mean anything Quent."

"Yes, thats true, but I also searched the mystery woman's name," I pause, taking in a deep breath, as I hear his breathing increasing in panic.

"And what Quent? Just tell me."

"Look Hunter I shouldn't say anything but you're my brother and..." Again I pause.

This is a lot harder to say than I thought it was going to be.

"Quent please just tell me," he begs.

"Um, Hunter there is no record at all of a Savannah Galison."

"What?" he spits back, as if he didn't hear me.

"Yeah I searched on Births, Deaths and marriages. She doesn't exist."

He doesn't reply. He's clearly shocked.

The last sound I hear before he hangs up is an exasperated sigh.

To say I'm incredibly worried about my big brother is an understatement.

I have to do something, starting with taking a drive out tomorrow to look at the car myself.

Sometimes if you needed a job done you have to do it yourself.

~~

First thing the next day I sign out a patrol car. I know I should tell someone where I'm going but the station is overly quiet and I don't want to waste any time.

The V6 engine of the patrol car rumbles contentedly when I start it. It's tempting to put the sirens and lights on and book it down the dirt road out of town but if I'm caught using the patrol car inappropriately I'd be suspended for sure.

And I love my job.

So instead I leisurely cruise through the town and out to dirt road that leads out of town and towards our family farm.

It's a cool day but sunny and the sun damn near blinds me. It makes the road blurry at times, as the heat hits it and dissipates.

I'm sure Hunter mentioned the car being about two kilometres from the farm on the left side, parked in the direction of driving out of town, but as I reach the farm gates I've not seen any cars along the side of the road.

Pulling up at the farm gates I tap out a text to Hunter,

Quentin: Bro are you home?

Hunter: Nah out checking the horse paddocks

Quentin: Oh i've just come by to check out the car

Hunter: Anything?

Quentin: It was about 2 kms from the farm yeah? On the fence side?

Hunter: Yeah definitely

Quentin: It's gone

Hunter: What?

Quentin: Yeah my thoughts exactly bro
Hunter: i'll keep my eyes out
Quentin: Thanks bro
That was certainly not what I wanted to hear.
This mystery is turning out to be a lot more in depth than we'd first thought.
It makes me think for a moment, as I spin the wheel to turn the patrol car back to head back to the station.

Is my brother going crazy from being out on the farm alone? Or had there really been a car there?

The appearance of the mystery woman in his farmhouse has to be connected.
There is no way she could have gotten that far out of town without a car in the middle of the night.
Back at the station I'll have to speak to the Sergeant to see if he'd managed to find out anything more about her or maybe I'll just head to the hospital to see Addison and suss things out myself.
Sussing out a good mystery is my favourite part of my job after all and I've certainly missed interacting with females lately, so visiting the hospital with the excuse of it being for work but also getting to see the ever beautiful Addison would make for a perfect day.

(14) Addison

Getting lost in work is my only escape from my stupidity, still not believing that I'd thrown myself at Hunter again.

To be honest I can't believe he'd actually played along, kissing me, teasing me and then rejecting me.

I should have driven off straight away, but a part of me wanted him to come out, to say he was wrong and to invite me back inside, but all did he instead was say sorry for rejecting me and said he wanted to take getting back together slow.

Knowing Hunter as well as I do though, that was a nice way of rejecting me without actually saying it and my heart is literally breaking because it means I have to let go but I don't want anyone else.

I only want Hunter Mackenney.

My phone buzzes in my pocket with a message and thankfully being on my break means I have a chance to read the message.

It's from Jett, my older brother, checking in on me as usual.

Jett: Hey hot shot doc

I laugh at this new nickname for me and quickly tap a reply,

Addison: hey yourself farmer Jett

Jett: lol what's cracking sis?

Addison: Not much

No reply comes after that and I know that means he's going to call instead.

He never was much of a text person as he likes talking and the sound of his own voice a little too much.

His picture flashes on my screen and I slide my finger on across the screen to accept his call.

"Hi Jett," I say trying to sound a little more excited about talking to him than how I actually feel.

"Hey sis. Is something up?" he asks, sensing the off tone in my voice.

"No, why do you say that?"

"Your reply to my text seemed off."

"I'm fine Jett. Just stressed at work," I complain.

"Addi don't lie to me," he says patronisingly.

I let out a sigh, knowing he isn't going to be happy if I tell him I'm trying to get Hunter back.

He'd never really approved of us being together, not liking his impressionable younger sister being with someone so much older than her, but it's not like they are best friends anymore and we are both adults capable of making our own decisions.

"I..um..."

"Addison," he says my name like my Mum calling me when I've done something wrong.

"I did something stupid," I blurt out.

"You're not pregnant are you?"

"No! What would give you that idea?" I say hastily and a little angry, as his tone suggests that he wouldn't be happy if I was pregnant, which kind of hurts a little coming from my brother.

"That would be something you'd think was stupid to do."

"Well, I'm not but I um..." I pause, thinking that there really is no easy way to say what I need to say to anyone, especially my brother, "I um tried to seduce Hunter to get back with him."

He's silent on the phone line, only the sound of his breathing coming through.

I know I shouldn't have told him.

He hates me.

I'm the worst sister ever for going against what he wants for me.

"You did what?" he asks suddenly breaking the silence.

"I threw myself at him and he rejected me Jett ok? Happy?"

"Addison, come on, thats crazy," he shrieks.

"What do you mean?"

"Hunter would take you back any day."

"Yeah, well not now."

Again he's silent and I'm confused at his reaction. He'd reacted as a protective brother and not with anger at me like I thought he would. It makes me realise how much I've missed him.

"Jett, look I gotta go. Could you maybe come visit soon?"

"Yeah Addi, I'll try. Bye," he says.

After he hangs up I slide my phone back in my pocket and try to fight the tears that are stinging my eyes.

There is part of me that is wondering why I'd even come back to Ridgehope now.

My family had long left, heading back to Adelaide to be closer to medical facilities for my Dad and Jett is a three hour drive away in the opposite direction.

It doesn't seem like much of a drive when you think about it, but since moving back and working at the hospital I barely have a day off and when I do I'm so tired I stay in my pyjamas all day binge watching Netflix shows. But honestly I can't kid myself, there is only one reason I came back to Ridgehope and that reason is for Hunter Mackenney.

And that isn't turning out like I'd hoped. It never occurred to me at all that he wouldn't want me back or that someone else would be in his life. I can't completely blame Savannah for that though.

I want it to be all her fault, but it isn't.

Leaving for the city to study medicine, I knew I'd broken Hunter's heart, but there was so much I never got to say as he didn't even say goodbye to me the day I left and it made the bus trip to Adelaide the longest six hour bus trip ever.

I don't think I'd honestly stopped crying the whole time.

Most people think that I'm heartless, and there was gossip on the town grapevine about why me, why would 'Addison Yorke' be studying medicine.

But not many people knew the real me or the real reasons I'd left.

I'd wanted to show Hunter the real me, to know everything and share everything with him but I let him go instead.

It really pained me to think of how things went downhill for him whilst I was gone.

He never told me anything about his Dad's death or his Mum being in the rest home.

It wasn't that I didn't want to know, but Hunter kept things close, never letting anyone in enough to see how he was really feeling.

He locks things that hurt and upset him deep inside and it sometimes makes me wonder what other secrets he keeps.

Since throwing myself at him, even though he'd been in the hospital everyday to see her, I'd not had the chance to speak to him about what happened between us.

Today he's absent from her room and I kind of wish he was there, just so I could see him.

It honestly doesn't make any sense to me about why he seems to be spending every waking minute here in the hospital with her.

She never says a word and he doesn't know her from a bar of soap, as far as I know.

I check her charts and her wound, noting that her stitches are ready to come out and leave without saying anything to her.

There is no point speaking to her when she isn't going to say anything back, but I have to be nice to her, as one of her doctors though.

It doesn't mean I have to like her and I most definitely don't like her, because anyone could see that even though she's not spoken a word there is something between her and Hunter.

And I can see my chances of being with Hunter slipping away.

Again my phone buzzes in my pocket.

I shouldn't check it whilst on duty, but I can't help myself.

I'm happy to find the message is from Hunter.

Hunter: Hi Addison. Didn't see you today. How's Savannah?

Scoffing I think, 'No how are you Addison? Let's talk about the other night?'

He wants to know about her, and I know it's now or never to try and set the rest of my plan to get him back into action.

Hopefully he'll think I'm being sincere in telling him about what happened to her and maybe he'll not see me as heartless anymore.

Addison: Sorry Hunter. Different shift. Savannah is doing a lot better. And I know I shouldn't but I'm going to tell you what happened and what we suspect.

No reply comes so I continue typing another message.

It isn't really making me feel any better though.

Addison: She had a miscarriage. We believe she was about 7 weeks. She also cut her leg in getting to your house. The bruises may have been related to that, but we believe they may be from physical abuse of some kind. Police trying to find out but doesn't help that she doesn't say anything.

He doesn't reply at all, so I leave it at that , slipping my phone back into my pocket to check on other patients and trying not to think about him as I walk around the hospital.

Caz May

Being back in Ridgehope and not being with him or even just talking to him is torture.

I can't help but think that maybe I've made the wrong choice in coming back as it sure feels like it now when he's rejecting me.

My heart knows though it isn't wrong but right.

Ridgehope is home.

(15) Hunter

Addison's text message about Savannah had been eye-opening, giving me some interesting insight into Savannah's past. It hadn't helped my guilt about the gash on her leg though.

I still felt responsible for that, because I am, as I'd not kept up with maintaining the fence.

But what gets to me the most about the message, is the mention of the possibility that she's been physically abused.

It made my heart ache for her and I know it means that maybe she is running away from someone.

It also means that she could be still in danger, and I'm scared for her as well.

I just can't imagine why anyone would want to hurt her.

It's making my protector instinct kick in and all I want is to care for her, to take all pain of her past away.

The only thing I can do now though is go to hospital and try to make her feel safe.

It's practically imperative that she speaks to someone as well. She needs to tell someone the truth about how and why she's ended up in Ridgehope.

Being six hours from the city and not really on the way to anywhere it isn't the place you come to out of the blue.

Despite my text message to Addison the day before making it seem as though I want to see her, I really don't.

She is actually the last person I want to see and entering the hospital I try to be inconspicuous, to hopefully not make it known I'm here again.

The wide hallways and bright lighting feel overbearing today as I practically sprint to Savannah's room, waving a quick hello to the nurses on desk.

I've been in so much lately they don't even get me to sign in anymore.

They know I'm coming in to see Savannah and thankfully haven't asked any questions.

Rounding the hallway near Savannah's room a hand grabs mine causing my body to tense up at the touch.

When looking up I find myself facing Addison and the look in her eyes is foreign.

It makes me feel even more tense.

Trying to snatch my hand away is futile as she has a serious grip on it that makes me feel like a wimp.

Opening a built in door nearby, she giggles as she pulls my arm, dragging me into the room.

Flicking the latch locked, she pushes me against some shelving, and pleadingly says, "Hunter, please."

The way she says my name makes me want to cringe and I want to say please for what, or something along that line but words freeze on my tongue.

I'm not even given a chance to speak actually before she fiercely presses her lips on mine.

Her kiss is demanding and quite frankly weird.

It's an odd way to describe a kiss, but I'd kissed Addison many times before and it had never felt like this kiss.

Initially I respond to the kiss, like any hot blooded male, but when she tries to undress me by placing her hands on the waistband of my jeans, I pull back, pushing my hands against her hips.

"What the actual fuck Addison?" I question.

"I...I missed you," she stammers.

"Well ambushing me in the hospital hallway isn't the best way to show me that."

"I'm sorry Hunter. But you've barely spoken to me since you know."

"Yeah, things have been a little crazy. But seriously Addison, I don't know if I..."

I stop mid sentence knowing she doesn't want to hear what I have to say. I don't want her back and playing along pretending I do is too hard. It makes me feel immoral and I was raised to be better than that.

She's still staring at me, as though pleading me to do something or say something and I have to continue what I was going to say or I know I'll regret it.

"I can't do this Addison. I can't get back together," I declare, feeling a rush of relief, but as soon as the words have left my mouth I feel a pang of guilt, seeing the tears stinging her eyes.

How dare she make me feel guilty?

"Please don't cry Addison. I'm sorry but I don't love you anymore," I inform her, feeling like such an arse when she replies, even though her reply is far from the truth.

"But Hunter, please, we're meant to be together."

"No Addison, we're not. Please just let us go," I demand as I step away from her, reaching to unlock the door.

Again she grabs my hand, pleading, "Hunter please wait."

"What for Addison? Please just let me go. I only came to see Savannah." Shocking me she smiles and says, "I know."

I don't know what to say to her now, feeling completely tongue tied. The silence between us is suffocating and being in the medicine storage room surrounded by shelving doesn't exactly help any claustrophobic feelings from surfacing.

Opening the door to leave, I breathe in deeply, inhaling the bleach smell of the hospital and trying not to cough.

Stepping out I head down the hallway to Savannah's room, hearing Addison's voice follow me, "Hunter, please I need to tell you something first."

Turning back towards her I can see a sense of worry cross Addison's face. Outside Savannah's door peering in I can see she's asleep.

The thought crosses my mind that maybe Addison hasn't told me everything about Savannah's injuries in her text and I have to know.

Addison has stopped in front of me at that point placing her hand reassuringly on my arm.

"You know in my text how I said about the physical abuse?"

"Yeah, is it true?" I ask worriedly.

"We don't know Hunter, but that car was registered to a male so maybe a partner or husband of hers."

Nodding I reply, "I know about the car. Quentin told me. Can we do anything Addison?"

She shakes her head, "You need to talk to the chief Hunter. The partner might be an emergency contact but you know if the patient is conscious we need permission to contact them."

The only response I can manage is an, "ok."

I don't want Savannah to have a partner, or be married.

I want her to be mine and even though I know nothing about her, I desperately want to.

Her arrival has taken me by surprise and I'm completely captivated by her.

Before Addison walks away she speaks again, "And Hunter, when you speak to the chief please don't tell him I told you anything."

"No worries Addison," I say, before reaching out to hug her, noticing that she practically melts against me before she pulls away and smiles at me as she walks away.

It appears that she isn't quite ready to let go of the idea of us yet.

But her response to my friendly hug, even though she melted against me a little seems like she is more open now to be friends than she was before.

She may have been naive at times but she's also smart and she knows me a lot more than some people.

I'm sure she's noticed how I'm feeling about Savannah, because a person would have to be blind to not notice that I'm feeling something for her.

I'm not really certain about what those feelings are, but I know one thing and that is that I want her more than anything.

(16) Herbert

Being the hospital chief isn't always an easy job.

I always found having to make decisions about how to run the hospital to ensure the best interests of the patients in our care a huge burden to deal with.

Not many people ventured into my office, as usually if anyone was in my office news of their family or friends was not pleasant.

And that was exactly how it was last time Hunter Mackenney was in my office.

The last time he'd been in my office was to discuss if turning his father's life support off was the right decision.

It was part of my job, however it never got any easier to discuss bad news and now seeing him in my office only makes me fear the worst.

Looking at the papers on my desk, I think for a minute about who in my hospital Hunter would be barging into my office to discuss, but I'm stumped.

He stands overbearingly by my desk, pressing his palms hard into the wood, as he tries to calm himself before he speaks.

His breathing is laboured and panicky so I wait to give him a moment to collect his thoughts before I speak, "Hunter, how can I help?"

"I...um...came to..." he stammers.

"Take your time, Hunter. Take a seat," I say calmly, gesturing for him to sit in one of the tub chairs in front of my desk.

He sighs deeply, running his hands through his hair before he settles into one of the chairs, taking another deep breath in before he declares, "I came to talk to you about Savannah."

Again I shuffle through the papers on my desk, scanning for any information about a 'Savannah'.

Finding it, I look up at Hunter and his face is wrought with worry.

"What about her?" I ask.

"Well, I..um found out some information about her."

"Oh?"

"You know, her bruises and stuff?"

"Yes, Hunter. But unless you're an emergency contact we can't discuss a patient with you."

"I know that Herbert, but I think; well I've heard that she might be married. Could we contact the husband?"

It's my turn to sigh, as I try to stifle my anger.

I have my suspicions as to how Hunter would have found information out about a hospital patient, and it's unacceptable, but so as to not rock the boat and upset him or my staff I know it's best to let it go.

The best course of action in this case, considering the history I have with the Mackenney family and the odd behaviour Hunter is displaying is to speak to the patient.

"Well, Hunter, considering she is conscious we would need her consent to contact him."

Before I can even think he's out the door almost immediately and I have to sprint to catch up with him in the hallway.

Patting him hard on the back causes him to stop dead outside her door and he speaks to me before he turns the handle to enter.

"She hasn't spoken to anyone Herbert."

"I know Hunter, but we have to try. We need to ask her," I say following him into the room, flicking the light on.

Her eyes flutter open, and she smiles wide seeing that Hunter has entered the room.

There is definitely something going on between them, which definitely worries me considering his barging into my office with information regarding her.

Looking at me on the other side of the bed though, her smile turns to a frown so I nod at Hunter. "Maybe you should ask her," I say, swallowing hard and shuffling my feet on the spot.

He pulls a chair to the side of the bed and takes her hand in his, "Savannah I need to ask you something," he says softly looking down at her.

She nods and squeezes his hand so Hunter continues, "We've found some information out and we'd like to contact your husband, is that ok?"

Time seems to stop, as the horror of the question Hunter has asked hits her.

She turns as white as a ghost and without warning screams out, "NO, NO PLEASE DON'T!"

Hunter is completely stupefied that she'd spoken, looking himself like he's seen a ghost.

He's still clutching her hand and lightly presses a kiss to her forehead.

He doesn't say anything, instead stands up and without even looking back at either of us he leaves the room.

Reassuringly I nod at Savannah before following Hunter, finding him leaning against the wall outside her room, his hands in fists like he's ready to punch someone.

"You ok Hunter?" I ask him in a friendly tone.

"Yeah, but Herbert you heard her."

"Yeah, but..." I start, unsure of what I'm actually going to say, as I've never been in a similar situation before.

"She hasn't said anything the entire time she's been here and now that."

His body tenses up more as he pushes his hand into the wall and grunts in rage.

"We have to respect her wishes Hunter but I'll look into it."

He takes a deep breath to calm himself down, extends a hand to me and shakes mine in thanks.

"Thanks Herbert. Please keep in touch."

"No problems, Hunter. You take care of yourself," I say turning to walk back to my office, leaving him standing by her room.

I'm worried about him, as Hunter Mackenney is almost like a son to me. His father had asked me to look out for him and his reaction to this stranger is definitely of concern.

I don't want to see him get hurt by another woman, like he had been when Addison broke his heart.

It would surely break him more and he doesn't deserve anymore heartbreak.

(17) Savannah

Blurting out my protest at the question of Dante being contacted was far from planned.

Naively I thought changing my name, or at least telling people a different name would make my past go away and that no one would find me.

I feel nothing short of an imbecile to think I could escape in his car.

I really had not thought about all the details when I'd escaped, but being stuck in this hospital bed for weeks, I've gone over and over leaving in my mind and I definitely had not thought some things through.

One being taking Dante's car; I should have hired a car instead but i'd panicked and the keys were there and it had far more petrol than mine did.

Now though I have nothing of my own with me.

No keys to the car, no clothes, no phone or ID.

Not that ID really mattered, as for all these people know I'm Savannah Galison and my ID suggests otherwise. I probably should have just gotten rid of it, to truly become Savannah.

Being released from the hospital is all that matters now though.

I will find a way to get out of this town and continue my escape from Dante.

But just thinking about leaving this town now and in particularly my sweet mystery man, Hunter, is so painful.

I don't want to leave, and face not seeing his gorgeous face again, however I need to.

My stitches have been removed and I'm just waiting for the day when they tell me I'm free to go.

A day has passed since Hunter had come in with the hospital chief to ask if they could contact Dante. He hadn't been back after my protest and it has made me feel really upset.

I want to say goodbye to him, to thank him for being so kind and for making me laugh during the endless days holed up in the hospital bed.

All the same though I'm glad he's not come in, because if he had I don't know if I could actually say goodbye.

The doctors had let me be a little more mobile in the last week or so which was extremely welcome.

Climbing out of the bed to head to the bathroom, a little sleepily I head out of my room and bump into a tall, rather muscular man wearing scrubs.

It isn't the chief but another doctor. He apologises and looks me up and down before he speaks, "Ms Galison?"

I nod.

After my outburst I haven't spoken again.

No words are better in my current situation.

"I'm Doctor Rivnay. I was just coming to see you to work out your discharge papers."

His words make me feel a little giddy.

Smiling, I point towards the bathroom.

"Thats fine. Go ahead. I'll just be in the room checking your charts."

Just as he'd said Doctor Rivnay is in my room when I return from the bathroom.

Hesitantly I sit on the edge of the bed, but there is an odd tension in the room.

He seems friendly enough but I still feel uneasy like he's about to tell me bad news.

"Well, Ms Galison," he begins, "You've certainly been through quite the ordeal."

My only response is a nod; I must not speak or i'll blurt out everything, so I cannot open my mouth.

"So, your leg and bruises have healed nicely and we are happy to discharge you, however..."

He stops talking.

Why does there have to be a however?

I need to get out of this town, like yesterday.

Looking directly at him I smile to assure him I'm listening.

"Without being able to contact someone you know we are a bit hesitant to just discharge you."

I can't help myself. I burst into tears.

This is not happening.

I want to get out of here, the hospital and the town and this new doctor is slashing all hope of that.

I'm a grown woman for fucks sake.

I don't need anyone to hold my hand, but obviously that isn't how it works out in the country or probably anywhere the more I think about it.

"I'm sorry Ms Galison," he apologises, breaking my thoughts, "Is there someone I can contact to come take you home?"

Home.

His words, the mention of home stab at my heart.

Do I even have a home anymore?

Shaking my head causes him to look at me with pity. This is hell, literal hell and I want out, now.

My feet make contact with the floor and without looking back at Doctor Rivnay I rush out the door. If they aren't going to let me go; then I'm going to escape.

Confusingly I run down the hospital hallways, looking for any signs that point to an outside the hospital exit.

'Carpark'; a carpark has never sounded so good.

Rushing up to the automatic sliding doors, I stop a moment, resting my hands on my knees and taking in a few deep breaths to calm myself.

When I feel ready to go I take a step back to make the doors slide open, about to walk out when a familiar figure walks in.

He smiles when he sees me.

Not smiling back I brush past him out the door, but he catches my arm and pulls me back.

"Woah, Savannah, where are you off to so fast?" he asks, even though he knows I'm likely to not answer.

I try to pull away, but his grip on my hand is too strong.

I know the tears have begun dripping down my cheeks and I feel so torn.

Torn between wanting to run away from the pain more and torn between wanting to stay for him; the amazing man gripping my hand tight.

Again I try to pull away, but his grip tightens and before I can protest he pulls my body against his in a firm hug.

I feel his kiss on my hair and can't help but melt into his embrace.

"Please Savannah, come back inside," he says looking at my tear stained face.

There is something in his eyes that gives me hope, that makes my heart skip.

Breaking away from his hug I don't hesitate or try to run when he tugs me back inside the hospital. Doctor Rivnay is standing at the nurses station, speaking to them, flapping his hands about frenziedly.

He turns towards us and sighs in relief.

"Oh thank god," he says exhaling a deep breath.

Hunter extends his other hand to him in greeting.

"Hunter Mackenney, you must be the other new doc in town?"

"Yeah, nice to meet you Hunter. I'm Doctor Zane Rivnay."

Neither man speaks for a minute, both a little tongue tied and not sure of the situation.

Zane looks at me and then down at my hand that Hunter still has a tight grip on.

"So I'm presuming you know Ms Galison then?" he asks Hunter.

"Well, not exactly. She was found unconscious in my farmhouse a month ago and I've been coming in to see her the past few weeks."

Zane nods as Hunter spoke, attentively listening.

I can sense something is ticking over in his mind and I'm not sure if I should be happy or scared.

"We haven't been able to contact any family or a partner for her."

"Yeah I'm aware of that," Hunter replies to the doctor, looking across at me.

"We can't discharge her without knowing her contact details, you know where she will be staying and such."

Hunter nods, giving Zane a look that is like an unspoken connection, as though he can read the doctors mind.

"I'd be happy to have her at the farmhouse with me. Just for a couple of weeks."

"That's not normal protocol Hunter, but..." Zane pauses.

Is he going to say 'yes' to Hunter's offer? More importantly, do I want him to say 'yes' to Hunter's offer?

Encouragingly I squeeze Hunter's hand. I do want to escape this town but to do that I need to get out of the hospital and I get the feeling that this is the only way.

"But I guess in the circumstances we can make an exception," Zane states, nodding his head slightly.

"Great!",Hunter beams, "So do I just sign the papers now?"

"Yeah just fill out the details with Maggie and all good."

"No worries Doctor Rivnay."

Hunter still has a tight grip on my hand.

He leads me up to the counter, letting go of my hand to fill out the paperwork.

Zane turns to walk away.

I could have turned to run again, but Hunter has made me feel safe and for the moment I'm not going anywhere but back to Hunter's farmhouse.

Hunter is being an absolute gentleman.

After signing the discharge papers he spoke to the nurses, buttering them up so he could search through the lost and found to get me some clothes to wear.

He whispered in my ear after I came from the bathroom wearing tracksuit pants that were a little too big for me and an oversized t-shirt that he'd take me shopping for some new clothes sometime.

It could have made me feel like a charity case but something about the way he looked at me wearing the ridiculous clothes made it seem more sincere and gave me the sense that Hunter is extremely genuine, as if I didn't already know that from the past few weeks.

Now sitting across from him in his Ute heading back towards the farm I have to tell myself to breathe.

Partly because just being so close to him does things to my body I don't want to acknowledge and partly because I'm scared.

He seems to be a nice person but I don't know him and I'm about to go to his house to act like I do.

I tug at the car door handle but it's locked.

Jumping out would have been crazy anyway and probably would have sent me straight back to hospital, which is the absolute last place I want to go to.

What I really want though is to get away from the tension between us. There has been some kind of connection between us ever since I'd woken up in the hospital and he was there.

His presence made me feel safe, not to mention a lot of other things that I'm too scared to admit to myself that I'm really feeling, about someone who is essentially a stranger.

We are getting closer to his farm now as he begins to slow the Ute down, pulling up to a gate.

A wave of nausea washes over me looking at the fence of his farm causing my leg to throb, as my thoughts wander back to climbing over it and I inwardly curse myself for not realising the gate was mere metres away from where I climbed over the fence slicing my leg from the knee to my ankle.

Before Hunter climbs out of the Ute he touches my thigh, asking "Are you ok?"

My nod reassures him, even though I'm not ok.

After closing the gate behind us the farmhouse quickly comes into view and I swallow the lump in my throat that surfaces from looking up at his rundown farmhouse.

I'm frozen, scared to go inside the farmhouse, just afraid in general.

Do I really want to go inside?

I can't think anymore about what is happening though as Hunter is at the door of the Ute, holding a hand out to me to help me out.

He slings the bag of found clothes over his shoulder and leads me up the verandah.

We are greeted by a scruffy dog bounding up to us.

He looks at me, cocking his head to the side and eyeing me as though he knows me.

Hunter speaks to him, "Yes Blitz it's her."

Blitz registers acknowledgement at Hunters' words, coming up and nudging my legs.

Bending down to pat him, he greets me with a sloppy, soggy, doggy kiss to the face.

"He must really like you," Hunter says smiling, "not even I get kisses like that."

Blitz happily follows us inside, eagerly wagging his tail and padding down the hallway after us.

Passing the first room the nausea rushes in again. I turn to look in as we past and the déjà vu hits.

I feel for sure that I'm going to have a major panic attack right there when the pain of the events a month ago come rushing back to my mind, but against the small of my back I can feel Hunters hand gently guiding me further down the hallway to another room.

He dumps the bag on the floor and when he speaks my stomach fills with butterflies, "This is your room. As long as you need it to be."

Your room.

Why do those words hit me like a tonne of bricks?

Caz May

Smiling in thanks at him doesn't seem like enough so instead I step closer to him and wrap my arms around his back.

He embraces me back, pulling my body closer to his and I revel in the way his arms around me feel warm and safe.

"Aww Savannah I..." he mutters before freeing me from his arms.

The tension between us is intense. In his dark blue, brown tinted eyes lust is evident.

He hesitates for a moment, like he's maybe going to cut the tension by kissing me, but instead he turns to leave the room, leaving me feeling a little taken aback.

"I'll leave you to freshen up. Bathroom is back down the hall on the right."

I exhale a deep breath, closing the door behind him. Bending down to pick up the bag of clothes I realise Blitz is still in the room.

"Hey Blitz, I'm Savannah," I say out loud, ruffling the fur of his head.

He barks in greeting, making me laugh.

Hunter must have heard him bark as his voice calling Blitz's name is ringing down the hallway.

I sneakily open the door and Blitz slips out, scooting down the hallway.

I'm hoping to slip into the bathroom but find myself stopping in the hallway outside Hunters room firstly and then the other spare room.

It isn't that I want to remember that night but just being there means I can't block it out anymore.

Reality hits me again however when Blitz comes skidding around the corner with a shoe in his mouth, Hunter close behind chasing him.

Blitz is obviously thinking it's game when it clearly isn't a game, as Hunter looks furious but I laugh anyway.

Blitz stops at my feet, dropping the shoe.

Picking it up I hand it to Hunter.

"Thanks," is all he says, with a slight smile on his face.

I find the words of reply are stuck in my throat and it frustrates me as I know I'll have to talk sometime but I'm just not ready to.

Hunter is looking at me like he's expecting a reply that I don't have.

We are so close to each other again that I could hug him again, could kiss him in reply but instead I brush against him as I edge away to head to the bathroom.

My movement isn't quite quick enough though as he pulls my body towards his and lightly touches my cheek, mumbling, "Savannah you have no idea what you do to me, I want to k.."

I panic at his words, feeling my body tense up.

He's going to say he wants to kiss me.

But I can't do that can I?

I can't kiss a stranger.

Mustering as much strength as I can manage I free myself from his embrace and stumble back to the guest room, slamming the door behind me.

(18) Hunter

Watching Savannah walk away from me down the hallway, close to tears from my actions makes me feel absolutely wretched.

The mystery of her past is really getting to me and it hurts my heart to see her upset.

It must have been horrible for her to have to escape from and I'm kicking myself for even thinking about kissing her, let alone actually almost telling her my intention of wanting to kiss her.

The need to be with her is becoming consuming.

There isn't really a minute that goes by that I'm not thinking about her and now having her in my house is going to make the need, the want to be with her even harder to resist.

I'm basically clueless as to whether she's feeling the same about me and her not speaking to me doesn't make it any easier, as it's not like I can just ask her.

After she'd slammed the door of the bedroom behind her, Blitz had retreated to his bed in the kitchen.

Going to lay in my own bed, I try closing my eyes to try to sleep, but the wretched feeling won't leave me.

My mind keeps thinking of Savannah lying in the hospital alone and now she's in my guest room, alone.

I'm sure she's scared, worried what might happen if she opens up to me but I know that if I was in her situation though I wouldn't want to be alone.

I'd not undressed, still in my jeans and flannel shirt, so sliding out of bed I walk down the hall to the guest room. I knock, even though I know she won't answer anyway, a habit of coming to a closed door.

Her sobbing tells me she's still awake.

Slowly opening the door, I find her curled up, clutching the bed covers and sobbing into the pillow. Looking at her breaks my heart.

She's too beautiful to be feeling so wretched.

Kneeling by the bed next to her I wipe the tears from her cheek.

"Savannah, don't cry beautiful. I'm sorry if I upset you."

She shakes her head.

"Please speak to me Savannah."

Again she shakes her head, and takes a sharp breath in through her sobbing.

"Savannah I want to protect you, please."

This time her response is different.

Her hand appears from under the covers, pulling the blanket and doona back before grabbing my hand in hers. It sends a rush of warmth coursing through my body.

"You want me to lay down with you?" I ask, nodding my head a little.

She nods smiling, as I walk around to the other side of the bed to slide in next to her.

Placing a hand across her stomach, hoping she won't flinch or pull away, I pull her body closer to mine. Her breathing is heavy and laboured, as though she has every worry in the world plaguing her.

It feels amazing to have her so close, but I have to control myself, knowing it isn't the time to make a move, no matter how much I want to. I'd already moved too fast for her.

All I can do is be content with just having her close and hold onto the hope that she will open up to me soon.

She needs to trust me, trust that I'm not going to hurt her, like she'd been hurt in the past.

Placing a soft kiss on her hair I close my eyes, trying to slip into sleep. But sleep never seems to come in this bed for some unbeknown reason, so behind my closed eyes I allow my mind to focus on trying to piece together what I knew about her so far.

It all pointed to her escaping from something or someone, a past that makes her withdraw and has left physical scars evident on her body.

I recall Addison telling me she was pregnant and had miscarried and I can't help but wonder if she'd known about the baby before she escaped. It's all so mixed up.

I just want answers.

I want to know her secrets.

She murmurs softly, as though she's trying to say something, but looking down at her in my arms I see her eyes are tightly shut in sleep.

Placing another kiss on her head I take my arm away from her side gently and climb out of the bed, pulling the covers back over her.

She is absolutely beautiful.

Leaving the room I leave the door open, tip toeing down the hallway to grab my phone from the kitchen.

I'd had enough of wondering, I want some answers about her and about her past and there is only one person who can possibly give me some answers, so I quickly dial his number.

I barely say hello when he answers, "Hi...any updates Quent?"

"Well, hello to you to Hunter and no I don't have any updates," he replies with a hint of laughter in his tone.

"Oh, so nothing?" I ask, a little deflated.

"No nothing Hunter. Why are you so keen about this case?" he asks, his tone laced with concern.

"She's staying with me Quent," I admit worried about what my younger brother is going to think.

"Oh," he says shocked

"Yeah and I kinda fucked up."

"What do ya mean?"

"I nearly kissed her Quent. She panicked and ran to the guest room."

"Seriously Hunter."

"I know Quent, but I don't know, I..."

"Hunter I don't know what to say, but maybe take it slow or you know leave her be," he says sounding wiser than his twenty-six years.

"I can't Quentin. I think i'm falling for her," I admit, surprising even myself.

"Hunter come on bro, thats crazy. She hasn't even spoken a word to you."

I sigh, hating to admit to myself that my younger brother is right.

How can I be falling in love with someone I've never spoken to?

"Yeah I guess. Um Quent?"

"Yeah Hunter?"

"Could you investigate the car owner more? I think he might be her husband."

"Yeah sure Hunter, but just lay low bro ok? Give her some space yeah?"

"I will Quent and thanks."

"No worries bro. Goodnight."

After hanging up I cross the kitchen plugging my phone in to charge.

Blitz had woken up when he heard me talking and he gives me one of his signature looks of disgust, like he'd understood what I was saying to Quentin.

"Don't judge me Blitz," I spit at him, feeling a little silly to be angry at my dog.

He lets out a grunt in response closing his eyes when I pat his head before heading back to my room.

It's another night that sleep isn't going to come easy, not from worry about the farm, but from thinking about Savannah and how she's making her way into my heart.

(19) Savannah

Waking up in Hunter's farmhouse is so much more pleasant than the hospital.

Sunlight shines through the windows, warming my body and making me feel so alive.

I feel more at home than I have in a long time, and that thought truly scares me.

I'd thought my home was with Dante, but what he put me through, the scars he left on my body and heart tore me apart and anywhere with him was hell, not a place to call home.

Rubbing my eyes from sleep, I look around the room, noticing the door is ajar. I can't help but smile thinking about Hunter coming in last night to comfort me.

It's blindly obvious that he wants me, from the way he looks at me lustfully, almost longingly. When he lay behind me last night, his body also betrayed him holding me so close.

He wanted to kiss me, I know that, and a part of me wants to kiss him too.

But I can't do that. I can't kiss someone who is practically a stranger. Cheating on Dante, after what he'd done shouldn't be an issue but it is. He's still my husband and I'd made vows to love him for better or worse. This is surely worse, but I'd still made the vows and even though i'd left him behind in Adelaide, my heart is still tangled up with feelings for him.

Banging sounds come drifting down the hallway from the kitchen, signalling that Hunter must be up making breakfast.

Caz May

Stretching my arms above my head to wake up and embrace the morning I put my feet tentatively on the floorboards and prepare to face him.

He's being truly kind to me and I feel underserving.

There has be some way to repay him for all his kindness, the most amazing thing being open to letting me into his home without knowing me at all.

But I want to find a way to repay him that isn't physical, as I'm not prepared to let him or anyone near me in that way.

Out in the kitchen, his back is turned as he cooks bacon and eggs on the stove.

He's humming a song I'm not familiar with and his back is bare, his only clothes are jeans that hang low on his hips.

He isn't wearing a belt like usual and unintentionally I let out a 'ahem' to clear my throat, but instead alert him to my presence in the room.

Turning and seeing me, a smile spreads across his face and his dimples nudge the corners of his mouth.

I gulp, my eyes not able to focus on his face, as him turning towards me shirtless bares his muscular chest.

God, he's gorgeous.

Staring at him, taking in his amazing body, muscular, peppered with dark brown hair makes me breathless. Stifling a whimper I shake the thought away of running my hands across his chest, feeling the muscle beneath my fingers, getting them tangled in the brown hair.

I can't feel this for him, I don't know him but God do I want to.

Catching me staring he grins, waving the spatula in his hand, greeting me, "Good morning beautiful. Hungry?"

I manage to say "mmm", hoping he doesn't realise it isn't actually a response to his question, but a response to his glorious half naked body. Turning back to the stove, he serves up a plate of bacon and eggs to me.

Could he get any more delicious?

He's gorgeous and cooks mean bacon and eggs, like a true domestic well raised gentlemen.

Shovelling a forkful into my mouth, I let it linger in my mouth, chewing slowly before swallowing it down hard and licking my lips.

He's standing next to me, watching me eat, so close I could reach out to touch him.

My eyes dart up to look at him when he asks, "Tastes good huh?"

"Does it ever?" I moan.

Hospital food really did taste like cardboard.

Again I lick my lips, shovelling more food into my mouth.

Hunter has not moved away from the table and is contentedly watching me with a devilish grin on his face.

Having him so close, watching me eat and grinning at me like a cheshire cat is making me feel things I shouldn't.

Needing to put some distance between us, I press a hand against his bare chest to try and push him away, which backfires.

He lets out a deep murmur.

Oh God, that was so hot.

In response I pull my hand back like it's on fire.

The tension between us is electric again, the feeling of warmth rushing through me from that single touch on his bare skin.

Caz May
I want him but it's wrong, isn't it?

Pushing my chair back from the table, I quickly get to my feet, wanting to run straight out of the room, away from him, but after standing up my feet will not move.

He touches my arm gently and the same warmth from before runs through my body.

There are words in my mind that I want to say, but I keep my lips tightly closed as I know once I speak, I won't stop and I can't begin to tell him, not yet.

That lustful longing look is still in his eyes, and it both excites and scares me, worried about what his next move is going to be.

Is he going to try and kiss me again? Do I want him to kiss me?

I don't want to know the answer to that question, so instead I pull him to me in a hug, finding my body melting against him.

I let out a deep sigh and revel in how his arms around me feel safe.

His kiss on my hair is soft and sends my mind again to wondering what kissing him would be like.

I have to stop thinking about kissing him though.

Pulling back from him, I feel the heat rising in my cheeks, just from thinking about kissing him.

I know that if I don't move, he will kiss me and as much as my body wants it, my heart isn't ready to take that step with someone else, even after all the hurt I've experienced.

~ ~

The days in the farmhouse have passed by in a blur and avoiding Hunter after our second almost kiss was easy enough.

Most mornings he was gone before I got up and left me be when he arrived back, as I was often engulfed in a book from the expansive bookshelf in his barely used study.

Some days Blitz went out with him and other days he was left at the house with me.

Those days were my favourite as being alone with a dog, having an animal to confide in had always brought me comfort.

It was the fact you could pour your heart out to them and they didn't talk back, content just to listen cocking an ear to listen as you ruffled their fur.

Blitz is sitting beside me now, watching me as I sip my coffee, waiting to see if I'm going to give him any of the biscuit I'm munching on too.

He can sense my unease too and I find myself talking to him again.

"I'm scared Blitz," I declare looking down at him next to me.

He cocks his head at me, whimpering in response, "Yeah, scared he's going to find me."

His response this time is a bark, "And scared I'm falling too."

He knows who I mean I'm falling for, a hundred percent knows I'm talking about his gorgeous owner. He puts his paw on my knee, showing me his approval of how I'm possibly feeling about Hunter.

I'm already in love with Blitz though and handing him the rest of my biscuit I whisper to him, "I've already fallen for you Blitz."

He devours the biscuit in one swift bite and barks in agreement.

My conversation with Blitz is cut short though when Hunter saunters onto the verandah, looking gorgeous as all hell in dark jeans, that are sitting low on his hips. If that's not enough to make my libido spike, it's paired with a flannel shirt unbuttoned to show just a peek of his muscular chest that's dotted with dark brown hair. I gulp down hard, practically overheating from how gorgeous he is.

Blitz runs straight to him, jumping up his legs to excitedly greet him.

"Hey buddy, how was your day?" he asks him, ruffling the fur on his head.

Blitz barks excitedly, before running back to me and sitting at my feet.

"You like Savannah buddy, huh?"

Blitz puts his paw on my knee again.

Hunter suppresses a laugh at Blitz's behaviour, instead lifts his akubra off his head and runs a hand through his luscious chocolate hair.

He looks incredibly sexy doing that and I find my thoughts wandering to wanting to run my own hands through it.

Stop it Savannah, seriously, you can't think such things

Smiling at me a little cheekily, he walks inside the farmhouse.

I can hear his footsteps stop in the hallway, and his loud voicing of the word *'Gosh'* which shows his approval of what I'd been up to the last couple of days whilst he'd not been home.

During the days when Hunter had been out busy on the farm I'd washed all the curtains and cleaned the farmhouse from top to bottom, until it was sparkling.

It was the least I could do for him, after he'd let me into his home, no questions asked.

He rushes back out to the verandah, leaning on the door frame, "Did you really do all that? For me?"

Come on Savannah, say something, talk to him.

Again, the words are tumbling in my head, but my tongue won't cooperate, stuck to the roof of my mouth.

Instead I nod as if that's enough to express what I want to say to him.

"Oh Savannah, thank you. You honestly have no idea how much I appreciate it," he says so sincerely my heart leaps in my chest.

Show me how much. No don't, oh God please don't.

He bends down to hug me in thanks and in response I stand up to wrap my arms around him further, again melting into his embrace.
I hate admitting to myself that I've missed him being around the last few days, but I have and again the electric tension between us sizzles.
We seem to constantly be caught in these moments together and every time my wall is breaking down little by little.
Without a doubt I will give into Hunter Mackenney, sooner or later.

Caz May

(20) Hunter

Savannah has no idea how much I'd appreciated her cleaning up the farmhouse.

She'd made it feel even more like a home than it honestly had in years and that wasn't just from her cleaning efforts but her presence.

Every day that passes made me want her more and she has no idea the little things she's doing that are driving me wild with longing.

Every time she wraps her arms around me in a hug, melting against me, it takes more and more willpower to not kiss her senseless, to take her pain away and turn it to pleasure.

I want her so much, it feels like it's killing me slowly, softly.

From her busy days, making the farmhouse spotless, she hasn't taken care of herself though and she looks a little ragged, although even with her hair dishevelled and the dirty old clothes she's still incredibly gorgeous.

As a way to thank her, I run her a bath, filled high with lavender scented bubbles.

She hasn't come in from the porch, so popping my head out the door I beckon her inside with a finger. Reluctantly she stands up and I grab her hand to lead her down the hallway to the bathroom.

Gesturing towards the bath I speak, my voice coming out husky, "For you gorgeous as a thank you."

A joyous smile lights up her face, a smile that makes my heart pound in my chest.

I'm not sure if I actually mean to stand there or even if she knows I'm still standing in the doorway but she begins to undress, not quite facing me.

111

Firstly, she puts her fingers in the waistband of her track pants edging them down her legs and I close my eyes for second, knowing I shouldn't be looking at her undressing but I'm not able to help myself from looking either.

Underneath the track pants she slipped down her legs she has on lace underwear that doesn't leave a whole lot to the imagination.

Now realising I'm standing in the doorway she turns to face me, smirking slightly as she starts to lift her t-shirt over her head before clumsily trying to cover herself and shoo me out of the room at the same time.

I'd seen enough to see my fantasies of being with her fulfilled for the next week anyway so shutting the door behind me I head to the kitchen.

I know she'd tried to cover herself as I walk out because underneath the t-shirt she had cheekily not worn a bra.

God I want her so damn much

But I can't take any step at making her mine, at least not yet.

She's still so vulnerable, some bruises and scars still evident on her body from whatever terrible trauma she'd been through.

It pains me to think about how she got them and how much hurt she had endured.

I want to take all the pain away and tell her she would never endure pain like that with me.

Blitz is on his bed when I enter the kitchen and he looks up at me like he knows something is up with me.

It fascinates me how dogs have a way of sensing emotions.

He knows what I'm feeling, and I'm glad he's there to admit it to, as I sure as hell can't tell Savannah yet.

Bending down to pat him, I say the words out loud that I'd been thinking for weeks, "I'm falling in love with her."

It feels good to acknowledge how I'm feeling, but I want to show her how I feel, which I obviously can't do.

Flopping down on the couch with a beer I flick on the TV to try and distract myself from thinking about Savannah naked in my bathtub just down the hall.

There is nothing decent to watch, as usual, so the feeling of my phone buzzing in my pocket is a welcome distraction.

Digging it out I gaze in disbelief at name flashing on my screen.

I really don't want to talk to her but she will keep calling if I don't answer so reluctantly I accept the call, swiping my finger across the screen.

"Hi Addison, what's up?" I ask, trying to sound happy that she's called.

"I spoke to Quentin about Savannah the other day," she declares like it's the biggest news to face the world as we know it.

"And you're telling me this because?"

"I thought you'd like to know that he's trying to find out about her husband."

I scoff.

What she's telling me isn't news to me and it isn't why she called either, only a fool would think that.

"I'm aware of that Addison. You forget Quentin is my brother."

She laughs. "And Hunter, you know she's out of the hospital yeah?"

"Yeah she's staying with me," I say, taking a sip of beer, waiting for her response.

"What? Zane didn't tell me that," She spits down the phone, obviously shocked.

"Yeah long story. So Addison?"

"Yeah?" she says with a hint of guilt in her voice.

"Is that why you really called me?"

She sighs. I'd caught her out.

"No."

I knew it.

"So really why did you call then?" I tease.

"I miss you Hunter. And I can't stop thinking about our kiss in the medicine storage room the other day."

Oh yeah, that horrible kiss that i'd not spent even one minute thinking about it, until she'd brought it up just now I'd literally erased it from my mind.

"Oh right yeah. Um Addison I honestly don't know what you want me to say."

"Oh I don't know Hunter, something. I still fucking love you."

Oh for fucks sake!

I don't need to hear it from her again, the same old excuse of still loving me, as usual she's too late in admitting her feelings.

She could have told me she loved me a year ago instead of refusing my proposal and running away.

I don't answer her.

I have nothing to say to her, nothing she would be happy to hear anyway.

Hanging up the phone I throw it down on the couch beside me, downing the rest of my beer.

The sound of water exiting the bathtub reverberates through the walls and jumping up quickly I throw the beer can in the recycling by the kitchen bench and dash to my bedroom, so Savannah won't see me.

It's going to be another night of no sleep, this time thinking wicked thoughts about Savannah.

(21) *Savannah*

Hunter Mackenney had literally not left my mind for barely a moment since he'd entered my life, or more so since I'd entered his life.
He was incredibly sweet and patient with me and so thoughtful.

Sitting in the bath he ran for me I giggle thinking back to the look he had on his gorgeous face, when I caught him staring at me as I undressed.
Consciously I covered myself but he'd already seen me.
The look on his face gave that away, the devilish dimpled smirk that sent desire rushing through me.
Soaking in the bath is absolute bliss, the water and bubbles have never felt so divine.
I run my hands over my skin, washing away the dirt from my cleaning efforts, but also subconsciously I know I'm washing away the pain of my past.
There's nothing more I want than to open up to Hunter and tell him what I'd left behind.
He's making me feel so vulnerable and I really want to let my guard down, to let him in to help me heal from the emotional damage.
Escaping from Dante I'd built a wall around my heart and tried to move on by making myself someone else, but I hadn't planned on meeting anyone, let alone someone like Hunter who is so genuine.
I know it won't be fair to him if he doesn't know the real me.
I get a feeling he's falling in love with me, as I am falling for him, but until I can open my mouth to tell him my past nothing can happen between

us. He needs to know the person I left behind, not the facade of Savannah Galison.

Climbing out of the bath, I pull the plug to release the water. The sound of the water exiting through the pipes practically shakes the whole farmhouse.

Wrapping a fluffy towel around my body, I step up to the door clutching the door handle listening out to see if Hunter is still up.

A slight crash sound drifts down the hallway, before the shuffling of feet and the bang of a door closing.

It's safe to say he's gone to bed, so wearing only the towel I tip toe down the hall to my room, the guest room.

It doesn't feel right calling it my room.

I don't live here.

I'm a guest in Hunter's home.

In the room I rub the towel over my body to dry my skin, flinching when I press too hard on some of my bruises that haven't quite healed.

Hunter would have seen them and is probably thinking about where I got them from, and where I got the large scar from my breasts to my hips, if he'd seen it in the dim light of the bathroom.

The day I got that scar was one of the most painful of my life to date, other than waking up in the back of my car bleeding from my miscarriage. That was painful for sure but it was what had led me to be in this room and in some ways I'm glad it happened, because it is maybe going to be time for my happy ending.

Slowly I dress in some cotton knickers and a granny nightie.

There wasn't a lot of nice, young clothing choices in the hospital lost and found, most likely because they came from lovely old ladies who had passed on.

Tears are stinging my eyes and I brush them away with my arm, cursing myself for thinking about being happy.

Caz May

How dare I think about happiness?

Dante had always told me that I didn't deserve happiness. To him my sole purpose was to make him happy. The only way I would ever find happiness was to escape and be on my own.

But since stumbling into this house, Hunter's home, I don't want to be on my own.

I want to be with Hunter Mackenney and that is both scary and dangerous, as something gives me the feeling that Dante is coming for me.

He isn't the type to let go without a fight.

(22) Quentin

Shuffling through the papers about Savannah, otherwise known as the mystery woman is useless.

The only thing I have to go on with the case is the registration of the car and the only details that gave me were the make of the car and the owner's name.

A search on him didn't render any results either, so it appears he has no criminal past to speak of.

It makes me wonder though especially after my conversation with Addison a week ago.

~~

Entering the hospital, I try to breath deeply to calm the pounding of my heart.

It's been about a year since I'd seen Addison and I should have hated her for breaking my big brothers heart, but I was still pining after her.

She'd never shown me any affection, no matter how much I flirted with her.

Still, stupidly, I kept chasing her, probably because she was the one girl I couldn't get, even after she broke up with Hunter.

I'd always wondered if she didn't want me because my reputation was one of the heartbreaker, too flirtatious for my own good and not one to settle into a relationship.

But what she didn't know was how I felt about her. I don't think she honestly knew how much I'd always wanted her and that if I had her I'd never look at another girl again. I didn't know whether that knowledge would change her mind about me.

To block out my feelings though I'd pretty much gone after every girl that showed any interest in me, and getting involved in other things I shouldn't have, which essentially hadn't gotten me anywhere, as here I am still single, pining after a girl I've loved since high school.

Stepping up to the nurses desk announcing my presence, the receptionist is a little taken aback, "Hello Maggie."

"Oh, Quentin, hello," she coos at me, her voice a few octaves higher than normal.

"Shocked to see me huh?" I say flirtatiously, before cursing myself.

God, have some dignity Quentin, she could be your mother.

"Well, um the Sergeants already been in, thats all."

"Yeah I'm aware of that Maggie. I'm here to see Addison actually."

"Oh, um I'll page her for you," she says, giving me a knowing wink, that makes me cringe.

Maggie, the old biddy must have a dirty mind.

Admittedly I most certainly do, and sitting down in one of the chairs along the wall whilst waiting for Addison my mind wanders to devilish thoughts about finally making her mine.

My thoughts are interrupted by the click clack of her high heels on the floor.

A smile spreads across my face at the sound. I'd often fantasied about fucking her with just those on and nothing else.

I know she's seen me when she blurts out, "Quentin Mackenney, aren't you a sight for sore eyes."

I stand up from the chair, running my hands through my hair, unsure what to do with them as she's standing directly in front of me.

"Likewise, Addison Yorke."

She giggles, deliciously.

Fuck, she's even more gorgeous than I remembered.

Without thinking I pull her into a hug, inhaling her perfume.

Seriously Quentin, settle down boy

She tenses up, so I let go and pulling away I press a kiss to her cheek.

All she does is stare at me, probably wondering why I'm even here.

It seems as though the chase is still on, hey?

Clearing my throat I bring myself back to reality and she asks, "So Quentin, what brings you in?"

"Just wanted to um, get your thoughts on our mystery woman," I say, a little too quickly.

She shrugs her shoulders, "Not much to tell Quentin. I told the Sergeant everything I know."

She isn't giving me anything, no insight into the case at all and standing so close to her is torture.

"Yeah but what do you think Addison?" I query, trying to butter her up to get her to open up to me.

"Quentin, honestly I don't know. I think maybe domestic violence, but it's not my place to pry."

"Ok, well thanks anyway."

I turn towards the door, she's still standing in the same spot, and calls back to me, "Has Hunter said anything about me?"

"Not exactly, why?"

"Oh no reason, I've just been trying to get him back and he keeps shutting me down."

Sadness is present on her face. It's kind of a relief to know I hadn't put it there but I feel a pang of anger towards my brother because he has.

To reassure her I say, "There are some things even brothers don't talk about Addison."

"Hmm ok, see you later Quentin."

This time I watch her walk away before leaving the hospital.

Maybe it's time to confess to Hunter about my unrequited crush.

~ ~

Granted, I had spoken to Hunter since, but hadn't confessed my feelings for Addison to him.

It seems as though he doesn't care anyway. He's too concerned with the mystery girl now and I'm a little worried about my older brother.

I don't think it wise that she's staying with him, but Hunter never did care what I thought. He'd always had my best interest at heart and was a protective brother, but never listened when someone tried to tell him that what he was doing was wrong.

My feelings are mixed though.

It's jealousy because Addison still wants him and not me and worry because he seems to be falling for Savannah and we know nothing about her.

It just doesn't compute in my head as to why my brother would be going after Savannah, when Addison wants him back.

Admittedly Savannah is beautiful, but she isn't Addison Yorke.

And I want Addison Yorke so damn much.

(23) Hunter

It'd become a nightly ritual when I wasn't out droving, that Savannah and I ate dinner together, one of us at either end of the large dining table that took up most of my farmhouse kitchen.

Oddly I enjoyed watching her eat, seeing her savouring every bite and loving every mouthful.

The feeling of wanting her only made more intense, as she licked her lips in delight as she ate.

Having her in my home for the last week, and not being able to touch her was driving me wild with longing. She seems happy, but I know that something in her past is holding her back from giving into me.

She still seems so scared and vulnerable.

She stands up to take her plate to the sink behind me.

Turning I look straight at her, truly dreading what I have to tell her, as I'm scared that this time when I return she won't be here. I don't know why that thought plagues me, but it does.

Tentatively I speak, "Savannah, I need to talk to you."

A look of worry crosses her face and it makes my heart constrict a little. She still hasn't spoken a word to me, only little mumbles or grunts at times.

"It's ok. Please sit down," I say pulling the chair out next to me.

Hesitantly she sits down, and looking straight at me she reaches out to take my hand in hers.

It's a sweet gesture and it takes me by surprise.

I can tell it's her way of showing me she's ready to listen to whatever I want to talk about, so I continue, "I have to go out droving again. For a few days this time."

Without warning she rips her hand from mine and covers her face with it instead, peering out at me between her fingers.

Tears are threatening to pour down her cheeks.

It certainly isn't the reaction I was expecting. She seems genuinely upset that I have to leave, but I have to wonder is she upset or if she's scared of being alone in my farmhouse.

Or even worse, is she going to run? And is pretending to put on a show for me even though she's happy she could now be free of me?

I gently pull her hands away from her face, wiping the tears away with my thumb.

My hand lingers a little on her cheek.

I don't want to leave her, but I have to.

"Oh Savannah, please don't cry. I'm sorry."

She shocks me when she abruptly stands up and bolts down the hallway.

I stall, not sure if I should follow her or leave her be, feeling so torn between wanting to comfort her but not knowing if she wants my comfort.

But when the sound of her sobbing comes down the hallway it tugs at my heart so much that I want to comfort her like the first night she came back to the farm.

This time though I need more than just a hug.

I slowly edge down the hallway towards the guest room, but stop outside my own room where a shadow catches my eye.

Savannah is lying on my bed, sobbing.

"Savannah?" I ask cautiously standing in the doorway.

She looks up at me with her tear filled eyes with an expression that is too hard to read.

Stepping further into the room, I sit on the bed next to her feet.

She sniffs through her tears, wiping her arm across her cheeks.

Her mouth opens as though she's about to speak, but just as quick she closes it, biting her lip instead.

I need to reassure her that everything will be ok and that I'm going to come back.

"I won't be gone long I promise. You'll be safe here."

Sniffing again she nods, clearly not convinced.

It really breaks my heart seeing her cry. I don't want to see her endure anymore pain, although this is nothing compared to what she's been through, I'm sure of that.

She sits up on the bed next to me then and I pull her to my side, touching her cheek softly.

"You're so beautiful Savannah."

Her arms are suddenly around me in a warm embrace.Holding her close feels so incredibly right and I truly don't want to be anywhere else.

But I want more. I need more.

Pulling back I look into her blue-green eyes intently, "Savannah, please I really want to..." I pause a moment, to try and calm myself, to stop my heart from pounding in my chest but it's futile and I have to tell her now.

"Savannah, I want to kiss you," I declare, feeling like I'm begging her.

But when she edges closer to me, pressing her lips against mine my heart stops a moment before pounding wildly.

Her kiss is soft, her lips taste sweet but it's so much more than just a soft meeting of lips.It's everything i'd hoped it would be and more.

Longingly, I deepen the kiss, wanting to taste more of her, for her to feel how much I want this, to feel how much I want her, all of her.

She lets out an impassioned murmur that drives me utterly wild with hunger for her. Never has a kiss left me feeling so overwhelmed. Reluctantly I break away from her kiss, breathless, and still a little spellbound at how just one kiss has made me feel.

A cheeky grin has taken over her face, that makes me feel even more overwhelmed.

"Savannah that was amazing."

She mumbles an 'mmm' that makes me desperately want to kiss her again and unlike the past few weeks I don't hesitate to pull her closer to me.

Zealously I press my lips on hers again, taking her cheeks between my palms to deepen our kiss more. Warmth rushes through my body and all I can think of is this, of her, of wanting so much more than just to kiss her. Again breathless we break our kiss, but this time I'm speechless, feeling completely tongue tied at how consuming her kiss was.

The look on her face tells me that she has wanted that as much as I did and I'm not planning on it being the last time I kiss her.

~ ~

I'd tried to sleep that night, holding Savannah in my arms after we'd shared the most amazing first kisses but having her close had just made my thoughts wonder to taking more of her for myself.

I want to know everything about her, every curve, every sweet spot and heartbreakingly every scar on her gorgeous body.

She murmurs, half asleep when I roll over to get out of bed at dawn.

"I have to go," I whisper.

Again she mumbles 'mmm',before cuddling the blankets to her chest.

Kissing her forehead softly I whisper to her, "But I really don't want to after last night."

She doesn't respond this time, having drifted back to sleep.

She looks so peaceful and so incredibly beautiful, it makes walking out the door so difficult for the first time in ages.

Grabbing my swag and clothes I load up the Ute to head off. It's going to be a long, hard couple of days alone out in the far paddocks. The farm work has to be done but it's the last thing I want to be doing.

After kissing Savannah I'd have much rather stay in bed entangled in her arms than be out in the freezing morning air.

Blitz is staying back at the farm this time around as it's easier to work the far paddocks with the quad bike and sometimes having him on the back with me was difficult, so it's me alone with my thoughts.

And from the moment I leave the farmhouse until arriving at the far paddock gates there is only one thing on my mind.

Savannah.

God I want her so damn much.

(24) Savannah

Waking up in Hunter's bed I shiver touching the sheets beside me and panicking when he isn't here.

I open my mouth to call out to him, the words on the tip of my tongue, but nothing comes out. I take a deep breath to calm myself and my mind wanders back to the night before, reliving the kisses we'd shared.

Pressing my lips to his was brazen, and even now I can still feel his lips on mine.

The feeling of warmth kissing him had filled with my body with had not left, even waking up without him beside me.

I recall him saying he was leaving, in my half awake state at dawn, and there's another thought in my head.

I'm sure he'd said, *'he wanted me'* but it could have been my imagination, in my dreams of him when he'd left for droving.

About to get out of bed, I sit up, clutching the sheets to my chest firmly when I hear footsteps padding down the hall.There's no one here, there shouldn't be anyone here should there?

In panic I freeze, shutting my eyes tightly to wait until the footsteps stop and they do stop, at the bedroom door.

I can't bring myself to open my eyes, as the footsteps appear to now be coming closer to the bed.

The intruder doesn't make a sound, instead bounds onto the bed and licks my face.

My eyes spring open and I laugh at myself for thinking Blitz was an intruder in the house, "You scared me Blitz."

He lets out a low bark, before putting his head in my lap. "You're not meant to be on the bed you know?"

He lets out a whimper, trying to make me feel sorry for him, and my heart softens. "We won't tell him buddy," I say stroking his head.

I'm not sure why Hunter has left him here, as I'm sure he would have needed him for droving, but nevertheless I'm glad he's by my side for some protection.

He isn't a big dog, but he's most certainly protective of those he cares about and for some reason he's shown a genuine care for me, from the moment I'd followed Hunter onto the porch a few weeks earlier.

His kennel and some toys are out on the verandah and I think back to the night I'd crawled onto the porch bleeding and in pain.

Blitz had not been there, obviously out with Hunter droving that night, but a memory of Hunter's voice in my head from the day after linked things all together.

Blitz had been there when Hunter found me, and for some reason the silly dog loved me.

"How about some breakfast, buddy?" I ask him, even though he can't respond.

He eagerly jumps off the bed and trots towards the kitchen. I follow him, stretching as I yawn and slowly climb out of bed.

My body aches, not from the bed, but because kissing Hunter has awoken something inside me.

Something I'm a little too scared to feel as it reminds me a little of the beginning of my relationship with Dante, when things between us were exciting and new.

He'd made me feel the butterflies too, but with Hunter it's different.

I was petrified to feel those things with Dante, like maybe I'd always known our relationship was toxic, but with Hunter the butterflies in my belly stir something deeper in me and even though I barely know him, I want more from him. I want him, all of the gorgeous Hunter Mackenney.

Out in the kitchen Blitz is hoeing into food like he's never eaten in his life. It makes me laugh out loud, but also floods me with the same feelings I'd had a few nights ago.

The feeling of not being able to deserve happiness. Kissing Hunter had been the first time in so long that I'd felt happiness and I'm beyond terrified it's all going to be taken away, just like in the past.

Quickly making a coffee I revel in the warmth on my hands and sitting down on the couch I try to calm myself, sipping the coffee and inhaling deep breaths.

No matter how uneasy it makes me feel, I know I have to tell Hunter everything.

I need to open up about my past to him if I truly want a future with him. Our kisses have made me yearn to give him all of me.

I just have to find the words.

(25) Hunter

Barely a minute had gone by that I hadn't thought of Savannah whilst I was away.

Her kisses had made me long for her even more. In some ways it had shaken me to the core. I'd never felt such intensity before with anyone. I'd truly loved Addison, but no kiss with her had ever sent the rush of warmth and electricity through my body like kissing Savannah did.

There's no doubt I'm falling in love with her.

But I'm frustrated that she hasn't spoken to me about her past. I know she's afraid to let me in, to expose herself to me but if I'm going to give myself to her completely I need her to trust me.

Without thinking when arriving home, I open the farmhouse doors, tugging off my shoes and putting my akubra on the hat stand, just like always. I'm feeling a little uncomfortable from still being in my dirty clothes so I tug at my tucked in t-shirt lifting it over my head and sighing as I walk into the kitchen, desperate for a coffee.

I don't even make it to the far end of the kitchen to make my coffee, as stopping near the lounge room I see Savannah on the couch, her legs draped over the armrest, engrossed in a book. She looks so happy and absolutely gorgeous.

Sensing I'm in the room she turns to look at me, blushing. There's silence between us and I hate it. I want to talk to her, have her greet me, kiss her 'hello' and have my wicked way with her right there on the couch, but that isn't going to happen, no matter how much I want it to.

Lost in my thoughts I don't even see her get up to come and stand in front of me.

She touches my bare chest, and my whole body tingles with the sensation of her soft fingers on my skin.

The look in her eyes isn't the same as when I'd kissed her and she seems edgy, as though something is wrong.

The only thing that crosses my mind is that she regrets kissing me.

"Savannah," I say, lightly brushing her cheek with my fingers, "do you regret the kisses we shared?"

She flinches, removing the hand she still has on my chest and shrinking back from me. My heart lurches in my chest.

This isn't happening.

I'm ready to give my heart to her and she's throwing it back in my face. I'm nervous to look at her now, but when I do she's looking straight at me shaking her head.

"So you don't regret kissing me?"

Her mouth opens, and then closes again.

"Please Savannah I need to know," I plead with her.

Again she repeats the same action, this time letting out a tiny grunt, that is like slow torture.

I just want her to tell me, use some words to tell me how she feels.

"Fuck Savannah," I say with a hint of anger and want all rolled into one.

There's only way to find out if she did regret our first kisses.

Grabbing her by the waist I pull her closer to me, wanting there to be no space between our bodies. Cupping her cheeks in my palms, I press a fierce hungry kiss to her lips.

She murmurs against my lips and that sound of her telling me she's loving the feel of my lips on hers, makes my body rise to attention.

I need her. I need all of her.

This kiss is wild, more intense than the ones we'd shared before and when she pulls away from me breathless I can't stop myself from confessing, "Savannah I want you so fucking much, please I need you."

She wraps me in a hug, but it isn't enough, kissing her isn't even enough anymore.

Grabbing her hand from around my back, I urge her to touch me, to know what she's doing to me. But feeling the desire in my pants, she snatches her hand back like it's on fire and her mouth opens to say, "I...I..ca.."

And then she's gone, racing down the hallway to the guest room.

Once again I've fucked it up again by moving to fast.

I have to give her some space and make it up to her but I want her so damn much, it hurts.

I let Savannah be, even though it's torture and all I want to do is run down the hallway to the bedroom and kiss her senseless.

If she needs space I'm going to give her that, as it's the least I can do after my crazy lust filled advances.

Honestly I don't know what else I could do, so plonking myself down on the couch I sigh, trying not to think about her like that again.

But I can't stop my thoughts, my head is filled of thoughts of kissing her, of so much more.

I think I need a damn shrink. I need to talk to someone.

That's what I need, a damn conversation with someone else , not a one sided one that has me wanting to bang my head against the wall in frustration.

Digging out my phone from my back pocket I dial my brother, hoping our conversation about Savannah this time won't have him thinking I'm a damn fool.

"Hey big bro. How's things?"

"Fucked Quent."

"Must be for you to swear."

I sigh, knowing that's most certainly true, as I'm not one to swear much at all.

"Hunter?" he queries, when I don't respond.

"Yeah?" I ask.

"Is something wrong? You're being weird."

"Oh god, Quent, she won't fucking say anything."

"Who? Savannah?"

"Who else Quentin?" I say a little angrily.

"Look bro I just think you should forget about her. Get back with Addison."

There's a hint of pain in his voice saying those words to me, that has me a little intrigued.

"That's the last thing I want Quent. I don't want Addison back. I want Savannah."

"Well bro I don't think that's a good choice but hey up to you."

"Yeah not going too well though."

"What ya mean?"

My younger brother is going to think I'm a total idiot and Savannah a cock-tease but what the hell, he wants to know.

"Every time I kiss her and try to take things further she runs off."

Just as I thought he laughs.

"Oh god Hunter. I'm so sorry but seriously that's crazy. Bro you could have Addison back and your chasing after some cock-tease."

There, he said it.

"What's with your sudden fascination with Addison?" I ask, wondering if something had happened between them.

Quentin hesitates before he answers, a different tone in his voice, "I'm in love with her Hunter. Always have been."

"What? That's fucked up, even for you little brother."

Again he laughs. I'm probably not being the most supportive big brother with that reaction but I'm seriously shocked to find out my flirtatious little brother had always wanted my ex-girlfriend.

He could have any woman he'd wanted and he did. But the one woman he actually loved he couldn't have. I can't help but feel sympathy for him.

"Well, you can have her bro," I say trying to be supportive.

"If only Hunter. She wants you."

"Um yeah that ship sailed about a year ago."

"Haha, good one so are you coming to the movie fundraiser tomorrow night?"

"That's tomorrow?"

"Yeah I'm on patrol duty."

"Sure I'll be there."

"Ok big bro, see you then."

He hangs up and I audibly laugh. How is it possible I'd not known he was in love with Addison all this time.

It's a good thing I'd never married her as she probably would have gotten bored with me and run off with him.

It doesn't matter now anyway, he can have her. I hope I have Savannah and to make it up to her for all my stupid advances I'm going to take her out to the movie fundraiser.

I hope it will make her see that she can be a part of my life, because I want her to be more than anything.

(26) *Savannah*

Hunter hadn't come rushing into the room to comfort me like he'd done before and I could have been upset about it, but I'm not.

I'm angry at myself for pushing him away when he confessed how much he wants to be with me.

I need him too, more than I care to admit and so much more than I could possibly show him.

Words are the only way I'm going to be able to communicate with him properly, but every damn time I open my mouth the words get caught on my tongue.

When he'd not come rushing to the bedroom, I sneak down the hallway to hear him talking on the phone about me.

The conversation is muted, only parts of it drifting to my hiding spot in the hallway but what I hear makes me uneasy.

Whoever he's talking to clearly doesn't like me and it doesn't seem like Hunter even defends me.

Does he even want me like he says?

He'd ends the call, saying that, *'he'll be there.'*

It leaves me wondering even more about who he was talking to.

I hope it wasn't her, the obstetrician, as she clearly has a thing for him.

Not that I can blame her.I feel something for Hunter Mackenney too but I just can't figure out what.It's lust, need, hunger and want.

It's all of that and more and sneaking back down the hall to the bedroom I curse myself for pushing him away and not opening my mouth to speak to him.

~ ~

Engrossed in my book I hadn't heard Hunter walking down the hallway, so I'm shocked when he clears his throat, announcing his presence.
Looking up from my book, I find him standing in the doorway with only a towel around his waist. His skin is still dewy from showering and his dark hair wet.

Oh fuck, he's gorgeous! Oh, I can't look at him!

I swallow the lump in my throat, from taking in his naked torso again, wishing I could lick the droplets of water from his bare chest.

Him, naked, well almost, right there in front of me, oh my god, but... Savannah thats just plain dirty

I can't help the blush that rises up my cheeks, can't stop my mouth from gaping and my mind from wandering to stripping him of the towel, but he shakes me back to reality when he speaks, a little too sexily for my overheating body. "Savannah, you can't wear that tonight."
I look down at my outfit, wondering what he means.

Am I supposed to wear nothing like he is? Come on Savannah, say something.

All I manage to let out is, "Huh?"
"We are going out and you need to get dressed."
Again all I can manage is a *'huh.'*

Hunter shrugs, sauntering into the room. A grin crosses my face when the thought of the towel dropping to the floor pops into my head.

Of course it doesn't and he grins back at me when he catches me staring. He has to know how much I want him.

Crawling onto my knees, I edge up the bed to where he's standing by the wardrobe in the corner of the room.

I stretch up to kiss him, but he presses a finger to my lips to stop me.

"Uh-uh, you need to get dressed. Wear something you like from here," he says, opening the wardrobe to show its contents.

I'm taken aback, shocked at why he'd made me sift through the old granny clothes at the hospital, when in this wardrobe there's an array of dresses, blouses and pants.

He steps aside as I eagerly jump off the bed, running my hand along the clothes, giddy, like a kid in a candy shop.

I let out an excited "Eeek." It makes Hunter laugh and press a soft kiss to my lips.

"I'd love to see you wear a dress," he suggests, a hint of that annoying teasing sexiness in his tone.

He leaves the room so I can find an outfit and kicking the door shut behind him I start to look through the dresses. There has to be about ten, in an array of colours and styles, some more elegant and others casual.

I have no idea where we're actually going so the choice of what to wear is a challenge but if Hunter wants me to wear a dress I will.

It needs to be a dress to capture his attention, more so than before, as it appears he'd want me even if I was wearing a potato sack.

The first dress that catches my eye is beige, with an array of colourful butterflies collected at the bottom and scattered over the bodice. The neckline is low, curved and it dipped low in the back. Luckily it also has a bra sewn into the front, as the back is so low it's sure to almost be at my butt.

Stripping from my shorts and t-shirt I step into the dress, tugging it over my hips, before I unclasp my bra, hastily throwing it on the bed to lift the dress over my breasts.

Hunter knocks on the door. "Savannah, are you dressed?"

I open the door, holding the dress at the front with my other hand.

He takes one look at me, words caught in his throat no doubt as he bites his lip and gulps hard, looking down at how low the dress is, grazing my butt.

Seeing I'm having trouble with the zip, his hand is swiftly against the top of my butt, hitching the small zip up. His hand lingers there, causing heat to rise up my spine. He also helps me clasp the hook and eye at the top, before urging me to turn and face him.

"You look absolutely stunning Savannah."

He doesn't look to bad himself.

Ok, that's an absolute understatement.

He looks absolutely devilishly handsome, as usual dressed in his signature look of dark jeans hung low on his hips, although this time they aren't worn at the knees, but crisp and they hug his legs tightly.

They're held up by a tan belt with a ginormous buckle bearing a horse on it. His blue and green check shirt is tucked in and his sleeves rolled up to the elbows, and a few buttons are left undone at the top, exposing some of his chest.

I really want to tell him how hot he looks but there aren't words. He'd be frustrated with me that I can't speak to him as I'm frustrated with myself but I know the time will come soon.

He's already broken down my defences in getting me to kiss him, so speaking to him eventually is inevitable.

Ready to go wherever he wants to take me I take his hand in mine, lacing our fingers together and squeezing his hand tightly as he leads me out the room.

The way he looks at me, not taking his eyes from mine, makes me feel weak at the knees. I'm falling in love with Hunter Mackenney.

Hunter is the perfect gentlemen with a little bit of cheekiness thrown in. Opening the ute door for me, helping me get in he shamelessly smacks my butt. He doesn't see that I noticed him also licking his lips in delight. It makes the butterflies flit even more in my stomach.

Trepidation is definitely rising in my body though as I can't shake the feeling that I'm getting myself in too deep. The feeling that I shouldn't be feeling so happy and that it's all going to come crashing down on me before I know it.

Hunter can clearly sense my unease as he drives into town smiling at me, and comfortingly placing a hand on my thigh.

"Relax, Savannah. It'll be fine."

He's right. I'm just panicking. Everything is going to be fine.

I manage to say softly, "Yeah."

And the smile on his face turns to a wide grin, highlighting his adorable dimples. One simple word is one step closer to actually talking to Hunter about my past.

We stop suddenly outside a large football oval that's abuzz with people everywhere, as though every person from the town and beyond is there. The uneasy feeling surfaces again and I gasp at the prospect of getting out of the ute to be surrounded by a crowd of people.

I can't do this, this is too deep.

Caz May

Hunter is already out of the ute, and opening my door, holding his hand out for me to take.

His smile turns to a frown when he sees how uneasy I'm feeling.

Comfortingly he presses a kiss against my forehead.

"It will be fine Savannah. Just relax."

Taking a deep breath, I nod, taking his hand and stepping out onto the soft dirt.

My heels slip under me causing me to stumble, falling right into Hunter's arms.

He laughs. "Careful, baby, people will think your drunk already."

Getting drunk right now seems like a great idea. It would at the very least make me let my guard down and take away the feeling of the world possibly crashing down on me.

But also getting drunk right now, out in the small town of Ridgehope with Hunter Mackenney would be a very bad idea.

With alcohol in my system there would be no way I'd ever able to resist his charm, especially when he calls me *'baby'*.

(27) Hunter

Driving to the football field I'd found it incredibly difficult to focus on the road ahead, with Savannah sitting in the passenger seat.

It really struck my heart that the dress she chose to wear was my mother's favourite.

Guilt had been plaguing me about visiting my mother more. She needed her son's in her life after Dad's death and I'd not been the best son, not visiting her anywhere near as much as I should have, and not even picking up the phone to call her.

I hadn't planned on introducing her to Savannah just yet, but seeing Savannah in that dress, I know I have to. Selfishly I also hope it might get her to open up, to see how much I want her in my life.

She seems apprehensive as we head into town, like the world is going to swallow her whole.

To comfort her I leave my hand lingering on her thigh as I drive. Part of me wants to pull the car over, and touch her all over, but there isn't time and she isn't ready for that either.

The fundraiser is starting at eight pm when the sun will be setting over the horizon and before then we need to head to the dinner I'd booked, but also pop into see Mum.

I'm a little tentative about introducing Savannah to her when she's hardly speaking to me, but I know it's the right thing to do. Mum had never really loved Addison and she'd never really told me why, but I got the sense it was to do with our family's past connection to the Yorke family.

Arriving at the football oval, helping Savannah out of the car, she trips on her heels in the dirt, falling into my arms.

I'd wanted to kiss her, but could feel the eyes of the town on me so it wasn't the time for PDA's. When she takes my hand I can't help but smile though.

"Follow me gorgeous," I whisper in her ear, leading her towards the main street.

The rest home is just down from the football oval and I love the fact that Ridgehope really is a one street town, that you can walk the whole main street in ten minutes and it's another ten to get to hospital.

Walking with Savannah's hand in mine is making me feel like a teenager again, the feeling of falling hard and fast.

Her guard is breaking down too and she has a sparkle in her blue-green eyes, that gives me the sense that she's starting to trust me.

Stopping in front of the rest home, she looks at me quizzically, wondering why on earth we would be here.

Squeezing her hand I say, "There's someone I want you to meet."

Just as she followed me down the street, she follows me inside the nursing home, not once letting her grip on my hand loose.

When I step up to the desk, she's right beside me, leaning against my side.

"Hunter, my dear, it's been too long. Here to see your Mum?"

"Yeah, it's been too long," I muse, hanging my head in shame.

Savannah encouragingly rubs her other hand up and down my arm.

It sends tingles all through my body.

Pressing a light kiss to her forehead, I say to the receptionist, "I wanted to introduce her to the woman I'm falling in love with."

Both Savannah and the receptionist let out excited giggles, that give me a rush.

"Grace will love that Hunter. Go on through. She's in the same room."

Savannah's smile has not left her face since my bold statement at the desk.

I feel utterly nervous about introducing her to Mum, especially as I haven't been in to see Mum for months and here I am showing up unannounced with a woman wearing her favourite dress.

Hesitantly I knock on her door. Her reply comes immediately, "Its open. Come in."

As soon as I enter, with Savannah behind me, still clutching my hand, Mum's face lights up with the widest grin I've ever seen her exhibit.

"Oh, Hunter, my darling. What are you doing here?"

"I missed you Mum," I tell her pressing a kiss to her cheek, "and I wanted to introduce you to someone."

Touching the small of her back and dropping her hand from mine, I urge Savannah forward.

"Mum I want you to meet Savannah," I pause, not sure if calling her my girlfriend is going to make her run for the hills, but I know it isn't going to when she bends down to kiss my Mum on the cheek.

I continue softly as my Mum's eyes lock onto mine, "My girlfriend, Mum."

"Oh Hunter," she coos, standing up from her wheelchair awkwardly to envelope me in a hug.

"Does this mean you got rid of that awful Addison?"

I laugh, not sure if Mum knew that Addison was even back in town.

"You know that was like a year ago."

She scoffs. "Yes dear, but I heard she's back and after you again."

I grab Savannah's hand, and look across at her. She hasn't run for the hills, she's still here and she looks happy.

"Yes, that's true Mum, but I don't want her back."

"Well, how could you when you are with this beautiful girl," she coos again, looking Savannah up and down.

"Hunter is this my dress?" she asks, touching a hand over Savannah's heart.

"Yes, Mum it is."

"Oh sweetheart," she says a little shocked.

"I felt bad for not coming to see you Mum, so I thought what better time to see you than to introduce you the woman I'm falling in love with, who happened to choose your favourite dress to wear."

Again, she hugs me.

"Don't feel bad darling. It's lovely to meet her and I'm glad to see you happy. It's about time my dresses had a night on the town."

"I'm sure they will now. We have to get to dinner before the fundraiser but it won't be so long next time Mum, ok?"

"No problems, sweetie."

Savannah has started walking towards the door. Mum pulls me back for a moment and whispers in my ear, "She's sweet Hunter but take your time with her. I can tell she's been hurt."

"Thanks Mum. I will."

She presses a kiss to my cheek. "And Hunter dear, you've already fallen for her."

I smile at her, blushing.

How do Mothers always know exactly how you are feeling?

Because she's right, I have already fallen for Savannah.

I'm absolutely head over boots in love with her.

(28) *Savannah*

After leaving from meeting his Mum, Hunter takes me to the only restaurant in town. It to is packed with people. Normally crowds make me anxious, but I feel safe with Hunter by my side.

His Mum is just as amazing as him and I truly understand where he gets his caring nature from.

My heart had swelled, pounding in my chest when he'd called me his 'girlfriend'.

It's all such a whirlwind and from Hunter's words completely unplanned. He wants me to be a part of his life, that's a certainty and more than I care to admit I want it as well.

I truly want to be his girlfriend more than anything but I'm technically still married. Hunter may or may not know this as I'm not really sure how much he's been told about my past and I'd left my wedding rings in my jewellery box when I ran.

Sitting down across from him in a corner booth I shake my head, needing to stop thinking about the past to focus on him and the thoughtful night he's planned.

Sensing my rising anxiety, he takes my hands with his across the table.

"I'm sorry if I scared you back there, but I want you to be my girlfriend Savannah, more than anything."

I beam at him, "I wwwa..." I start to say the words, but as usual they get caught in my throat.

"Its ok, you don't have to tell me Savannah. I know already."

He leans across the table, kissing me softly.

Caz May
God, I really am falling in love with him.

Quite suspiciously, an older woman wearing a name badge that says, 'Squeak' has appeared at our table, like she has been watching us from the moment we'd walked in the door and was waiting for the most inappropriate moment to come over to our table. As soon as her mouth opens I find her rude.

"Well, Hunter Mackenney, it is true."

"Sorry?" he questions her, with a hint of rudeness.

"What everyone's been saying? That your with the likes of the town mystery woman here."

"Yes, I am with Savannah," Hunter says winking at me.

"So thats your name," she squeaks, giving reference to her name badge. Hunter is clearly annoyed at her insolence. He's defensive when he replies, "How about you just take our order and mind your own god damn business."

She goes to open her mouth to reply but only a squeak comes out. Clearly her name badge is right.

"We'll take two of my usual and two coffees," Hunter almost demands. She scribbles on her notepad, squeaks a *'yes, ok'* and turns to head to the kitchen.

I look across at Hunter and we both burst into a fit of laughter. He starts imitating her squeaks causing me to laugh so hard I damn near wet my pants.

It takes me back to the days in the hospital when he was telling me jokes, or funny stories about growing up on the farm.

I'd started to fall for him then, and now I'm falling even harder for him. It's impossible not to.

When our food comes, we eat in silence, trying to not glance at each other so as to not burst into laughter and spit food everywhere.

It isn't an uncomfortable silence though. It's just like the nights at the farmhouse when we'd eaten dinner together.

It didn't matter where I was I felt comfortable in Hunters presence.

Putting down my knife and fork I lick my lips.

The food had been utterly delicious and I hadn't noticed that Hunter had finished. He's watching me as I finish eating before he reaches across the table to touch my cheek, grabbing a stray piece of food from my cheek.

"That was delicious," He says, giving me a wink.

I know he isn't talking about the food, so as to tease him I lick my lips again.

It works.

"Fuck Savannah. Don't you dare tease me like that," he swears, squeezing my thigh under the table. Naughtily I do it again as his gaze locks on mine.

"Oh no you didn't," he jeers, grabbing my hand and pulling me up to rush out the door.

Squeak had come by to clear our table, clearly flustered about our exit. She has her hands on her hips when Hunter calls back as he pushes the door open, "Put it on my tab Squeak."

Outside the door, breathless he grabs me around the waist, his face close to mine and teasingly he says, "You're fucking delicious Savannah and I'm..."

I cut him off by hungrily pressing my lips on his. Clasping his hair between my fingers I deepen the kiss, wanting him as close as possible.

He pulls back, breathless, "Baby as much as I want more, we can't do that here."

"Mmm," I muse in response, but he's right.

The gossip wheel is probably already in full swing about us and we don't need to fuel it with the fire burning between us.

Hunter glances at his watch, realising the movie fundraiser is going to be starting any moment.

"You still want to go to this?"he asks me.

I hesitate. Yes, I still want to enjoy what the rest of the night has in store but there's a small part of me that wants to run back to his Ute, speed back to his farmhouse and see where the fire inside my belly is going to take us. But that fire has me scared.

This is too deep. Meeting his Mum was too deep, making out in the street. I'm in too deep. But when he looks at me like that?

That look is a grin, with his dimples on full display like he's deep in thought.

"The movie baby, yeah?" he asks me again.

Him calling me baby makes the fire burn harder, and I need to use some words this time.

"Yes," I say, as he takes my hand to walk back to the football oval.

The movie has just started to play when we arrived. Hunter excuses himself to go get some popcorn and drinks, telling me wait for him before finding a spot to sit.

My eyes are scanning the grassy oval for the best spot when I hear voices behind me.

'She's certainly pretty,' 'yes but not like dear Addison,' 'I hear she hasn't spoken a word' and 'yes strange choice for Hunter'.

I turn to face the voices, to find three women in their sixties gawking at me and continuing their gossip session.

Their words are making me feel sick in the pit of my stomach. Their eyes are on me, eyeing me as they point at me like I'm a piece of meat.

Where the fuck is Hunter? I need to get out of here.

Tears are stinging my eyes and without thinking I run straight towards the old biddies, to run away from their torture as the sobs come out, the tears then streaming down my cheeks.

Not looking where I'm going I bump into someone. A tall muscular man in a police uniform.

Looking up at him, my eyes scan his face and my recognition is immediate. It's clearly Hunters brother.

"Savannah?" he asks.

Through my sobs I manage to let out a *'yep'*.

I'm really getting somewhere with my one word answers. Baby steps I guess.

He looks over at the old biddies. "These lovely ladies bothering you?"

I shake my head. They are bothering me, yes, but I don't want them to know how much they'd really gotten to me.

Maybe he only said something because it was his job or maybe it was because he was Hunters brother but he raises a hand as if to say stop and firmly says, "How about we leave the young lady alone tonight."

They all back down at his request.

"Oh yes Quentin. We didn't mean any harm."

So that's his name.

"Sure ladies. Go off and have a good night."

I smile at him in thanks.

"So we meet Savannah," he says more as a statement than a question.

He holds out his hand to me. "Quentin Mackenney. Little brother."

Shaking his hand I laugh. I can see that Hunter is heading back towards us, arms full with popcorn and drinks.

Quentin, seeing his brother nudges me and leans down to whisper in my ear, "I hear my brothers got it pretty bad for you."

I gulp. I have it pretty bad too.

Hunter is standing in front of us now and awkwardly hands me a drink before looking at his brother.

"Quent you trying to steal her too?" he jeers.

"No, she's all yours Bro. Just had to scare the old biddy gossip club away. They had her quite upset."

Hunter frowns, kissing my forehead, mouthing *'I'm sorry.'*

Balancing his popcorn against his chest he shakes his brothers hand.

"Thanks little brother."

"No worries. Just doing my job," Quentin replies before he walks off.

"So where are we sitting?" Hunter asks me. I don't have a free hand to point so start to walk to the edge of the oval, near the back.

Hopefully sitting back from the main crowd will mean that not all the eyes of the town will be on us.

Plonking myself on the grass is far from lady like in a dress. Clumsily I fall backwards spilling half my popcorn everywhere. Hunter laughs at me like a hyena, as he sits down beside me.

"You seem to be falling head over heels a lot tonight baby."

There he goes again , calling me baby. Cue fire in belly.

I grunt at him.

"Sorry baby," he muses, pressing a soft kiss to my lips, "Let's watch the movie huh?"

"Hmm," is all I manage, but it's something.

Soon I'll be able to talk to him, I'm sure of it.

Concentrating on the movie when Hunter is sitting next me on the grass is damn difficult. I can feel his eyes burning into me and I want him so damn much.

The fire in my belly has somehow intensified in the last few days, and even more so being out with him in the town.

He's letting me into his life, and as much as I want to let him into mine, I still have the anxious feeling plaguing me.

Trying to tell myself to breathe isn't helping calm my nerves at all as scanning the crowd around us, I shiver feeling as though I'm being watched.

"Are you cold baby?" Hunter asks.

Shaking my head I mutter, *'no'*

"Are you sure baby?" he asks me again. I'm not cold. I'm on edge.

Hunter's arm wraps around me, pulling me closer to him.

"You're so tense baby."

I'm beyond tense. I really want to let my guard down, just like I did at the restaurant, but the feeling of being watched just won't leave.

Hunter presses a kiss to my forehead, touching my cheek before pulling me to his lips in a lingering kiss. "Ok, now baby?"

I need to use words now. I don't need Hunter to see my unease, to think it's to do with him, because it isn't.

It's all me.

Softly I mutter, "I'm ok."

That felt good, baby steps, small words. But untrue words. I'm not ok.

The moment the words leave my mouth I'm not ok, because standing at the edge of the crowd I see *'him.'* The reason for all my anxious feelings, the reason for not opening up to Hunter is here.

Panic stricken, I gasp for air and pain crosses Hunter's face.

"Savannah what's wrong?"

I let out deep sharp breaths, focusing on the in and out, "Not ok," I manage to say through my strained breathing.

He pulls me close to his body in comfort.

"Do you want to go home?"

I pull back from his embrace, finding it hard to hide the fear in my face. Even though I haven't answered him, he helps me up from the grass.

I lean into his body as we stumble back to the ute.

In his gentlemanly manner he helps me in, clicking my seatbelt and shutting the door, before going to his side.

My breathing is still laboured, trying to focus on calming myself I notice that we are already out of the town and on the way back to the farm.

Sensing my obvious still unease, Hunter glances over at me, brushing my cheek with his coarse hand. It sends the tingles coursing through me, but doesn't do much to calm me.

I jump in my seat when Hunter speaks, "You need to talk to me Savannah."

His voice is hard, hinted with anger and I can't help but break down into tears.

Hunter is staring at me, wanting me to speak to him, but all I can say is, "Him."

It came out so meekly I don't even think Hunter heard it, as again he cuts the silence in an angry tone, "Savannah, please fucking talk to me."

I have to say it louder. I have to find my voice.

"I...ss" I stutter, looking across at Hunter.

His face is almost emotionless, but it gives me a sense of comfort and I stutter again, "I s..saw...h...him."

The car has stopped. We are at the farmhouse and like that first night I saw it the relief washes over me.

Hunter hasn't jumped out to open the gate, instead he brushes a finger across my cheek.

"Oh Savannah. Don't cry. You're safe with me."

Am I really? Am I really safe?

I want to be, but if I had truly seem *'him'* I'm far from safe.

(29) Quentin

This is truly the worst part of my job. I absolutely fucking hate patrolling town events.I'd much rather have a beer in hand, and get blind drunk with my mates.
Not all the time, but at least now thats what I need. Hunter hasn't said anything to me about my confession of being in love with Addison and I wasn't sure if that meant I had his blessing to pursue her or if he honestly didn't really care.
Since I'd barged into the hospital to see her, she'd not left my mind.
She had no idea what thoughts of her did to me.

Speak of the fucking devil.

"Hey Quentin," she coos at me as I run my eyes up and down her, loving how her short sundress extenuates her legs, making them seem even longer and the neckline is just low enough to see her cleavage damn near ready to burst over the top.
I can feel an uncomfortable strain in my pants.

God Quentin, get a hold of yourself.

"Hi," I say, running a hand through my hair flirtatiously.

Quentin, what the fuck are you doing? Don't fucking flirt with her while you're on duty.

But I can't help myself. I want her so fucking much.

"Have you seen Hunter?" she asks, causing my insides to constrict in anger.

I want to scream at her, *'yes I've seen my fucking brother. He doesn't fucking want you, like I do.'*

But of course I don't say that. I'm not that stupid.

"Yeah I saw him with Savannah before, but they left about twenty minutes ago."

I almost tell her about the old biddies upsetting Savannah too, but Addison doesn't really need to know that.

She's clearly upset that Hunter had brought Savannah here as it was.

I want to make her forget about my brother, take her back to my house and fuck some sense into her.

It's never going to happen but hey a guy can dream.

Breaking my thoughts she speaks again, "Is he serious about her then?"

Do I tell her? Will it make her maybe give into my advances?

"Yeah I think he's in love with her. I've never seen him like he is with her."

"Oh," is all she manages to say, the pain of my words cutting her deep.

She still loves my brother and I just want her to love me.

It's time to be nice Quentin, not horny I love you but want to get into your pants like right now Quentin.

"I'm sorry Addison."

She scoffs, "For what?"

"I don't know. That he doesn't love you back," I say wanting to finish the sentence with confessing to her how I feel about her.

"It's ok," she muses, looking at me confused.

Oh fuck she's on to me.

"You can't help who you fall in love with."

Damn right Addison, I love you

"Yeah, true."

She stands next to me for a moment in silence. Seeing her in pain, that my fucking brother has caused makes my heart constrict.

If I wasn't working, patrolling this fucking fundraiser I'd kiss her, damn hard.

"Well, um, I gotta go, um catch up with Zane," she stutters.

Maybe she's feeling the same as I am? Hot and damn bothered. Nah i'd have to be my brother for her to feel that way.

"No worries Addison. Enjoy the rest of the night yeah?"

"I will," she says, a little happier and before she walks away she presses a kiss to my cheek. Instantly I feel the heat rise up my face.

Only she could make me blush by just kissing my damn cheek.

In an effort to try and calm myself down I start patrolling the oval, ready to make sure nothing goes down.

Ridgehope is usually a quiet town, just humming along with everyday life, but things like the mystery of Savannah turning up always got the gossip wheels turning.

I have no idea what the old biddies had been saying about Savannah but it really got her upset.

She was clearly unsettled the whole night and they'd left only about twenty minutes into the movie, in a major hurry.

It didn't seem as though they were leaving for dirty reasons at all.

The food stands have started to close up, and the movie is nearing its end. I've stopped at the back of the oval to wait for the credits to roll, when I first see him.

He's wearing dark jeans, a white shirt and a brown leather jacket. He's definitely not a local. His arms are folded and his stare is cold and calculating.

He appears to be looking for someone, but at the same time it's as though he's trying to blend into the crowd instead of standing out like he does.

Instantly the moment the credit start rolling, most of the town begins getting up and leaving the oval.

A few give me nods, and 'heys' as they pass me, but my eyes are locked on him.

He seems to wait until a few people have dispersed before he begins walking away from the oval to the far right, heading in the direction away from town.

Slowly, keeping a safe distance, I follow him. He glances around before he gets into a car that has no registration plates.

He spins the car tyres as he speeds off towards the next town.

I know I should rush back to the patrol car and pursue him, but my head is spinning from my encounter with Addison still, as well as his foreboding presence in my quiet town.

He doesn't seem like a nice guy and yeah, I should be used to dealing with not so nice people in my job but something about him has really gotten to me.

It all seems a bit uncanny, first Savannah turning up, her possible car goes missing and another stranger turns up in town.

These are definitely not any mere coincidences. Without a doubt that strange mystery man is connected to Savannah somehow and if my suspicions are right she's in danger.

That means that my brother is too and I have absolutely no idea what I'm going to do about it.

(30) *Savannah*

As usual Hunter had been his sweet caring, loving self. He hadn't pushed me to talk anymore after my breakdown at the fundraiser.

I desperately wanted to talk him about it more, but I was just being silly, as there wasn't anything else to say about my crazy feelings.

It's stupid even thinking that Dante is here. There is no way Dante is here, in Ridgehope.

It just isn't possible, but still I feel the anxiety though. I feel like I'm not being told everything about what happened to me and I had noticed my car had disappeared but as I was to scared to open my mouth so I'd not asked about anyone about it.

~ ~

The days have just seemed to flow into each other and even though I've had the uneasy feeling plaguing me I push it aside.

I'm just happy to be spending more time with Hunter, like now sitting across from him to drive into town; he's stealing glances at me and his dimpled smile is on his face.

It makes the fire burn in me more. I hadn't been able to tame that fire since it started.

Not even kissing Hunter is enough to quell it, instead kissing him fuels it. After our kiss that night outside the restaurant for the first time I'd wanted to give more of myself, all of myself to him but that was shattered when I thought I saw Dante.

It's that feeling again of not being deserving of happiness and only Dante made me feel that way.

Hunter gives me the feeling that I do deserve happiness and I want it desperately, just like I want him, more than anything.

"Penny for your thoughts, baby?" he asks me, breaking me away from my trance like state.

"Um...I was just.." I stop talking, swallowing hard.

Too many words. Breathe Savannah breathe.

"Just thinking about me huh?" Hunter says in a seductive tone.

Yes I was thinking about you

He lightly touches the skin of my thigh and licks his lips as he gazes across at me.

That has become our new thing, a naughty little signal to each other, hinting that I want to kiss you right now.

I lick my lips back, right as he hurriedly parks in the Main Street. He'd noticed my tease and grabs my cheeks in his palms.

"Oh really Savannah," he murmurs before he crushes his lips to mine.

Every time he kisses me it's all consuming, like he can't get enough of me. Sneakily this time, he licks my lips urging me to open my mouth to taste me more.

The fire is intensifying in my belly and is heading south. I need this and him so much.

Responding to his teasing gesture I open my mouth, licking his tongue and biting down on his lip.

He murmurs in pleasure, pressing his lips harder onto mine before he pulls away breathless.

"Fuck Savannah you sure know how to drive me wild."

So do you Hunter.

He'd jumps out of the Ute and is at my door before I can even think about kissing him again.

I'm kind of glad though as kissing him again with the fire burning lower in my body would not have been a good idea considering where we are.

He takes my hand to help me out and thankfully I don't stumble due to wearing more appropriate footwear. If thongs can be considered appropriate footwear that is.

Pressing a kiss to my forehead as he shuts the door behind me he points to the supermarket a few doors down the street. I grab his hand, not wanting him to leave me alone.

For some strange reason, a feeling per se, I don't want to go into the supermarket on my own, but he squeezes my hand.

"Baby, just go in. I'll meet you there. I just have to go to the farm supplies first. Ok?"

I nod. I'm ok. Nothing is going to happen. It's Ridgehope.

~ ~

Walking into the supermarket I'm greeted by the young checkout operator. I just nod, grabbing a basket as I pass through the entry gate.

It seems stupid having a security feature like that in a small town as it doesn't seem like there would be a lot of theft.

Looking up to read the overhead signs I inhale a deep breath.

Something definitely feels off in here as that feeling of being watched is surfacing again.

I look back towards the checkouts, only to find her reading a magazine, clearly not watching me.

You're just being paranoid Savannah. Take a deep breath. It's just a
supermarket. There's no one watching you.

But there is.

I stop dead. My feet are glued to the floor, the basket falling from my
hands making a loud clatter as it hits the tiles. Surely I'm seeing things.
There is no way he's here. Dante is not here standing in front of me.

He's six hours away in Adelaide isn't he?

I literally cannot move as he's coming towards me, a finger over his lips to
say, *'shh'* .
I open my mouth to scream, but no sound comes out. His arm forcefully
grabs my waist, digging his fingers into my diaphragm making me gasp.
His other hand is over my mouth.
"Don't you even fucking think about screaming Trinity," he breathes
huskily into my ear.
I cringe at him saying my name, my real name. It's like a knife, stabbing
me all over.
"You're going to calmly walk out of here with me, ok?"
I shake my head, trying to say something with his hand still pressed to my
mouth.
"Ok Trinity?" he asks again driving the knife of my old name further in.
"If you don't Trinity you'll regret it." He takes his hand from my mouth.
"Trinity?" The way he says my name is making me feel violently ill.
I have to say, *'no'*. I can't walk out of here calmly, pretending like
everything is ok.
Meekly I protest, "No, Dante, no I can't."
"Don't be a fucking bitch Trinity," he seethes, reaching into his pocket.

In his hand he now has a knife and he presses it hard against my neck. "If you don't play nice, and do as I fucking say I swear Trinity I will slit your fucking throat."

I'm utterly paralysed , completely speechless and absolutely terrified. This isn't the Dante I loved; but it's him and his threat is ringing in my head.

I have to play along or his face will be the last thing I'd ever see and even in death that would haunt me. More calmly he says, "Going to play nice now Trinity?"

"Yes, Dante. I'll do whatever you want," I say softly as he pulls the knife back from my neck, sliding it back into his pocket.

"You look hot baby," he says teasingly grabbing my hand.

Him calling me *'baby'* made my insides tense up, but I have to play along. Slowly he leads me down the aisles, clutching my hand so tight it hurts. Walking past the checkout operator I fake a smile, as Dante drags me out the doors and around the corner.

His grip on my hand makes me wince in pain and now out of view of the Main Street he presses me up against the wall.

"I've missed you Trinity. Why'd you run off on me baby?"

I want to get it all out, to scream at him and make him feel the pain I did. Instead I break from his grip, beating my fists against his chest in anger.

"That ain't gonna work baby. You can't resist me baby."

Yes, I damn well can.

I push him away as forcefully as I can, but trip in my thongs, stumbling to the ground and grazing my knee on the concrete.

Wincing in pain try to get up and run again but he grabs me again by the waist, again pressing me against the wall. His hands are now at my throat gripping my skin so tight it's sure to bruise.

"You can't fucking run from me Trinity, " he seethes at me.

Still clutching my throat he forces his lips on mine. His kiss tastes of whisky and cigarettes, and I have to stop myself from gagging.

I'd kissed him before, and even when I hated every second of it, it had never literally made me feel like vomiting or had taken my breath away in an unpleasant way.

Sensing his rising anger I force myself to respond to his kiss, biting his lips like he always loved. His grip loosens on my neck and he pulls back.

"Thats more like it Trinity."

He's looking at me with hot lust in his eyes. I want to get far away from him and run to find Hunter, but I need to say something.

"Fuck off Dante. Leave me alone," I try to say as menacing as I can.

"Oh baby used a swear word," he taunts back.

I feel anger rising in my chest, pushing my palms into his chest, in an effort to push him away.

"No, Dante, just leave me the fuck alone."

"Not a fucking chance Trinity."

He's at my throat again. I'm terrified he's going to pull out the knife and follow through with his threat.

"You're mine Trinity."

Gasping, I respond, "No Dante I'm not. I love someone else. I'm not yours ."

"Yes, you fucking are."

"No, I'm not!"

"Seriously Trinity I told you not to do this."

His grip loosens again from around my neck, but instead he grips my hand just as tight and whispers in my ear, "If I can't have you Trinity, no one fucking can."

(31) Dante

Seriously I'd always thought Trinity was a stupid bitch but she had really confirmed it with her little stunt, thinking she could fucking run from me and I'd not find her.

I couldn't even believe she'd taken my car; that was seriously beyond moronic.

After I'd made her mine by marrying her like she fucking wanted I'd planted tracking devices in the glove boxes of both our cars. I knew her every fucking move and she had absolutely no idea.

The day after she left, stumbling out to go to work a little hungover I found she'd taken my car because hers had literally no petrol. She didn't need it, the daft bitch.

Where was she even going to go?

Well, apparently six hours away to some shit hole called Ridgehope. God, I'd laughed so fucking hard when the tracking device signalled she stopped for an extended period of time, in a town with hope in the name.

Did she honestly think she was going to find some hope here?

What a fucking imbecile! She was always going to be hopeless and utterly fucking useless, but even so I let her have some time to think I wasn't coming after her, gave her some hope that she'd escaped from me.

To be honest I should have taken the car away a long time ago, when she first resisted me, but I was a fucking half-wit for not thinking of that. She didn't even really need a car but I let her keep it as she seemed attached to it but I think she just didn't want to let go of life before me. Now she thought she could have a life without me, with someone else. Not a fucking chance.

Seeing her with him had made my blood boil and my anger seethe. Little does she fucking know, that now her life is fucking over.

~ ~

Whilst attempting to drag the stupid fucking bitch to the car, she has the audacity to try and get away again.

I seriously want to follow through with my earlier threat to her, right here in the middle of this fucked up little town but I'm not that foolish.

The fucking cop had seen me drive off from the fundraiser as it was.

They'd link the act back to me in a heartbeat, so instead of giving into the anger, I grab a fist of her hair as well, leaning into her so she can feel my breath and words on her face. "Don't you dare fucking run Trinity. You're never gonna run again."

She whimpers. It's the same scared whimper she'd make when I fucked her that drove me dangerously wild.

God I fucking love her

Her whimpering intensifies and she speaks, "Dante, you're hurting me."

"Shut the fuck up, Trinity. Do you hear me?"

She mutters, *'mmm'* and I can't control myself anymore, pressing my body into hers, slamming a kiss on her lips and fucking her mouth with my tongue.

She is mine, forever mine. He better not have fucking touched her more than those sickly sweet kisses he was giving her.

Pulling away from her, she grimaces.
"Didn't like that baby?"
She spits at me.
"Well, I did you feisty bitch."

God her resistance is driving me insane, Maybe I'll have to change my plans, just to have her one last time.

We finally reach the car that I'd parked around the back in a deserted carpark. Grabbing both her hands in a wrist-lock after opening the back passenger door I shove her in the backseat, kicking her delicious arse before slamming the door closed. When in the drivers seat I hold her head down.
"Stay down there, and don't make a fucking sound, Trinity," I threaten, before gunning the engine and speeding out of the carpark.
I'd driven out of this half-arsed excuse of a town a few times in the last week trying to find the perfect place to carry out my plan.
I can't deny I've gotten off on the whole idea, but the thought of having her one last time is only fuelled by her devious resistance of me.
I gun the engine harder when she starts making noises, little whimpers and moans like she's hurting. I couldn't care less about how much pain she's in.
Inflicting pain on her, my little fucking bitch always feels good and turns me on so fucking much.
The scrub all around has started to get more dense, and we're probably a good fifty kilometres away from the town, with not another town or signs of life for kilometres.

"We're here baby," I jeer at her, opening the passenger door and forcefully flipping her body over, slamming her head against the headrest. Stretching over her I kiss her, so damn hard.

"You gonna resist me baby?" I ask her.

She shakes her head.

"Good girl," I tease, yanking down her shorts and lacy underwear.

God, she's fucking beautiful.

"Do you want me Trinity?"

Biting down on her delicious lips she shakes her head. I don't give a fuck what she wants. She has no fucking choice.

"Too bad, I want you. No one else can ever have you like this, Trinity."

I fumble with my belt and fly, finally getting them to cooperate.

I push them to my knees along with my boxers. Grabbing her around the waist, gripping her arse cheeks I slam my throbbing cock into her tight body.

She flinches, gripping the carseat with her hands.

Thrusting harder into her I whisper in her ear, "You don't like me inside you baby?"

Her inviting whimper escapes her lips. She's in pain but it makes me delirious and hot with desire for her.

I take ahold of her hands and force them above her head, slamming my body further into her.

I'll forever remember this feeling, fucking her so hard in my car before I cast her aside like the fucking garbage she is.

Her voice breaks my thoughts and I stop thrusting hard for a moment to hear her.

"Dante, please stop, please."

I scoff. "Not a fucking chance of that happening Trinity. I'm going to rip you apart."

I fucking love how innocent she looks. It reminds me of our first night together, when I'd slammed her so hard taking away her innocence that the bed was soaked red with her blood.

Uncanny it is that now she's far from innocent but she will still bleed. Harder and faster I thrust deeper into her, not giving a fuck about her moaning out, *'No, please stop'*.

It just makes me thrust deeper and harder until I finally come undone, exploding inside her when she bites on her lip trying to hold out from screaming in pain.

Pulling my pants up I climb off her and throw her clothes at her.

"Put these on and get out of the fucking car."

She follows my direction, slipping her knickers and shorts back on and sliding out the door behind her.

I've gone around to the drivers side to unhitch the boot. The sound of it unlocking is thrilling.

She hasn't moved, except for squirming on the spot, obviously aching from my lovemaking.

Again I grab her hands in a wrist-lock and push her towards the back of the car.

Lifting the boot up I grab the jerry can of petrol and the ropes out. Putting the petrol down beside her feet I tie the rope around her hands first, forcing them behind her back.

I force her to sit on the boot frame and tie her feet together as well, pulling the knots extra tight until they're straining against her skin causing it to redden.

"Get in."

"No, Dante, please don't do this," she begs looking down at the jerry can.

"Don't make me fucking gag you too, Trinity."

She follows the direction I've given and lies down in the boot, curled up like a baby.

I press a soft kiss to her forehead and then to her lips before forcefully slamming the boot down, tapping it with my fist.

"Goodbye, Trinity. I hope you go to fucking hell!"

I can hear her whimpering and screaming as I walk off with the petrol can in hand.

I've opened the cap and slowly pour a thin trail from near the boot of the car out into the bush.

This will just look like an accident, and her body will be so burnt they'll never identify her.

Once the petrol is spent, I grab the matches from my pocket, revelling in the sweet hiss as I light a few, throwing them into the dry scrub.

Back at the car, I grab my wallet and the keys, even though I'll never need the keys to the shit box car again.

Locking the doors I press an ear to the boot to find she's silent and soon she'll be forever silent.

Grabbing the petrol can I head back down the road to town a bit. The smoke is starting to drift in the air and the smell of it hitting my nostrils is thrilling.

A few kilometres up the road I flag a truck down, holding the petrol can up. He pulls over, winding down his window as I climb up the step to get in.

"Need a ride mate?"

"Yeah, I've run out of petrol down the road."

"I can take you to the petrol station in Ridgehope if you'd like."

"Yeah, maybe the motel. Might crash there for the night and hitch out tomorrow."

"No worries mate. Get in."

Great, all is going according to plan. Time to get back to Ridgehope and get the fuck out of the shit hole.

I don't say a word to the truckie the whole way into town. He keeps looking back in his mirrors at the increasing fire and I have to try to hide the wicked grin that wants to cross my face.

"Motel," he says, bringing the truck to a sudden halt.

"Thanks mate," I say jumping out, landing on the ground with a hard thud.

I brush the dirt from my jeans, run back to the room I'd been staying in to grab the rest of my stuff. Closing the motel door behind me I don't go to the reception.

I need to make a quick getaway now, as the fire will be taking hold of the scrub.

Quickly I drop the key in the after hours box and pulling my black hoodie over my head I head towards the bus station to buy a ticket back to Adelaide.

The only thought in my mind now is *'Burn baby, burn.'*

(32) *Hunter*

Having finished at the farm supplies store I return to the Ute, lugging one huge bag of dog food over my shoulder whilst trying to push a trolley with some wood, paint and other related supplies to finally fix up the outside of my rundown farmhouse.

Savannah had made the inside so perfect I thought the outside could do with a lick a paint and some new boards to replace the cracked ones.

Throwing the dog food in the back of the ute I look in the window expecting to see Savannah waiting in the passenger seat.

We'd only needed a couple of items from the supermarket and I'd only been gone for about fifteen minutes.

She has to still be in the supermarket. It isn't like she could get lost in Ridgehope.

I can't help but shake the feeling that something is wrong though and that I was crazy for telling her she was safe with me, after she saw him; Him most likely being her ex-husband.

It isn't that I don't believe her but I just can't wrap my head around it.

How would he know where to find her?

With panic rising in my chest I rush to the supermarket, bypassing the security gate and racing through the checkout line instead.

In panic I search the aisles of the small supermarket but she isn't here.

Trying to calm my breathing I rush back up to the checkout line and press my palms into the conveyor belt.

Taking deep breathes in and out I start to ask the checkout chick, "Was there a.."

"Sorry sir? I can't understand you. You need to calm down."

Focus Hunter, breathe, in, out.

"Was there a dark haired woman in here before?" I ask as calmly as I can. The checkout chick thinks hard.

"Seriously how many customers would there have been in the last fifteen minutes?" I scream at her.

She hesitates, scratching her nose. "Um yeah there was. She didn't buy anything though."

"Is that all? She's not fucking here," I seethe at the poor girl, even though it's not her fault.

"Um yeah, I think. I'm sorry."

"So she left? Without buying anything?"

"Yes, sir that's right."

"And?" I ask, not even sure why I said it but sure she isn't tell me something.

"And she left holding hands with a guy. He had dark hair and green eyes I think. Kinda hot looking. She seemed happy walking out with him."

I know my mouth gapes open at her words. What she's telling me doesn't make any sense, but at the same time makes complete sense.

Maybe Savannah had been right and her husband was here.

But why would she willingly leave with him and be happy about doing so?

Hastily I race back to the Ute. The police station is next to the hospital and only a ten minute walk but still I jump in the Ute and reverse out of the Main Street like a bull out of the gates.
I gun the engine fast, pulling up at the police station in record time.
Inside I slam my hands on the desk.
"Gail, I need to speak to Quentin urgently," I demand.
"Regarding what Hunter? Is it a police matter?" she questions me in a patronising tone.
"Yes, Gail it's a fucking police matter."

Stupid old biddy, she should retire.

"Don't you use that language in here Hunter Mackenney."
I'm angry with her. She's wasting my time. I just want to speak to my brother.
"Just buzz him please Gail,"I beg.
"Ok," she says rudely, before pressing a finger to the intercom mic,
"Quentin Mackenney to the desk. Your brother is here."
I start pacing the room, waiting for Quentin to come out.
He takes one look at me when he comes from the office halls and he knows something is wrong.
To stop me from pacing he places his hand on my shoulders, looking me straight in the eyes.
He's direct and professional when he speaks to me.
"Hunter you need to calm down and tell me what's happened."
I run a hand through my hair sighing.
"I don't know Quent. I'd just gone to the farm supplies and.."

Oh how am I going to say this? I feel so god damn guilty.

He directs me to sit down on the hard chairs in the foyer, sitting next to me and rubbing my back.

This isn't exactly a professional thing to do; it's a brotherly thing to do. He gives Gail a scowl for looking at us like Quentin isn't doing his job, because he is. He looks me in the eyes and asks, "So you went to the farm supplies and what Hunter?"

"Savannah..." I stop speaking again.

This is so damn hard. I don't want the words to be true. She could be hurt or worse be dead, because of me.

"What about Savannah?"

You can do this Hunter. Tell him what happened.

"She went to the supermarket and when I went back to go home she wasn't there."

"So maybe she went for a walk or something?" he says trying to calm me.

"No, Quentin she left the supermarket with a man. I asked the checkout girl."

Shock crosses my brothers face and I know that it's bad news. He's about to ask me more when we first hear the siren. The fire truck siren blaring as it tears through the town. It's a sound that always makes everyone tense.

Quentin stands up, and grabs his police radio from his belt, pressing it to listen for an announcement and what we hear shocks me to my core, stabbing me straight in the heart.

'Bushfire Back Ridge Road. Fifty kilometres out. Suspected arson. Car involved.'

I can't hold back the fear that Savannah is involved. Tears are stinging at my eyes.

It's my fault. She's going to die out there because of me. I left her alone for a god damn minute and she's going to die. She can't die without hearing me tell her I love her.

"Hunter I've gotta go out there. Might be a homicide."
I stand up next to him, a little wobbly on my feet.
"I'm coming with you Quentin. What if it's Savannah's car?"
He pushes me back down on the seat, his hands on my shoulders again.
"We both know that's not possible Hunter. And you can't come with me."
He's right. I can't get involved in an emergency situation. Even if the woman I'm in love with is involved.
"Stay here, calm down and I'll let you know the minute I find out anything."
"Ok," is all I manage to say, standing up and pulling him into a hug.
Patting his back I say, "Thanks little bro."
He walks out the door, calling back to me, "No worries Big bro. Just doing my job."

~ ~

There's no point in sitting around waiting for Quentin to call. It's only going to torture myself more. The guilt is plaguing me and it's overwhelming.
Jumping back in the car I head back into the main part of town.
I shouldn't really be driving in the state I'm in but I need to get back to town fast to drown in alcoholic stupor.
If I've lost Savannah because of one idiotic choice I'll never forgive myself.
The anguish that something has happened to her is hard enough to deal with. The thought of her actually being gone is unfathomable.

I've not even told her I love her or made love to her and my world is shattering with the thought of her not being a part of my life.

I find myself inside the pub. Fortunately 'happy hour' hasn't descended yet so it's relatively quiet.

I park myself on a stool and wave at the bartender.

"Mick, whiskey straight up."

He pours it out in a glass, sliding it across at me down the bar.

"You don't look so good Hunter."

"Not feeling so good, Mick."

"Drink up mate. It's on the house."

"Thanks, but I shouldn't."

The look he shoots me then is both concern and wonder. Sculling the whisky in one gulp I slide the glass back down the bar and signal him for another.

Like any good bartender he serves me another whisky. I know getting drunk is a bad idea. It isn't going to take the pain away and it certainly isn't going to take the damn guilt away. Propping my elbows up on the bar, I sigh, my head in my hands.

"You sure you're alright Hunter?" Mike asks.

I nod. "Yeah all good. Just a rough day."

The door creaks open with a person entering. His next words literally tear my heart out for a moment, before it constricts in disgust.

Mike happily says, "Your girl just came in. I'm sure she'll lift ya spirits."

It isn't possible that Savannah is here. It can't be her. She's gone isn't she?

Slowly I turn my head to door and I'm right. Savannah isn't here at all. The person who's entered the pub is Addison. Yes, once my girl and the girl most of the town had thought I'd end up with, but my girl now is Savannah and she's gone.

In disgust I sigh again, as Addison saunters up to the bar. A look of misery crosses her face, mirroring my own face when she looks at me.
Yeah, I know I'm a fucking wreck right now.

"Hunter, what are you doing here?"

"Drinking away my guilt."

She sits down on the stool next to me pulling it a little to close for comfort.

Her legs in her too short and too tight mini skirt are pressing against my thigh. Much to her disappointment having her that close does nothing to my libido.

"Guilt? What did you do Hunter Mackenney?" she says with a flirty tone.

"I lost her."

She has the gall to laugh, throwing her head back to spray her hair around like in those stupid shampoo commercials. It isn't going to work. She's trying to flirt with me when I'm utterly heartbroken.

"Lost who?" she asks as if she honestly has no idea who I'm talking about.

"Savannah. Who else would I be fucking talking about?"

"Oh, maybe it's for the best Hunter," she coos, placing a hand a little to high on my thigh.

I smack it away, shoving my hands into the bar and throwing the stool from under me away in anger.

"Seriously, Addison, seriously."

"What Hunter? Why are you so angry?"

"Because I fucking love her, thats why and she's gone."

She stands up from the stool, grabbing me by the shoulders to try and calm me and lighten the moment.

"What are you saying? Gone?"

I look up at her, her eyes are focused on me and not lust filled like usual.

"Hunter what are you saying?"

"Didn't you hear the sirens before?"

"Yes, but whats that got to do with Savannah?"

"It was for arson with a car involved."

I collapse, falling to my knees on the floor.

This is not happening.

Saying the words out loud makes it real. Addison bends down in front me, balancing on her heels.

"Hunter please, I can't stand seeing you like this."

Her arm wraps around my shoulder and it's nice to see this caring side of her.

Helping me up, she ushers me over to the booths in the corner and slides in across from me.

"Tell me everything. I'm asking as a friend Hunter."

She touches my hands softly and I blurt out everything, just like I had with Quentin.

When I finally shut my mouth, her words are caring. "I'm sure she'll be fine Hunter. She's a strong woman and i'm sure you'll get to tell her you love her."

I smile at her. "I hope so."

"You will," she says standing up. "Look Hunter, I have to go meet Zane but please take care of yourself."

"I will," I promise her, even though I'm not really feeling the sincerity those words imply.

And walking away she stops and looks straight at me, her hair flipping across her shoulders. "And Hunter I'm sorry."

"For what?" I ask.

She doesn't have to apologise. I know what she's saying it for and it makes sense to me. What happened in the past between us was as much my fault as it was hers. I just want to put it in the past now and move on.

"You know what for."

And with that statement she walks to the other side of the bar, sliding into a booth with the new doctor in town. At least it appears like someone is going to get their happy ending.

(33) Savannah

I have never been more terrified in my entire life, locked inside the boot with the smell of petrol and smoke drifting in.

I feel absolutely wretched knowing I've taken my last breaths and that I'm going to die out here in the middle of nowhere.

Time had seemed to stop after I'd heard Dante's voice telling me to go to hell.

Those words were knives stabbing me repeatedly all over my body, everywhere he'd inflicted pain on me.

The pain now in my body is engulfing me, threatening to pull me under, for each breath to be my last.

But I don't want that.

Even though Dante is still out there I want to live.

I don't want Dante to be the last person I remember, the torture he inflicted on me to be my last memory.

I don't want to die out here remembering the feel of his torturous kisses or worse the way he'd...

I can't even bring myself to remember it, even though my body is throbbing in pain because of his depravity.

I try to focus on remembering my last kiss with Hunter, the giddy feeling it gave me, the rush and warmth being with him gave me.

I try to think about what seeing him again would be like, and how he would react when I tell him I love him.

I have to tell him my past and I have to tell him what Dante had done.

Still, after all this I want to be with Hunter, and give him all of me.

Yes, I'd need time to heal, but I still want it more than anything.

Caz May

I cannot let my eyes close, I cannot give into the pain.
The pain that is so overpowering.
I could just close my eyes and it would be all over.
But in the distance I hear sirens, getting closer and closer.
I have to hold on.

(34) Quentin

Arriving at the scene of the fire my heart is pounding in my chest.

This shouldn't have happened as there's absolutely no doubt in my mind about who started this fire.

I should have gone after him the night of the fundraiser, I know that now without a doubt and I'm cursing myself for not doing that.

If my unwise, moronic decision has caused Savannah to die, there would be no way I'd ever forgive myself. Hunter would fucking kill me.

Thankfully though, the fire hasn't reached the car, like the emergency call out suggested.

Pulling up next to it, by the fire truck, I slide out of the car. The smell of smoke and petrol fills the air, thick and assaulting to breathe in.

The flames are licking the bush, only a mere five hundred metres from the car. The only thing stopping the petrol from igniting further is the density of the undergrowth and fallen leaf debris.

It had been an incredibly dry summer and this was fire fuel.

Seeing my arrival the chief firefighter, my mate Hugh rushes over to me.

"Hey Quentin," he says with a hint of relief in his tone.

"Hey Hugh, whats the details?"

"Definitely arson. Appears to have been started about two kilometres down the road."

"Surprising it hasn't reached the car yet then."

He runs a hand through his hair, sighing. "You have no idea Quentin. We rushed out here almost immediately when we got the call from a truckie passing through."

This whole thing is sounding more and more suspicious.

"Truckie?" I ask, not really sure how to phrase what I want to ask.

"Yeah, he said he could smell the smoke and could see the fire, so called it in."

I put an arm on his. "Hugh, is there anything else? Do you know anything about the car?"

"Nah, mate, I don't know how the car is involved but he did say something else to dispatch."

"Yeah, possibly about the arsonist?"

"Yeah, he picked up a guy with a petrol can a few kilometres after he saw the fire."

"Did he give a description?"

"I don't know Quentin. Dispatch didn't fill me in on all the details. Just said to head out."

"Thanks, mate."

I don't need a description to know who the arsonist is. And I feel so incredibly guilty. I've failed at my job.

I've let my brother down and possibly caused the woman he's in love with to be gone from his life.

He doesn't need that. He's always taken guilt so hard.

Needing to check out the car, I grab some supplies from the patrol car for fingerprinting and collection of any other evidence.

Slowly I begin dusting the door handles for prints which come up instantly. I'm going to make this right. With a tissue in hand I try to open the door, but it's locked.

Peering inside I can see what appears to be bodily fluids on the backseat, blood and semen. I cringe, my heart constricting in my chest. I know what that means.

When I'm about to call out to Hugh to open the doors for me is when I first hear the banging and muffled almost screams.

It's coming from the boot and I put my ear over the boot to hear it better. It's a woman and I know it has to be Savannah.

I call out to Hugh, "Hugh, man, come over here. I think there's someone in the boot."

He's at the car straight away, listening intently.

"Fuck mate. I think you're right. I'll grab the lock kit and a crowbar."

Panic is rising in me.

If it's Savannah in the boot, how long has she been in there? What had he done to her?

In what feels like mere seconds Hugh is back with the equipment, getting to work skilfully and in a damn hurry. He picks at the lock, but it won't budge.

So instead, he edges the crowbar under the lip of the boot and yanks hard. The metal bends back and he wraps the crowbar around the lock to pull it out. It doesn't work and he sighs in frustration.

"Man, I'm gonna need the jaws for this."

The next five minutes are an absolute blur. Hugh had returned with the jaws of life, prying the boot open and cutting the lock. I could hear her whimpering in fear. I wanted to comfort her but I didn't know what words she needed to hear. The minute the lock was cut, the boot springs up and my eyes can't focus on what I see. The image of Savannah in that car boot will stay with me forever.

There's no way in hell I'm going to tell Hunter how she looked when I found her. It would damn near break his heart.

After helping her sit up on the edge of the boot, I untie the knots from her hands and feet.

They had been so tight, they'd left marks on her skin and her legs are bleeding.

"Savannah, it's going to be ok," I soothe.

She doesn't say anything, but stumbles forward pulling me into a hug.

I wrap my arms around her too. I know it isn't professional, but fuck it. My brother loves this woman and that means professional or not I need to be here for her.

When she pulls away from the hug a couple of minutes later, she softly mutters, "Thank you. I was so scared."

"It's my job Savannah. But you were damn lucky that fire didn't take hold and the firies got out here so quick."

Her face is emotionless, her whole body shaking. I can't even begin to understand what she'd gone through.

Hugh had gone back over to the other firefighters to see what was happening.

Again I call out to him, "Hugh man, hows it's going with the fire?"

"All clear man. Fucking lucky."

"Damn right, could we get some medical assistance for her?"

"Yeah no worries," he replies, before grabbing a first aid kit from the fire truck.

Returning to Savannah, he cleans up the rope wounds and bandages her ankles up. She writhes at the pain, still shaking in terror.

"Are you bleeding anywhere else?" Hugh asks her softly.

She nods but she doesn't need to tell us with words. It's written all over her face and from what I'd seen on the back seat I know anyway without her having to use words to tell me.

"Was an ambulance dispatched Hugh?"

"Nah, didn't know any people were involved."

"No worries. I'll take her in the patrol car."

"No worries mate. See you back in town."

Carefully I help Savannah walk to the patrol car, letting her lean on my shoulder with my arm around her waist for support. Every step putting pressure on her ankles she sniffles trying to hold back the tears from the pain. I help her slide into the front seat, picking up her legs gently before closing the door.

My heart is truly aching for her.

The whole way back into town she sobs. It's my job to ask what had happened but it's clear she's in no condition to do so. Nothing like this has ever happened in Ridgehope and I'm completely in the dark about how to be professional about it, but also show genuine care.

I look across at her and say, "It's going to be ok Savannah, I promise."

I can only hope that I'm not making a promise I can't keep.

(35) *Hunter*

I'd stumbled out the pub about an hour after my talk with Addison, having had a few to many whisky's. I needed to sober up so as to get back home and collapse in bed, to wallow in my sorrow from losing the woman I love.

It seems like the world is against me and I'm going to be doomed to be with Addison, in a loveless relationship, at least from my side.

The song that was playing in the pub, *'You are the reason,'* keeps repeating in my head.

Savannah had become my reason for living, for breathing and she's gone. Other than her there's only one person I need to see right now and punching myself in the stomach, in an attempt to sober up I slowly walk to the rest home.

The doors open and Maggie at the desk gasps in shock when she sees me.

"Hunter, you look terrible. Is something wrong?"

"I just need to see Mum," I say, trying not to slur the words.

"Visiting hours are over honey."

"Please Maggie. I need to see her."

"Hunter I'm sorry we can't allow that."

No! I need to see her. I'm quite literally dying here.

"You don't understand Maggie, I'm dying. I need to see my mum."

She looks at me concerned. Probably wondering if I'm really dying. I know I'm not but the pain is real and my heart is constricted for sure.

"Ok, Hunter. Go on through but don't tell anyone I let you in."

I bolt down the hallway to my Mum's room, knocking violently until she meekly says, *'come in'* and when she looks at me as I open the door the pain on her face breaks my heart even more.

"Hunter sweetie, whats wrong?"

"Savannah."

"What about your dear girlfriend sweetie?"

Hearing her say, *'girlfriend'* literally yanks at my heart.I clutch my chest and fall on my knees in front my Mum's feet.

I'm not much of a cryer normally but the tears that had been threatening to fall for hours break through and I'm sobbing into my Mum's knees.

She kisses my hair and lifts my head up to look at her. "Hunter my dear boy. This doesn't seem like a mere breakup."

I shake my head, wiping the tears away with my sleeve.

"She's gone Mum."

"I don't understand what you mean Hunter."

I have to break through the grief and tell her.

"You know the fundraiser night, when I brought her to see you?"

"Yes, dear, did something happen then?"

"No, not really but she freaked out because she thought she saw her ex-husband in the crowd."

Mum nods, so I continue, "Turns out she did, as he came to get her in the Supermarket earlier."

"So she's gone back to him?"

I shake my head, the tears threatening to break through again. "

No Mum. Did you hear the fire truck sirens earlier?"

"Yes, dear, no doubt a bushfire."

"Yes, Mum a bushfire lit by him. He killed her Mum."

God, those words hurt like a bitch, more than that, there are no words.

The shock that crosses my Mum's face is indescribable. She pulls me closer to her, rubbing my hair to try and soothe the pain.

Abruptly she stops and asks, "Sweetie are you sure he?"

She can't bring herself to say the word *'killed'*. We both know the shock of that word in our family but I don't want to think about that now. Her words hit me though and I shake my head. I don't know if Savannah is gone. I just presumed and I've not heard anything from Quentin so maybe it's a case of no news is good news.

Soothingly my Mum says, "Well honey get out of here and go find out. And tell her you love her."

~ ~

In obvious no condition to drive and to clear my head I run towards the police station, scanning my surroundings as I run. In what I first think has to be the most cruel but amazing mirage a police patrol car is driving into town, driven by my brother with Savannah in the passenger seat.

I have to be dreaming and if I'm dreaming, then running out in front of the car would be a good decision, not a damn stupid one.

So I do it.

I run out onto the street, waiting and hoping for Quentin to realise it's me who's running out in front of the car, waving my hands in panic.

He screeches the car to a stop, mere centimetres from my feet.

"What the fuck Hunter?" he curses at me through the open window.

"Why didn't you call me and tell me, Quentin?"

"Because I had to make sure she was alright first. I'm taking her to the damn hospital."

He isn't going to tell me this time that I'm not allowed to go with him; he'd have a better chance of seeing pigs fly.

Walking to the passenger side I yank the door open.

"This time I'm damn well coming with you."

"Just get in before I say no," he squawks at me.

I slide into the back seat and my heart lurches seeing how much pain Savannah is in. She turns to look back at me, and smiles through the pain. I lean forward, lightly caressing her cheek.

"Oh Savannah, I'm so sorry."

She presses a kiss against my hand taking me by complete surprise when she speaks, "It's ok."

It isn't ok. It's far from ok.

I don't even want to think about what he might have done to her for her to be in so much pain.

"It's not ok Savannah. You're obviously in pain baby."

She doesn't take her eyes off me the whole few minutes drive to the hospital, the pain and trauma evident in them.

Quentin cuts the engine when we arrive, and we are both at her door helping her out of the car to take her inside.

She leans on our shoulders between us, writhing in pain with each step on her badly bruised and cut ankles.

My heart is breaking for her.

I sit with her in the waiting area whilst Quentin fills the emergency nurse in on the details.

I can't really hear much of their conversation, but one word sticks out and it cuts me deep inside.

'Rape'. How could he have done something so vile to her?

I pull her against my body and kiss the side of her head. I really want to tell her *'I love her'* just like my Mum had said to, but it isn't the right time.

A nurse comes up to us, bending down in front of us.

"Savannah, we're going to admit you, just to check your wounds and do some tests for the police. Is that ok?"

She nods a *'yes'* and squeezes my hand that I hadn't realised she'd taken in hers.

Helping her up I lead her to the exam bed, lifting her up by the waist and setting her down on it.

The nurse comes in, handing her a gown to put on. She grabs my hand again when the nurse asks if she needs help.

"I'll just be outside the curtain baby. Let the nurse help you."

Waiting outside the curtain is torture, as all I can hear is her sobbing from the pain and I just want to take it away, by wishing I could turn back the clock on today and start it over.

I would have gone with her into the supermarket and taken the low life down, but as much as I want to I can't change what has happened.

I just need to be there for her, to love her.

The nurse comes out addressing me sternly, "She's in a lot of pain. The doctor will be here in a moment."

"Thanks," I say slipping back behind the curtain. Seeing her back in a hospital bed again breaks my heart into pieces.

Again a part of me feels guilt for putting her there but I know that it isn't really my fault.

It's the fault only of the low life she calls her *'husband'*, an absolute tool I don't know, but who's obviously not worthy of being called a *'husband'* to anyone let alone someone as beautiful as Savannah.

At the bed next to her I take her hand lifting it and pressing a kiss to it.

God, I want to tell her I love her so much.

(36) Savannah

Doctor Rivnay appears around the curtain with a look of concern on his face. Hunter had been so sweet, but I could tell he was heartbroken for me and that he heard Quentin say words to the nurse that he didn't want to hear.

I have no idea how I'm going to begin telling him what Dante had done to me, but I have to. The way he's looking at me makes it clear how he feels about me and I know I feel the same about him but after what I've just been through it's going to be incredibly difficult to express it to him like he needs me too.

Part of me wants to run again, to escape from the hurt I'd experienced in Ridgehope, but it's only because I'd see the pain every time I step foot in the supermarket or every time I went to the to oval.

It would surround me, but more than ever I need to brave and overcome the fear and pain.

Granted I'm also torn between wanting to let Hunter in and wanting to run.

After what I'd been through, I should be traumatised, barely able to function, move or speak, but I've been through it all before.

Dante taking me for himself, tying me up as he forced himself on me, not caring how much pain he inflicted.

The only thing that was different this time was being in the boot of the car, able to smell the smoke and hear the hiss of fire looming.

I was terrified for my life, feeling as though the scars and pain would never leave, but at the same time I knew the moment Quentin found me in the boot, the way he looked at me with genuine concern that being in Ridgehope with Hunter is where I'm supposed to be.

He makes the pain fade away just with one look at me, that shows me how much he loves me.

The trauma of the day is coursing through my body, the physical pain almost unbearable, but I'd learnt to block out how Dante had made me feel.

I wouldn't have been able to get through a day if I focused on everything Dante put me through, both physically and mentally, not only this day but all of the days before I left.

Lying in the car boot, terrified for my life, I'd thought back to all the good times I shared with Dante; the first time I'd seen him in the bookshop, our first kiss that was so sweet and how he never seemed to pressure me at first.

I thought back to how everything suddenly changed the first time he hit me, the slap across my cheek for embarrassing him in front of his friends. Maybe I should have run then, and saved myself from the pain.

But then I wouldn't be here, I wouldn't have found Hunter, the man who makes me feel like I could love again, who could take all the pain and trauma of my past and today away with just one look into my eyes.

Doctor Rivnay is speaking and I have to focus on his words, even though my head is spinning with thoughts of the past.

"Savannah we need to take a swab for DNA testing."

I gasp, looking back towards Hunter.

"Let the doctors do what they need to baby."

Him calling me *'baby'* makes me feel better, it doesn't cut deep like when Dante said it.

Hunter's tone is caring, loving and makes me feel like his arms are around me.

"No!" I scream out, realising what that means.

"Savannah, it's important we do this," Doctor Rivnay points out.

Violently I shake my head, screaming out, "No! I know who it was. What he did!"

Doctor Rivnay appears shocked, "Oh so you can identify the perpetrator?"

This is going to be incredibly difficult. I hate how he makes it seem like it isn't a big deal, and the word perpetrator is so clinical.

Saying the words I need to are made even more difficult with Hunter sitting beside me still clutching my hand.

"Yes, it was my husband Dante Haslett."

Saying husband, saying his name makes my heart constrict in pain. The expression on Doctor Rivnay's face changes to concern again when he speaks, "I'm so sorry, Savannah. I'll get the nurse to check the wounds on your ankles and we will let you go with Mr Mackenney. Is that ok?"

I nod a yes as I would have done anything to get out of the hospital again, except take the swab test for the police.

Doctor Rivnay starts to slide the curtain back. "You will need to give an official statement about what happened but maybe tomorrow. Speak to Constable Mackenney."

Hunter squeezes my hand.

"Oh Savannah, I can't believe he did that to you. I'm so fucking angry at myself."

"Don't be. It's not your fault. I don't want to think about it."

"I know baby. Are you sure you're ok?"

"I can't say it doesn't hurt like hell, and yes I was terrified, but..." I pause sighing deeply.

"Oh baby, I can't stand seeing you like this. How can you block out the pain?"

"Because I have to Hunter. I couldn't even breathe if I didn't block out everything from today or the past years."

"How are you so strong in the face of something so traumatic?"

"Because I learnt to be. And in that car boot I blocked out the pain and thought about seeing you again. It was the only thing that made me hold on until Quentin found me."

He presses a kiss to my forehead, about to say something else when the nurse comes back in. She doesn't say anything, just looks at me with genuine concern on her face as she dresses my ankles properly with tight bandages. The cuts are not deep enough for stitches but truly hurt like knives have been dragged across my skin.

She hands me some clothes to wear, grabbing my discarded clothes from the floor and putting them in a plastic bag. I know what they were taking them for and feel glad there's another way to test for DNA than swabbing me when I'm clearly bleeding and in obvious pain.

I wave Hunter out of the room for the nurse to help me dress.

"Ms, I think i'm bleeding, could I have some pads?"

"Did the doctor not check for bleeding?"

"No, I didn't want him to."

"No worries, lovely. I understand, this must be very traumatic."

"Yeah," I say softly, as she turns to the drawers on the other side of the room, handing me a packet of pads.

"Take them all sweetie. And please look after yourself. Hunter will take care of you, so let him in."

I smile at the nurses sweet statement. I have no doubts that Hunter will look after me. He's the complete opposite of Dante, and has a bit of a protector instinct that makes me feel safe with him.

The nurse helps me dress, holding me up as I stand on my aching ankles. She helps me slip some new underwear on, sticking a pad onto it, before I slide the knickers up my legs.

I'm definitely bleeding, and it seems a lot heavier than I would have thought given that I'd never bled any other time Dante had his way no matter how forceful he was. I shake the thoughts away when Hunter returns after I've dressed with a wheelchair for me.

I don't deserve him. Why does he love me?

It had felt so good to talk to him. It was the only good to thing to come out of the whole ordeal.

He helps me into the wheelchair and we proceed out to the nurse station for discharge. I watch him as he signs the papers and the nurse hands him a jar of painkillers. Her instructions to him sound like mumbling and without realising I'm doing it I press a hand to my forehead to quell the pain of the headache that has surfaced.

I really just want to go back to Hunters and collapse in his bed.

I feel safe there.

~ ~

Even though I'd just spoken to Hunter and now want to tell him everything I don't have the words.

The silence in the ute on the way back to his farmhouse could have been stifling, but at the same time it isn't.

Being in Hunter's presence makes me feel protected and I don't really want to think about the what if's, but I can't help but let my mind wander to them.

What if had Hunter been in the supermarket with me? What if Quentin didn't come to rescue me?

I shake my head to shake away the thoughts. It's all too much to think about, making tears sting my eyes. The pain is overwhelming me, my ankles throbbing, cramps in my belly and the feeling as though blood is gushing out even though I know it isn't.

Sensing I'm lost in my own world, Hunter comfortingly places a hand on my thigh and smiles at me.

"Baby, are you in pain?" he asks softly.

"Yeah, it hurts all over."

"We're nearly home. I'll try to make it better yeah?"

He smiles again, and seeing the obvious love in his eyes, and loving the way he'd said home, I know he'd do anything to take away the pain and trauma of the past hours.

What happened was horrific and I can't change the fact that it'd happened and how it made my world literally come crashing down, bringing unbearable pain but I know I have to focus on the future with the gorgeous man next to me.

If I'm being honest with myself and how I feel about Hunter, then gorgeous doesn't even sum him up. Yes, he's gorgeous, handsome, any of those words, but he's more than that.

His amazing personality, his caring nature and his charm make him the total package.

He's everything any girl would want and for some reason I can't decipher why he wants me.

~ ~

Arriving back at the farmhouse we're eagerly greeted by Blitz. He turns his head to look at me as though he's asking if I'm ok.

I'm not ok, but I will be once this whirlwind of a day is over and I can escape the physical pain by sleeping it off.

It doesn't seem like it has just been a day though, as time had ceased to exist for the most part of it and the sun still being up because of daylights saving makes it seem like it isn't as late in the evening as it is.

Hunter takes my hand, helping me inside the farmhouse as I lean against him struggling to walk on my aching ankles.

"How about a cuppa tea?" he asks once we're inside and he places his hat on the stand by the doorway.

After his reaction in the hospital I feel more comfortable around him so softly I reply, "Sounds lovely and maybe some painkillers to."

When in the kitchen he drops my hand and proceeds to make a cup of tea for me, waving at me to go and sit on the couch while he does so.

I stumble towards the lounge room, trying not place too much pressure on my ankles. The sound of the kettle boiling and the scuffle of his shoes on the floorboards are the sounds I focus on as they are sounds of being home, and being with Hunter is starting to feel more like home than being with Dante ever did.

Hunter enters the lounge room with my cup of tea in his hand. Carefully I take it from him and lift it to my lips, taking a slow sip.

"Take these baby," he says softly, handing me two Panadeine Forte tablets. The tea seems to seep through my veins, making me feel as though things are going to be ok.

I mutter an '*mmm*' as the warmth of the drink made with love fills my body.

Hunter has pulled up the ottoman to side of the couch next to me, opening the beer he's clutching and sipping it, his gaze on me.

He has one leg on either side of it and his legs are spread. He catches me staring between them, and smiling asks me, "Taste good baby?"

"So good. I needed this for sure," I say, licking my lips as I look straight up into his eyes.

Being locked in the boot and essentially ripped apart by Dante not even twelve hours ago I'd honestly thought I'd not be able to feel anything like how Hunter makes me feel again, especially so soon.

But he makes me want to feel those things just by being him.

He shakes his head at me in response to my tease.

"I'd love to baby but you need to talk to me first. What you've experienced today is beyond traumatic and I'm not going to do anything to hurt you."

He's right that I do need to talk to him about what happened, not just the recent events but the past that led me here.

I have so many thoughts in my head, tumbling around I don't know where to start, but I have to say something, as muddled as it may be.

I don't want to remember the trauma, but I know it's important to let Hunter in. It will take away some of the pain, verbalising it so it isn't just in my mind.

"Hit. Me. Abuse. Rape."

No, I can't tell him anything. He won't love me anymore.

I close my eyes.

I can't do this. I've already gotten myself in too deep and now I'm going to spill everything. I just can't do it.

My eyes shoot back open though when Hunters hand brushes my cheek.

"It's ok if you're not ready, baby, but I really think you need to open up to me."

"It's so hard. I don't want to think about it, let alone say it."

"I know baby. Take your time. I'm not going anywhere."

The tears sting my eyes then as Hunter looks up at me, and I can see his heart breaking for me.

He brushes my cheek again. "Baby, please don't cry. I don't want you to think about the pain now."

"But...I..want to tell you Hunter."

"Not tonight, baby. You're not ready. I appreciate your teasing but I can't take advantage of you tonight."

The tears break free then, cascading down my cheeks as I look at him. He's so obviously in love with me, and he genuinely cares about me too.

"Oh Hunter i'm sorry, I just...I just..." I stutter, not even sure what I'm going to say.

"Don't you dare say sorry Savannah. You have nothing to be sorry about. Come here, you need a hug," he says standing up next to the couch in front of me.

Standing up next to him, I fall against his chest, his arms wrapping around me as I melt against him.

"Hunter, I..."

I want to tell him how I feel, but the words are stuck in my throat, the trauma of the day taking over.

"Don't speak Savannah. Just breathe," he says softly kissing my hair.

"Will you come and lie down with me until I fall asleep?"

"Of course baby," he muses, slipping his hand lower towards my butt, scooping me into his arms to carry me to his bedroom.

I wrap my hands around his neck, feeling safe in his arms as he carries me.

Reaching his bedroom, he places me softly down on the bed, pulling the sheets back and helping me crawl in. He undoes his jeans sliding them to the floor, but leaves his t-shirt on as he climbs into bed next to me. He pulls me close to his side and I flinch when he touches a sensitive bruise.

"Sorry baby, did I hurt you?"

"No, no it's ok. It's just a bruise."

He looks across at me. "I'm so sorry you had to go through this Savannah. I should have been there with you."

"Please Hunter, I just want to forget about it, please," I beg, snuggling into his side.

"Ok, Savannah. I'm here for you though. I want you."

"I know Hunter. I want you too, but right now I just need to sleep and erase this all from my mind."

He doesn't reply at first, instead presses a soft kiss to my forehead as I close my eyes.

The room is silent for a moment, and as I drift to sleep in my half asleep state I swear I hear him say, "Goodnight Savannah, I love you."

Part of me wants to open my eyes and tell him *'I love you too'* but I don't want to startle him, and I'm not ready to admit how I feel about him out loud.

~ ~

A couple of weeks have passed since the whole ordeal with Dante. My ankles have healed enough to not have to bandaged and my bruises have started to fade.

Hunter has been super sweet, asking me constantly if I'm ok, holding me close to him as I slept, comforting me when I woke up from nightmares reliving that day. At times it's easier to block it out than others.

I'd bled for a few days, and once that subsided I felt a little more at peace with what had happened, as though that was a cleansing process and part of my healing.

Hunter had just been there for me, truly showing he cared for me every day and it was making me fall more in love with him.

Walking into the kitchen, rubbing my eyes I find him at the stove cooking oats for breakfast.

"Morning," I say softly, as I hug him from behind.

"Good morning, baby. How are you feeling today?"

"A little better I guess."

"Only a little?"

"Yeah."

"Baby? What are you thinking about?"

"Hunter, I'm ready," I declare, sighing.

"Ready for what?" he asks, pouring the oats into two bowls, and handing me one with a spoon.

I inhale it, speaking softly, "Ready to tell you about my past."

"Are you sure?"

"Yes, can we eat this in the lounge room?"

"Of course."

He follows me into the lounge room and I sit up on the couch, crossing my legs with the bowl in my lap.

Hunter sits next to me on the couch, looking at me sweetly.

"Eat first baby, and tell me whenever you're ready."

I lift the spoon to my mouth, moaning softly as the warm oats slide down my throat. They'd never tasted so good and I know it's definitely time to open up.

Putting the spoon down I touch Hunters leg lightly, looking up at him, taking a deep breath as I begin to talk, "Well, it all started about five years ago when Dante came into the bookshop where I worked. He was so incredibly good looking and he flirted with me."

I sigh, thinking back to how nice Dante had been when I first met him. My heart lurches for a moment thinking that maybe Hunter will be the same, but I shake the feeling away. Hunter has clearly shown me already he's nothing like Dante so I continue, "He kept coming in and after a few times he asked me out and he was really sweet. He completely swept me off my feet." I pause, looking for some acknowledgement in Hunters eyes. He brushes my cheek softly, urging me to continue.

"He showered me with gifts and I fell hard and fast. We only kissed, nothing else and had been together for a couple of months when he asked me to marry him."

Hunter is now looking at me confused. I can't read the expression on his face at all. I spoon another mouthful of oats into my mouth, savouring the taste, but I want him to say something, so I let out a deep sigh. He knows what I mean.

"So he changed after you got married?" he asks me worriedly.

"Yeah on our wedding night, he took my virginity so forcefully he left bruises and scratches all over me."

"Oh Savannah that's horrific," he almost yells in disgust.

"And then after that he started hitting me for little things like forgetting to buy milk, or dinner not being ready as soon as he got home."

Tears begin to trail down my cheeks. Hunter leans forward, wiping them away with his thumb and pressing a soft kiss to my cheek.

"Savannah I just can't even believe it, what your telling me."

"It got worse." I start sobbing.

Hunter's words comfort me. "Take your time and only tell me if you want to."

I do want to. Telling Hunter all the pain I'd been through just seemed to make it feel better.

"I want to," I say softly, taking his hands and holding them with mine on the edge of the couch.

"So one night I got home late from a very rare night out with friends and I hadn't been able to tell him why I was late because my phone battery was flat."

I withdraw my hand from his and lift up my t-shirt to show Hunter the scar from my breasts to my hips.

"And he did this to me, telling me if I ever did anything like that again he would slice me right open."

There are tears in Hunters eyes now and I've only told him the half of it, nothing about how against my better judgment I put up with sleeping with Dante just to have a baby, but it failed time and time again, only to work through IUI. I need to tell Hunter more, as much as it will hurt him. His head is down and I touch his cheek to get him to look up at me.

"Hunter did the doctors tell you anything about what happened?"

"About when I found you?"

"Yeah."

"No nothing because I wasn't family."

He half scowls, showing that he's angry about not being able to know what happened when he cares about me, but I get the sense that he knows something but wants to hear it from me instead.

"I was pregnant."

"What? With his child?"

"Yes, and the bleeding was from a miscarriage."

"Oh, Savannah that's so horrible. Why would you want to have his child though?"

"I don't know. I thought it would make things better."

He doesn't reply but I know he's thinking I'm a little naive and stupid for doing that to myself amidst all the trauma Dante put me through. I know I had been, but I'd wanted a baby so desperately I didn't care at the time.

"And well you know what he did after that."

"I don't even want to think about that baby."

(37) Hunter

I was absolutely shocked at Savannah opening up to me about her past. I'd wanted to take the pain away before, to show her how much I love her, but now I feel her pain, like my heart has been ripped out it hurts so bad.

I can't fathom how anyone could do such heinous things to her or to anyone for that matter. I have no words I could say that would even begin to comfort her or take the pain of her past away.

I want more than anything to be her future and telling her I don't even want to think about what he's recently done to her only a couple of weeks ago is the only way I can help her block it out and deal with it.

I don't know all that happened but I don't need to, don't want to.

I stand up from the couch for a moment to stretch, my shirt untucking a little from my jeans exposing the skin of my hips.

Savannah is looking straight at me, and lets out a little moan.

It feels wrong that after her ordeal her little moans are sending signals to my pants and I want to act on them.

To try and control myself I sit back down on the couch, looking across at her again.

"Are you going to be ok baby?"

I expect her to reply but instead she leans across towards me on the couch pressing her lips onto mine. It's unlike any kiss we've shared before.

It's loving, emotion filled and I find myself melting into it.

The feeling of her lips on mine sends warmth through my veins and I curse myself for wanting more than her sweet kiss after what she's been through.

I can't do that to her, so pulling back from her kiss I press my hands into the couch so as not to push her away.

"Savannah, are you sure?"

"Yes, Hunter. I want you."

"But after whats happened?"

"Take it slow," She murmurs licking her lips.

She knows that drives me crazy.

"Oh Savannah you didn't just do that," I tease.

She giggles and a delicious teasing smile spreads across her face.

I fumble with the hem of my t-shirt lifting it over my head before leaning over her and pushing her down on the couch.

Our bodies are so close, our faces just a whisper apart. I brush a stray hair from her cheek, and kiss it softly before I start trailing kisses down her neck.

In her ear I whisper, "Savannah you are breathtaking."

Her amazing little moan escapes her lips again and she grabs my cheeks in her palms pulling me to her mouth in a passionate kiss. She runs her tongue along my lips, forcing me to smile as I deepen the kiss.

I can feel the desire for her rising in my jeans but she doesn't flinch, instead she breaks the kiss and lifts her t-shirt over her head. I let out a gasp seeing her scar up close and the bruises that haven't quite healed still dotted over her milky skin.

"Savannah, you're so god damn beautiful."

I begin to kiss over the lace of her bra, loving how her body responds. I continue the trail of kisses down her scar, kissing every inch of it until I reach her hips.

She bucks her body in response and I stretch back up to her mouth kissing her again fiercely.

Pulling back from our kiss again, I wrap my arms around her waist, lifting her to carry her to my bedroom, like I'd done that night.

Putting her body down on the bed I lay next to her trailing my fingers across her scar.

"I don't want to hurt you baby."

"You won't."

Grabbing her again, she flinches when I touch a bruise.

"Are you sure baby?"

She nods rolling over to face me. She unclips her bra letting it fall off her body. Seeing her naked takes my breath away. Teasingly I kiss her nipples, loving how her body responds.

Pressing a passionate, heated kiss to her lips my hand wanders down to run across her hips. I know it isn't time to take things further, so instead I deepen the kiss, teasing her with my tongue. Just having her in my arms and kissing is enough for now.

Pulling away even though my body is aching for her is so incredibly difficult. She looks at me with a mixture of fear and lust in her eyes.

I know she wants me but after what she's been through she's scared and I completely understand. Her body needs time to heal and her heart needs time to let me in.

"It's ok, baby," I say pulling her body closer to mine. I want so much to tell her I love her, and have her actually hear it this time but she speaks first, shocking me with her words.

"My name isn't Savannah Galison," she blurts out, turning her head to face me, "Its Trinity Haslett."

Her body feels tense in my arms when she says her actual name, but still I say, "Well Trinity Haslett it is then."

She cringes, hearing me say it, like it's a verbal reminder of her painful past.

"Call me Savannah, please."

"Is that what you want?"

"Yes, I want to focus on the future with you, not the past."

Her words make complete sense but a part of me is afraid that she's still going to run away from the pain more.

"Promise me you'll stay with me Savannah."

"I will, I promise."

I press a soft kiss to her lips. The words I want to tell her are on the tip of my tongue again, but I keep my mouth shut, knowing she's still awake and not ready to hear them.

I close my eyes, falling asleep holding her naked in my arms.

It doesn't get any better.

(38) *Savannah*

Telling Hunter about my past is a weight lifted off my shoulders, as cliched as it that is.

He'd shown genuine care about me in his responses and it had made me fall harder for him.

There's no doubt in my mind that I'm falling in love with him. I was actually already in love with him really, before everything that happened with Dante and how Hunter had reacted to me telling him about it made me fall deeper, if that was even possible.

I'd felt a little giddy, despite the fact that my whole body was in pain, when Hunter had kissed me on the couch. The way he'd kissed every inch of my scar had sent shivers all through my body.

If it wasn't for the pain and the image of what Dante did still so fresh in my mind I'd have given myself to Hunter completely.

Hunter has a sweet way of knowing what I'm really feeling though. Even though his kisses and his touch were warming my body I could feel his desire pressing into me, even more so when we moved to his bedroom. He didn't take things any further and I was glad for that self control.

I need to heal more in body to take that step.

Letting him know my real name was definitely letting myself in deep, but I know it's the right time to tell him. It's clear Hunter's in love with me and I want him to know the real me, not just the facade of Savannah. I want to be Savannah more than anything now.

Trinity doesn't exist anymore because the way Hunter says *'Savannah'* makes my heart soften and it sounds right, just like being with him is.

~ ~

Hunter has gone out droving again, taking Blitz with him and the house feels a little lonely without him around.

It really has come to feel like home though; as I'd really enjoyed pottering around and giving the inside of the farmhouse a womanly touch.

I'm more comfortable going into Hunter's room now too; it isn't painful to remember the first night I'd been in there anymore, because going in there now reminds me of the nights I'd spent lying in Hunter's arms and his sweet loving kisses that take my breath away.

Wanting to tidy the bedrooms to make if fresh for his return I'm sweeping under the spare bed, completely shocked when I find that not only dirt comes out from underneath, but attached to the broom is also my phone and car keys. They slide out slamming against the wall and the phone screen cracks a little.

Dropping the broom, I pick up my phone, brushing the dust off of it. I'd honestly forgotten even bringing it in from the car the night I'd stumbled into Hunter's house.

With the ambulance coming in it must have gotten kicked under the bed and I'd not even given it a second thought.

Racing out to the kitchen I rummage in the drawers to find a charger. I'd seen Hunter with the same phone as mine so I know a charger has to be around somewhere. I touch first a photo and a tear leaves my eyes looking at it. It's a picture of Hunter holding the obstetrician in his arms spinning her around, looking at her whilst she's looking at the camera. It looks like he really loved her and it doesn't seem like that long ago, either. I hold it between my fingers, about to rip it in half, the thought coming to mind that maybe he does still love her.

I'd seen the looks she gave him at the hospital and she'd warned me to stay away from him.

Hastily, I throw the photo back in the drawer continuing my search for the charger.

Eventually I strike 'gold' finding one and plug it in to fire up my phone. I'm scared for it to turn on; scared to read the messages that will no doubt be on it.

The thought had crossed my mind of getting a new one before I left but I didn't have the time nor the money to do so.

As soon as the phone switches on and thankfully finds signal the message tone sounds a number of times. My heart lurches in my chest as I press the screen.

I know who the messages will be from.

No one, other than *him*, usually sent me text messages these days.

The first one gets to me the most.

If I'd only found my phone earlier, I could have prevented everything that happened to me. It reads:

Dante: Trinity how dare you run from me? I am coming to get you and you'll never run again. If you reply I'll play nice.

My heart is aching. It was sent a day before the fundraiser. I'm kicking myself for not thinking of finding my phone earlier but stupidly I'd thought I was free of Dante when I ran. I was letting myself get too involved in Hunter's world and the simple mistake had led me to a world of hurt.

It isn't a mistake though, being with Hunter is far from a mistake. He'd made me feel more alive, more free and more loved than I could have ever imagined.

The first message was painful enough, the second causes my heart to pound even harder.

Dante: How the fuck are you still alive?

It was sent only a day ago. I have no idea how Dante knows I'm alive but the fact he does know truly scares me and I know I have to do something to get him out of my life forever.

Many thoughts crossed my mind, many ways to rid my life of Dante, some of them highly illegal and so wrong I could never do them.

No doubt Hunter probably would have a gun around somewhere but shooting Dante isn't the answer.

I know there is only one thing to do and I hope it will be the right choice, to make Dante go to hell just like he'd said to me.

Not literal hell, but hell on earth is the only place he deserves to be.

He'd made my life living hell and now I want his to be the same.

He doesn't deserve happiness.

He doesn't deserve to live but it isn't up to me to take his life away.

He thought he had the power to end my life, but life had other plans and now I have to stop my heart from pounding in my chest to execute a plan to rid my life of him. Thinking of the word execute makes me shiver as he'd essentially tried to execute me.

I've always thought it was such a horrible word; it always sent shivers through me when it was mentioned on the news.

Dante deserved to suffer for the rest of his life, not be executed and for his miserable life to be over.

So my plan has to be one that will ensure he suffers and thinks about all the pain he put me through everyday for the rest of his god damn life.

My finger is resting on the *'reply'* to message on my phone.

I have to do this, but I'm terrified about what is going to happen.

The decision to go to Dante could be stupid, and he'd follow through with the earlier threat of slitting my throat to end my life, but I can only hope that maybe if I go to him voluntarily he'll be different.

Slowly I type a message.

Trinity:Yes I'm alive. Your plan to kill me failed.

I send it and then immediately try to delete it.

Why did I just do that?

Deleting it is futile as his message of reply is on my screen before I even have a chance to press yes to deletion.

Dante: I asked how the fuck are you alive?

What the hell am I supposed to say to that?

It seems blindly obvious to me how I'm still alive. I can't understand how he could be so stupid.

Trinity: The car didn't burn like you planned.

His reply again is instant and it shocks me.
It only says, ***'Fuck'***
There's obviously something I don't know about the car, as there seems to be a reason he wanted it gone as well as me.

Trinity: What's that mean?
Dante: Meet me @ the motel the town over from Ridgehope tonight @ 7pm. Don't you dare tell anyone

I hesitate, not sure if I should even reply. What he's asking means he's already back and was going to come and find me again regardless of my next move.

I know what I have to do and I know it's also going to be the hardest thing since running in the first place.

I quickly tap a reply.

Trinity:I will be there baby

He doesn't respond this time so I grab a pen from the counter top, frantically searching for paper to no avail.

My mind flashes back to the sickening photo of Hunter with the obstetrician that I'd wanted to rip to shreds. I pluck it back out from the drawer, trying not to focus on the image and the knot it causes in my stomach. Flipping it over I write Hunter a note:

'Hunter, I have gone to find Dante. It's for the best. He'll get what's coming to him. If this is goodbye then thank you for being you. You're amazing! Savannah.'

Dropping the pen next to the note, I yank my phone from the charger, tug on my shoes from by the door, noticing the keys to Hunter's Ute hanging on the hallway stand.

Thank God he's taken the quad bike out this time, as I hadn't even thought about how I was going to get to town.

Racing out to the Ute I jump in, annoyed and frustrated remembering it's a manual.

How the fuck do I do this again? Think Savannah think. Clutch, brake, gear.

I turn the key in the ignition, with my feet on the pedals, hand on the gear knob just willing my brain to kick into gear and instinctively know what to do. The engine roars to life and I slowly let out the clutch to ease the Ute to the gate.

Thankfully Hunter had left the gate open, so I lurch the car forward crunching the gears as my feet fumble to cooperate with the pedals. Once out of the gate I slowly start to get the hang of it again, and crunch the gears into second and third as I speed up.

The clock on the dash says it's 4:30 and I know I'll have to exceed the speed limit if I'm going to catch Quentin at the station before five pm. He's the only one I trust to help me as he knows how much I care about his older brother and he'd saved my life once so I'm hoping he'll do the same again if it comes to that.

Focusing on my driving, I think back over the last couple of months since I'd stumbled into Hunter's farmhouse.

I'd never believed in crazy things like love at first sight but the moment I'd opened my eyes when Hunter walked into my hospital room I honestly think I'd fallen in love with him. There was something about him from that very first moment i'd looked at him, and it wasn't just his insane physical attractiveness but the confidence he exhibited and his devilish charm and humour.

He'd never expected anything from me, but opened up his whole world to me before I'd even said one word to him.

He'd told me secrets from his past and let me in so deep into his world and heart, that I don't ever want to leave Ridgehope.

Part of me knows this is where I'm supposed to be and that Hunter is who I'm supposed to be with.

I'd just had to go through hell and back to get to him.

Realising I've arrived in town, I brake suddenly, crunching the gears to come to a grinding halt outside the police station.

It's 4:50. I'd made it , but that was only half of the plan.

~ ~

"Hello Constable Mywer. Is Constable Mackenney still here?"

"Your Ms Galison, yes? Hunter's girl?"

My heart skips at her words, hearing that I'm known as *'Hunter's girl.'*
Those simple words make my heart smile.

"Yes, I am but please can I speak to Constable Mackenney? It's urgent."

"No problem, Ms Galison. I'll buzz him."

She calls through to Quentin, announcing that I'm here to see him. I sit
down in the foyer, tapping my feet in a rhythm on the floor to try and
calm myself.

I have to keep telling myself I'm doing the right thing and more
importantly tell myself that this isn't the second time I'm facing the
possibility of never seeing Hunter again.

Breaking my thoughts Quentin appears from inside the station.

"Savannah, what brings you in?"

I take in a deep breath, exhaling it as I let out the words I know Quentin
needs to hear.

"I know where he is. And I'm going to help you arrest him."

His mouth gapes in shock. I'm not sure if he's shocked about knowing
where Dante is or that I'm going to assist somehow in his arrest.

"Who? Dante?"

"Yes, I found my phone and he'd texted me."

Quentin nods.It's comforting to know he's listening.

"And I replied and he told me to meet him at the motel in the next town
over at seven pm."

"Ok so we'll get the guys out there right away then."

He turns to head back into the station but I grab his arm to pull him back
a minute.

"No, he told me not to tell anyone. I need to go on my own first."

"Savannah, that's not wise. We can go straight in and arrest him. We have the warrants."

I shake my head, needing Quentin to understand that I have to go alone if they are ever going to be able to arrest Dante.

He'd make a quick getaway if the cops turn up as he'd evaded them in the past, when they turned up on our doorstep after I'd called triple zero one night when he was blind drunk and he'd taken his rage out on me.

He knew what to say then, making the cops step down and this time he wasn't going to get the chance to do any such things.

I'm setting him up to fall.

"I'm going to go first and play along."

"I don't understand Savannah."

"I'm going to trick him. Make him think I'm going back to him."

"Ok, I get you. Could you text me the room number when you arrive?"

"Yes."

"Ok, please be careful Savannah."

He once again turns to walk away and I hesitate for a moment before I say, "Quentin please come as quick as you can. I don't know what he's going to do to me."

He smiles at me, without saying a word but his smile is sincere and it gives me comfort.

I'm ready to face Dante to complete the first step in ridding my life of him, forever.

(39) Hunter

Returning from droving, the moment I walk in the door with Blitz at my heels, something feels off.

It's eerily quiet in the farmhouse and my heart sinks, knowing the silence means that Savannah isn't there.

Blitz had raced down the hallway, sniffing the floor to try and find her, but comes back looking forlorn. He loves her just as much as I do.

Sitting down at the table I notice the photo on the edge of the kitchen counter.

I don't remember leaving it there, nor my charger plugged into the wall.

Jumping up I grab the photo and see it's of Addison and I taken right before I proposed. Right before she rejected me, ripping my heart out.

Flipping the photo over I find a scrawly handwritten note from Savannah and it to rips my heart out.

She's saying goodbye, after all we've shared in the last couple of months she's going back to him.

It appears from the casual tone in her note that I meant nothing to her, as calling me amazing doesn't tell me how she really feels. Anyone could have said that to me, anyone.

I'd thought from the way she opened up to me, the way she responded to my kisses that she was falling in love with me, just like I am with her.

Actually I'm not falling in love with her; I am in love with her, desperately and hopelessly in love with her.

I have been for weeks, practically since I first time I'd laid eyes on her.

I'd never believed in love at first sight but it almost seems like this is a case of that.

I'd wanted her in my life from the moment I found her in my farmhouse, despite not knowing anything about her and the beautiful person she is inside as well as out.

Scrunching the photo in my fist, I feel anger rise in my chest. I'm not going to let her get away. She doesn't deserve the pain he forces upon her. She deserves to be loved and I know I need to find her and tell her I love her before it's too late.

~ ~

My keys are not on the hallway stand where I'd left them so it's clear she'd taken the Ute to wherever she was going.

I'm a little angry at her for thinking she could take the Ute without asking me but it was a pretty smart plan on her part and I laugh at her perceptive behaviour.

Maybe she thought I wasn't going to come home before she came back. It doesn't make any sense at all.

Her note was clearly a goodbye to me, but I'm not going to say goodbye and there is only one person who can help me find her.

Running out of the house I jump back on the Quad bike, making sure to shut the gate behind me or Blitz will be out like a shot behind me.

My anger at her leaving only fuels my haste and I'm glad that the Quad bike can really get going when you give it a few revs.

It isn't the best vehicle to be driving on the open road with however, especially without a helmet, but it's all I have and I need to book it into town if I'm even going to make it before the police station closes.

The speedo dial shakes violently when I reach eighty kilometres an hour but as long as I make it into town I don't care less if the Quad bike breaks down, never to be ridden again.

Straddling the bike as I gun it into town I think about the last kiss I'd shared with Savannah, with her lying in my arms and confessing her real name.

Her body cringing in my arms when I said her real name really tore at my heart. She wants to be Savannah with me.

I think Savannah suits her better anyway because she belongs with me, out on the farm amidst her namesake of the never-ending Savannah of the land.

The last kiss we shared still occupies my thoughts and arriving into town my heart lurches in my chest hoping it wasn't the last kiss we would share.

Stopping the Quad bike abruptly outside the police station I run in, glad to find the doors not locked and Gail Mywer sitting at the desk.

She isn't really who I want to deal with after my last encounter with her, but I need to speak to Quentin to report Savannah missing.

"Hi Gail. Is Quentin in?"

"I'm afraid not Hunter. He's gone out."

"But it's knock off."

"Yes, but this was an urgent case."

I'm confused and worried that Savannah had not actually left my house willingly. Nothing is making sense at all.

"Well, I have an urgent matter to report as well."

"Yes?"

"A missing person."

She taps her fingers against the computer keys and looks straight through me.

"Missing persons name?"

"Savannah Galison Or Trinity Haslett."

I cringe saying her real name. It definitely doesn't sound right.

"What are you saying Hunter?" She was here like an hour ago talking to Quentin."

"What?" I gasp at her in shock. I'm angry now. My head is spinning. This doesn't make sense.

"Tell me where she is Gail or I'll.."

"Hunter, dearest, please calm down. I can't discuss case details with you."

I literally feel like tearing my hair out. I need to know where she is. I can't let her go, not now, not ever.

"Gail you will tell me where she is or I'll...seriously I just need to know. I fucking love her!"

Yes, that's it!Appeal to the old biddies sensitive side.

She sighs. "Ok she has gone to the motel the town over. Something about meeting someone there."

"Thank you Gail," I call back, already half out the door.

I kick the tyre of the Quad bike, cursing at it. There's no way it's going to make it another five kilometres, let alone another forty to the next town away from Ridgehope.

I know I could get arrested for what I'm about to do, but the keys are in the ignition so it isn't really like I'm stealing it per se. I smile at the trust of a country town at its best.

Jumping in the drivers seat of the V6 patrol car I reverse it out at full speed.

In the rear view mirror I get a glimpse of Gail running behind me waving her fists in the air.

Sorry Gail this is a matter of life and death.

There's something about being behind the wheel of a powerful car that makes you feel invincible. The speed limit out here is a hundred an hour but if I want to get to Savannah I need to gun it hard and fast. Pushing my foot to the floor the engine roars, the speedo climbing until I reach a hundred and thirty. Opening the window a little I let the breeze blow in, to try and calm my nerves and deflate the anger in my chest.

Pulling up to the motel there's a number of other patrol cars, and a few police officers including Quentin surrounding the area with their guns cocked ready to shoot.
Standing in the doorway of one of the motel rooms are two people.
One with a gun to the others head.
When my eyes focus on them my heart falls to the ground.

(40) Dante

Hearing the old Ute rumble up to the carpark I'm at first worried she hasn't keep her promise. Worried that she'd opened her big mouth and had told the cops where I am or brought *him* with her. I don't even know him and I fucking hate him. He cannot have her. If I can't have her, no one damn well can.

She walks casually up to the motel room door, after staying in the car for a minute longer than I think she'd needed to.

It looked like she was sending a text message and I hope to God it isn't to *him*.

She wraps her fingers in a knock on the door and opening it I pull her inside, checking the surroundings before shutting it behind us.

Pulling her into a tight embrace I whisper in her ear, "I should have known you wouldn't die."

She shrinks back from me, cringing slightly and her eyes are expressionless.

"I needed to come back to you," she muses softly, taunting me.

I can't tell if she's sincere or is just playing with me. She'd always been feisty and a tease.

I want her so fucking bad.

The plan of killing her hadn't been my wisest choice. I know now I should have gone after him instead, so she'd have been forced to come back to me and the pain of losing him would have been far worse than any I inflicted on her.

"I missed you baby. I'm sorry," I say to her, trying to seem sincere, even though I'm not.

I'm not sorry either for what I'd done but I need her to think that she's made the right choice coming back. I press a kiss to her mouth and much to my delight she responds back, eagerly biting my lip. She still knows how to drive me wild with lust for her. I'm going to miss that if I do end up trying to take her life for a second time.

Deepening the kiss I edge her closer to the bed, her legs crashing into as she falls against it. I lift my shirt over my head, ready to undress myself and devour her again, glad she isn't resisting me like last time.

But that's when I hear the sirens and the voices.

There are cops outside the motel and they're saying my name, urging me to surrender myself on multiple warrants.

Arson, rape and attempted murder.

Raking my hands through my hair I try desperately to quell my anger.

"Did you call them Trinity?" I yell.

She hesitates, breathing in deeply.

"Yes, I did."

"Seriously, Trinity. You really are a fucking idiot."

"I had to."

"No, you didn't! I was going to change things, make everything better for us. But you can't let things be."

"I..I.."

"Fuck up," I spit at her, opening the bedside drawer and rummaging around until I feel the cold metal in my grasp.

Holding it in my hands I have all the power, even more so than I'd had before.

This is truly goodbye.

I put it to the side of her head, pressing the cold metal against her temple and she cowers in terror again, just like the day I had the knife against her throat. It's so thrilling having this power over her.

"You're going to go to the door and tell the cops to rack off or the last thing you'll hear is me blowing your brains out."

She mutters something that I can't hear but slowly stands up and walks to the door.

Opening it, still with the gun pressed against the side of her head I yank her closer to me with my other arm, a grip on her so tight she can't move an inch.

"If you fuckers come any closer I'll shoot her," I seethe loudly at the cops. That's when I see him arrive ,getting out of the car and looking straight at us.

A look of absolute terror and shock crosses his face and he seems stuck in his tracks seeing Trinity with the gun to her head like it's going to be the death of him.

Little does he know what his arrival has triggered in me. I'm beyond angry now. There is a better way to end this than to shoot Trinity.

"What's he doing here?" I seethe in Trinity's ear.

"I don't know," she answers meekly.

"Don't fucking lie to me Trinity."

"Ok, I love him," she declares, "But I didn't know he was going to be here."

Her words cut me like a knife. And she's lying to me. I fucking know she's lying. Her words are like vipers biting me.

Before I can even think a second, as though time has stopped with Trinity's words he's running towards me yelling, "NO! Please don't shoot her!"

I'm not going to shoot Trinity now. She needs to suffer and experience true pain.

I turn the gun towards him, the man Trinity declared she loves moments ago. Pulling the trigger I snarl into Trinity's ear, "Then say goodbye to him baby. I told you know one else could have you."

The sound of the shot ringing out from the gun is like nothing I've ever heard before. It's absolutely thrilling.

I watch, sniggering as the bullet hits him in the lower chest and he collapses to the ground in agony. Trinity is squirming in my arms, muttering a wretched *'NO, NO'*.

I loosen my grip on her, calling back, "Go watch him die baby," as she runs to his side.

(41) Savannah

As soon as Dante frees me from his grip after the shot rang out from the gun he'd held against my temple, I rush to Hunter's side.

It's all a blur.

I can't focus on anything but getting to Hunter as time had stopped the minute Dante pulled the trigger of the gun.

His words in my ear to say goodbye to Hunter are the most painful words I've ever heard in my entire life.

I can't lose Hunter now, like this, not at the hands of Dante.

I'd not told Hunter I love him; not had the chance to express to him without words how much I love him.

Dante knew that after I confessed loving Hunter that nothing would hurt more than losing him and I hate him more than ever for that.

At Hunter's side, I press my hands against his chest to quell the blood that's spilling out below his heart. Frantically I search nearby for the bullet but it's nowhere to be found. I don't know if that's good or bad, the fact the bullet is still inside his chest, or even if it isn't and I can't see it nearby.

Maybe that means his blood loss will be less with no exit of the bullet, but honestly I have no idea about gun shot wounds.

He's in absolutely agony though, trying to not wince from the pain and it breaks my heart seeing him enduring so much pain, as this pain is far worse than any I've ever been through.

"It's ok. I'm here Hunter."

He mumbles something softly that I can't understand. The pain evident on his face is breaking my heart so much.

I need to tell him the words I should have said months ago, because if this is goodbye I want those words to be the last thing he hears.

"I'm sorry Hunter. I love you."

I press a soft kiss to his lips and can't help but grin when he smiles back at me with his adorable dimples.

His smile whilst he's in pain and after telling him I love him makes my heart swell. He starts mumbling again, not able to form any coherent words because of the pain.

"It's ok. You don't need to say anything," I muse, brushing my other hand against his cheek.

He lifts his head up a little to look right at me and breathe in as deeply as he can with the pain in his chest to focus on what he wants to say.

"I love you too."

My heart pounds in my chest, finally hearing him officially say he loves me too. I don't want this to be our last moment together.

More than anything I want to be able to tell him over and over again that I love him.

He's turned my whole world upside down, made me feel alive and made me feel that I deserve happiness and without him I will never truly be happy again.

Silence has seemed to envelope us but in the distance I hear a police officer report into his radio *'yes man down. Shooting. Ambulance.'*

Pressing a kiss to Hunter's forehead and squeezing his hand in mine I urge him, "Hold on, please baby, hold on. The ambulance is coming. Don't say goodbye. Please don't say goodbye Hunter."

(42) Quentin

My heart is pounding after hearing my brother scream out to not shoot Savannah.

He shouldn't have even been here, let alone have been in the crossfire of a deranged man like Dante Haslett. Hearing the shot ring out from the gun Dante had a grip on made time stop and seeing my older brother collapse in pain was my worst nightmare, a flash of the past crossing my mind.

If he died it would be entirely my fault.

I would have failed him as a little brother and failed in my duties as a police officer, all because I'd let Addison effect my better judgement.

Loving her unrequited has always gotten me in hot water, even during our high school days.

A memory surfaces in my head of a time I snuck into Hunter's room when she was staying over and creepily watched her sleeping half naked.

She woke up to find me jerking off in the chair by the bedside, moaning her name.

She cursed at me, and told me to get out or she'd tell Hunter.

I kissed her cheek as I left and she slapped my cheek softly in warning.

Granted Hunter didn't find out but Addison never let me live it down and I'd always felt guilty for thinking that way about my brothers girlfriend.

Now my brother is lying on the concrete with Savannah at his side, quite possibly taking his last breaths. Time is in slow motion and I can barely focus on my job, the task at hand, a deranged idiot with a gun cocked and loaded, pointing it towards the police officers surrounding the area.

Sirens are now approaching, so evidently an ambulance has been called, but no ambulance would be able to help tie up this scene if we can't get Dante to stand down and arrest him on the outstanding warrants.

He's up for Arson, rape and attempted murder and once in custody he'll be given a long sentence of jail time. He honestly deserves to rot in hell for what he'd done.

He doesn't deserve to live honestly but shoot to kill isn't an option, even though I desperately want to pull the trigger of my gun, aiming at him like he'd deliberately done minutes ago when aiming the gun towards Hunter. Glancing over at my brother the pain he's in is clear and it warms my heart a little seeing Savannah whispering to him. She's trying to keep him calm with her hand pressed against his chest to quell the bleeding.

The look in her eyes, the tears that have stained her cheeks are evidence that she has fallen in love with my brother and the thought of losing him would break her heart. I can't let Dante win this.

If his careless action of shooting my brother to get back at Savannah causes Hunter to die he'd be up on a murder charge too.

It's all to much, too overwhelming for a little town like ours to deal with. It has to end now, before the ambulance and no doubt the press arrive to create more panic at the scene.

Urging my colleagues forward I yell out to Dante, "Put the gun down! And your hands up!"

Starting to walk closer I cock my gun towards him, my finger teetering on the trigger. I've never had to actually fire my gun at someone.

I'd only ever shot targets in practice and animals when out beating around the bush as kids.

I know I'm a good shot but in the circumstance I don't think I'd even be able to actually go through with it. My colleagues are closer now, tentatively walking towards Dante, afraid he'll pull the trigger of his gun on them at any moment.

They have handcuffs ready to make the arrest and I shut my eyes for a moment, hearing the ambulance pull up behind us.

Their voices are panicky, but methodical as they grab the needed equipment out to help Hunter.

Opening my eyes, I hope it isn't to late. My eyes blur as I open them though, not believing the very sight emerging right in front of me.

Dante now has the gun to the side of his head, his eyes darting towards us and to the ambulance.

His plan of killing Hunter most likely now has failed and he'll never have Savannah back.

The reality of what he'd done and the consequences of his actions that will most likely see him spending the rest of his life behind bars are probably spinning in his head.

In that final moment, I wish my eyes were closed again as the image of him depressing the trigger of his gun into the side of his head, the bullet coming out the other side and the blood that spatters everywhere as he falls to the ground is a sight I will never be able to erase from my mind.

Silence envelopes the scene as the other officers run to check if he's dead.

It would be a fucking miracle if he was alive after that brutal shot to the head.

I can't focus on that though. I need to get away from the whole scene and be with my brother, just in case I'm not going to see him again. The thought of losing him is to scary to think about.

Sarge is surveying the scene, and making notes to tell the press who are now arriving at the scene. I'm hesitant to ask him if I can leave as it isn't protocol to leave a crime scene, but I don't want to be there at all when my brothers life is on the line.

"Sarge, can the others tie up the scene? I'd like to go with Hunter to the hospital."

He pats me on be back and his tone is almost fatherly, "Go Quentin. I wouldn't expect you to be anywhere else than with your brother."

Racing over to the ambulance I climb in the back with Savannah as they hoist the stretcher with Hunter strapped on it into the back.

It's a little cramped with myself, Savannah and the ambulance officer in the back with the stretcher between us. Mark closes the door before getting in to drive away.

Ridgehope is the closest hospital, forty kilometres away, so in the hopes of getting there quicker I tap on the barrier cage to alert Mark.

"Gun it Mark! Do one forty mate."

He nods, slowly depressing his foot on the accelerator as we edge onto the highway.

The officer in the back is attempting to calm Hunter down. There's nothing they can give him for the pain at this point and even with the oxygen mask on his breathing is shallow.

Savannah appears to be in another world, not believing what's really happening. It must be truly heartbreaking to finally be able to be with the person you love and have the possibility of losing them looming.

She's clutching Hunter's hand in hers, afraid to let go.

I lightly touch her arm in comfort and when she looks up at me with tears in her eyes I soothe, "Savannah he's gonna be ok."

"I hope so. I can't lose him."

"You won't Savannah."

I grab my brothers hand in mine. "Please big bro, hold on yeah, I'm sorry I failed you."

He winces in pain, looking across at me. He tries to speak but with the pain and the oxygen mask he can't form the words. He squeezes the hand I'm holding and that's enough to comfort me as we pull into the Ridgehope hospital emergency bay.

Caz May

He's made it here and I can only hope that we've gotten him here in time.Losing my brother in this hospital would be my own literal hell on earth.

(43) Addison

The absolute worst part of being a doctor, especially in a small town is the possibility of having to work in other departments of the hospital when short staffed. The worst department being emergency.

I hate the smell of it, it's a more overwhelming stench of bleach than the rest of the hospital and it always makes me want to gag.

The emergency department of Ridgehope hospital generally isn't that busy, usually only the occasional woman in labour or someone involved in a car accident as it's the only hospital for a couple of hundred kilometres.

So when the unmistakable sound of sirens echoes around the hospital, it becomes a hive of activity as preparation for whatever case came through the double doors.

Zane is head doctor in charge today and he barks orders at me. His tone really irks me, and how he's looking at me with a gaze so intent I feel like he's stripping me of my scrubs with his eyes.

We've definitely gotten a little closer in the past couple of months, going out for drinks after work and attending the fundraiser night together, even sharing a few kisses that made me feel things I know I shouldn't. But even so, in my eyes we are just friends.

I don't really have any other friends in Ridgehope so it'd been nice to have that closeness with someone again.I know still pining after Hunter at this point is ridiculous.

He's clearly in love with Savannah, he'd confessed as much to me and I still can't let go.

The air is still always thick with tension whenever the Mackenney brothers are anywhere near me, even Quentin.

I'm still going over my last conversation with him at the fundraiser and can't shake the feeling that he wants something more from me than just being friends, but I've never seen him in that light before. He's always just been Hunter's little brother.

The thought had crossed my mind that maybe I should be with Quentin, considering we're the same age and he's just as good looking as Hunter, but I can't make my heart feel that way for him.

Right now though I have to concentrate on the emergency at hand, and get the Mackenney brothers out of my head. Again Zane barks at me, "Addison, you need to focus. We have a gun shot victim coming in stat."

Great, some idiot shot himself.

It's not some idiot though that comes through the double doors, with the ambulance officers and two others at his side. It's Hunter.

My heart falls to the floor, my jaw gaping looking at him on the stretcher barely holding on.

There's no way Hunter had shot himself. He rarely ever used his gun, unless it was to put a sick animal out of their misery.

By his side Savannah and Quentin both appear in a complete panic and I can tell they were both involved somehow. They're ushered out into the waiting area by a nurse.

"Addison?" Zane asks me, questioning why I'm not moving. I'm frozen and again Zane speaks to me, "Addison, saline, gauze, seriously now!"

I can't focus on his words. Hunter is being put on the bed.

His shirt is covered in blood and I want to vomit at the sight. Blood never has that effect on me, normally.

"What?" I muse, brushing the tears from my eyes.

"Get over here and do your job," he yells at me.

The tears are pouring down my cheeks now. I want desperately to help Hunter, but I can't, afraid that I'll do something wrong and he'll be gone from my life because of a mistake I made when upset.

"I can't. I can't," I sob wretchedly.

"Addison, I'm not asking. We need to stabilise the patient for surgery."

Those words ring in my head. Surgery means only one thing. The bullet is possibly still inside and to save his life it needs to be removed.

My breathing is now panicky, my head spinning like I'm about to faint.

"Addison, please," he says looking at me questionably, but also with an emotion on his face I'm not sure of.

"I c..can't," I stutter, breaking further into uncontrollable tears.

Zane nods at the nurses to keep preparing Hunter for surgery, stepping a little closer to me before putting his hands on my shoulders and looking straight in my eyes when he speaks, "Addison I'm sorry. I know you're attached to the patient, so I'm going to ask you to step back. Please go out with his family."

I nod, shuffling out of the emergency department to the waiting area. Savannah is pacing the room, clearly as upset as I am. I don't hate her, but if Hunter dies because of this, I'll never be able to forgive her for her possible part in his death.

There will always be tension between us, as long as we both love Hunter. Quentin is seated on the waiting room chairs, his head in his hands. Walking up to him, I stop, standing in front of his legs, and through sobs I speak, "Quentin, w..what h..happened?"

He doesn't say anything, instead he stands up and pulls me into a hug. I cry into his shoulder, grateful for the comfort of someone who cares about me. Pulling back, it's evident he has been crying too and sighing deeply he speaks with anger, "Dante happened. He fucking shot him."

"Dante?"

"Savannah's husband," he says, just as angrily.

"Oh."

"I don't want to talk about it."

I don't either.

"Is Savannah ok? Was she there too?"

"I said I don't want to talk about it Addison," he spits at me again, not looking at me but now focusing on the gurney being wheeled from emergency towards the surgery doors. Savannah is by it straight away, kissing Hunter's forehead.I can see her lips moving, but can't make out the words.

This is just not happening.

We all watch as Hunter is wheeled into surgery. Savannah comes to sit down on the waiting room chairs. The air is strained and thick with tension between us all wanting to say something but there are no words to say.

I should be the calm one in this situation, comforting his loved ones but I can't comfort her knowing that Hunter wants her, knowing that Hunter loves her.

I feel terrible that I want her to lose his love but I don't want him to be gone but her. I feel cruel but the hurt is so real. Tears are still stinging my eyes, from never having been in this situation before, having someone I love in danger of losing their life. I don't know how to feel or what to do. Without warning Quentin pulls me into another hug, "Are you ok?" he asks with a friendly tone.

"No," I sniff, "I don't know if I'll ever be ok."

He doesn't respond, instead shocks me by taking my hand in his and leading me in the direction of the main doors.

Walking past Savannah he asks her, "Savannah are you going to be ok here?"

'Yeah, I'll just wait here. I don't want to go anywhere."

"Alright if you're sure. I'm going to take Addison home," Quentin says, looking at me with care evident in his dark eyes.

Quentin Mackenney isn't his brother, but I feel a little better having him around and his offer to take me home is genuinely caring.

The hospital is the last place I need to be right now, as I'll only go more crazy thinking about Hunter in surgery.

I'm most likely the last person he'll want to see when he wakes up and I hate to admit it to myself but I really do need to let him go, for him.

(44) Quentin

I've never seen this side of Addison, emotional and vulnerable. She's absolutely distraught from Hunter arriving in the hospital and clearly she still loves him. It makes the ache I still feel for her intensify.

I want her so damn bad, to take away the pain she's feeling and turn it to pleasure, but at the same time I don't want to be that guy, taking advantage of her just because she's feeling vulnerable.

Arriving at her house, which is only a short walk away from the hospital, she fumbles with the door knob.

Tears are still evident on her cheeks and I want to lean in closer to kiss them away. I follow her inside towards the kitchen.

"Coffee?" she asks softly, grabbing the kettle.

"Yeah coffee sounds great," I reply.

There's definitely something going on between us right now, a strange tension hampered by the fact that I can't read her emotions.

If only I could read her mind, to know what she's thinking when she looks at me like she's about to burst into tears again at any moment.

If she was able to read my mind though I'd be in trouble.

Yes, I'm thinking about my brother in surgery but I'm also thinking about where in the house her bedroom is as I want to take her to it and strip her of the scrubs that envelope her body.

I know underneath her scrubs her body is delicious and I find myself licking my lips at the thought of tasting her skin, of kissing her and connecting her body with mine.

Instead all I'll be able to taste now is the coffee she places on the table in front of me. She sits in the chair opposite me and sips her coffee, her gaze not leaving mine.

I can feel the lust for her rising in my pants and curse myself.

How dare she fucking tease me right now?

I have to say something or I'll do something else that I know isn't right.

"He's going to be ok Addison."

"You don't know that Quentin."

"We have to hope that he will be."

She lets out an *'mmm'* that shamelessly sends a further jolt to my pants.

I pull my chair closer to hers, my knees brushing against hers.

"Come here," I say wiping the tears from her eyes with my thumb.

As if we both know what the other is thinking we stand up at the same time and I envelope her in my arms in a tight hug. This hug feels different to the ones in the hospital, as I can feel her melting into me and it's driving me crazy. I've never wanted her more.

She pulls back from the hug, her eyes glancing down to the desire in my pants.

"Quentin," she murmurs softly and teasingly.

God, I shouldn't want this so fucking bad right now.

But I do and when she suddenly presses her lips to mine in a fierce kiss I could damn explode. Her kiss is more than I'd ever imagined.

Her lips on mine make my whole body tingle and I never want to stop kissing her. To deepen the kiss I pull her body closer to mine, biting her lips and playing with her tongue.

She pulls back breathless.

"I'm sorry," she says with a sexy tone in her voice.

"Don't be sorry for that." I laugh, trying to hide how much I'd enjoyed it.

"Really?"

"Just fucking kiss me again Addison," I demand.

She lets out a little moan, licking her lips teasingly. She's driving me wild. My eyes don't leave hers, even when she pulls her scrub top over her head, exposing her lacy bra.

Taking her cheeks in my palms I smash another kiss to her lips and curse myself for the fact that now I've kissed her again I'm not going to stop until she's moaning my name whilst my dick is buried inside her.

Addison pulls away from my kiss, and begins fumbling with the buttons of my shirt. I have to question her as no doubt I want her but I have to be sure that she wants me.

"Addison, are you sure you want this?"

"Yes," she says with a raspy tone, breathless from our hot kisses.

"You sure? You want me?"

"Yes, Quentin, I want you," she announces dropping her scrub pants from her body to the floor.

I watch her lustfully as she steps out of them, and kicks her high heels off.

Fuck, she's gorgeous.

Frantically, keeping my gaze on her I unbutton my shirt, discarding it to the floor. Underneath my bullet proof vest feels stifling all of a sudden, as she's biting her lips as she watches me undress.

Pulling at the velcro of my vest I lift it over my head throwing it on the table beside us.

I've been shirtless in front of her before but now I feel more exposed than ever, especially when she reaches out to touch my bare chest with her palm and lets out a delightful giggle.

"Fuck Addison," I groan.

She again moans and I need to have her now. Grabbing her around the waist I scoop her up, bridal style and stumble down the hallway.

She points towards her bedroom and as soon as we enter the overly girly room, I throw her body onto the bed, stretching over her to kiss her.

Leaving her lips, I start to kiss her neck, trailing kisses down towards her breasts, kissing the pink buds through the lace of her bra.

Her nipples rise to attention at the graze of my lips over them. Continuing to kiss down her torso, towards her lace panties, I put my thumb in the elastic to push them down her legs to the floor.

She's clean shaven and I just want to drive into her waiting body, but also want to tease her more and enjoy every fucking second I have with her.

Plunging a finger into her body, I tease her, rubbing her clit to feel her desire increasing.

Stretching up to kiss her for a moment, my breath against her face I say, "Addison, please, I want you so bad."

She sits up a little, reaching behind her back to unclasp her bra, tossing it aside without a care.

With her body fully exposed she's even more breathtaking than I ever thought she'd be.

I'd fantasised about being with her so many times, but actually seeing her naked and pleasuring her is a thousand times better than any fantasy.

"Tell me you want me Addison."

She smiles, giggling. "I want you Quentin."

I fumble with my belt, shoving my pants and boxers down my legs. She grabs my length in her grasp, causing me to gasp.

"Do you have a...?"

She nods, reaching to open the drawer beside the bed, extracting a shiny square packet and holding up to me between her fingers. Ripping the packet open with her teeth, she stretches it onto my dick.

I push her back down on the bed again kissing her hard, my throbbing dick pressing into her torso.

Still kissing her frantically I thrust into her waiting body, pulling in and out slowly.

Oh fuck, oh fuck, she feels so fucking good.

I break the kiss, looking into her eyes as I push further into her body. She starts moaning, her hips bucking underneath me, meeting mine with each thrust. I can feel my climax building and want nothing more than to hear her moan my name as she comes for me.

"Addison, I want you to come for me."

As if my words are a cue, her body begins to twitch. She throws her arms behind her head and her climax is strong as she screams, "Oh Quentin, fuck!"

Her juice squirting over me drives me to a hard climax, filling the latex inside her. I collapse against her bare chest, panting, but completely satisfied.

Pulling out of her body I feel like something has changed between us. She's still looking at me lustfully and it makes me desperately want to fuck her again, but I don't want to be greedy.

I'd settle for holding her body against me, and kissing her again.

Standing up I discard the condom in the bin by the door, stepping out of my pants still around my ankles. She's gotten comfortable in the bed, and is still gazing at me like she'd honestly enjoyed every second as much as I had.

I yank my shoes off diving at the bed to kiss her and pull her close to me under the covers. Having her close after finally being with her feels like a dream come true. I'm in a complete daze and know I have to tell her how I feel about her.

Brushing a stray hair from her cheek I muse in her ear, "Addison, I love you."

She turns her head towards me. I don't expect an answer, instead I'm thinking she's going to kiss me, but the lustful look that was in her eyes is gone and has been replaced with shock. I'd fucked up, by admitting my feelings.

"I'm sorry Quentin," she states.

I don't want to her say what I know are going to be her next words. I've honestly just had some of the best sex of my life and she's still going to reject me.

"I don't feel that way about you."

Her words are like a knife to my heart, even though I knew that was exactly what she was going to say.

She'ss still hung up on my brother, and it hurts so bad, even though I know her rejection was inevitable. Anger rises in my chest. I'm seething. I just can't believe her, don't want to believe her.

Getting out of the bed, I grab my clothes from the floor and turning to leave I spit back at her, "I can't believe you Addison, after what we just did, you still don't fucking feel anything for me."

"I'm sorry Quentin, I just can't."

"Yeah, whatever. But thanks for the best sex ever."

She starts to respond but the words freeze on her tongue. Tugging my pants on, I take one last look at her sitting naked on the bed before running down the hallway to grab my vest and shirt. I can't get out of her house fast enough.

Feelings of regret are overtaking me. I'm regretting telling her I love her and I'm having mixed feelings about sleeping with her too.

I'd wanted nothing more than to have her for years, and I can't deny it was absolutely fucking amazing, like I'd said to her, the best sex ever, but I had to open my fucking mouth and tell her how I feel.

I could have had her again if I'd not told her how I feel. But now, as I trudge back to hospital to hopefully find my brother out of surgery and alive, I can't help but feel as though I've completely lost any chance of being with Addison for real, forever.

I'll probably never get the chance to be with her again, unless my brother is no longer with us and she'd again take comfort in my arms and I can't bear to think about that.

(45) Savannah

Even though I'd told Quentin I was going to be fine waiting in the hospital alone I'm not. Pacing up and down in the waiting area is doing nothing to calm my nerves.

The last few hours are a complete blur and the image of the bullet in the air flying towards Hunter is still so vivid in my mind, his body falling to the ground is something that will be possibly forever etched into my mind. The pain of possibly losing him is far worse than the pain Dante inflicted on me.

I can't believe Dante is gone. Hearing the shot he inflicted on himself was a shock to the ears but at the same time a sense of relief washed over me. I feel guilty for being happy he'd shot himself but I'm glad he did as I'd not have to endure months of court time, testifying against him for all I'd endured at his hands.

He's not going to sit in a jail cell, only to be released early on parole to offend again; no he's going to burn in hell and no doubt he deserves as much.

Glancing up at the clock on the wall I can see that only half an hour has passed since Hunter had been wheeled into surgery. It has seemed like eternity and I have to get out of there, or I'm going to find myself passed out on the floor from the stifling hospital air.

Rushing outside I take a deep breath, inhaling the cool night air. It feels strange to be outside at night in Ridgehope; the streets are deserted, lit dimly by tall streetlights that seem out of place.

I feel safer then ever knowing that Dante is no longer around the corner, about to lurch out of the shadows and grab me at any moment.

It's more than that though; it's the town itself. One street with everything you needed and more and I've never felt more at home. Adelaide is not home anymore.

I start to walk down the street back towards the main part of town. I've only been to my destination once but being blessed with a photographic memory I recall details like landmarks in my head easily.

Arriving at the double doors I push them open and walk up to the front desk a little nervous as I know visiting hours will most likely be over but in the present situation I'm hoping for some leeway.

"Hi, I'm here to see Grace Mackenney."

"And you are?"

"Savannah Galison," I declare, liking the way my *'new'* name sounds rolling off my tongue.

"I'm sorry, but visiting hours are over sweetie. We can only admit family after hours."

I sigh. I want to be family.

"I'm Hunter's girlfriend."

She looks at me like my relationship status means nothing to her and I know it probably doesn't but I'm not going to take no for an answer.

"Hunter is in surgery right now. I really need to see his Mum."

"What? Surgery? Is he ok?"

"I don't know. But I really need to speak to his Mum."

Her face softens to my plea.

"Ok Savannah, go on through. Room five."

She presses the door buzzer and pressing my hands against it the lock clicks open. I feel nervous coming to see her without Hunter, especially as the last time when I met her I didn't say a word. So much has changed since then.

I could tell he loves his Mum so incredibly much and she definitely has a soft spot for her eldest son which I can't blame her for. I feel like I should be thanking her for raising him to be the amazing man he is.

He's only been in my life for a few months but I'd fallen for him from the start, like I'd known him all my life.

I know that I want to share the rest of my life with him and knocking on the door of his Mum's room I take a deep breath hoping that I'll get to do just that.

Her voice is low and sad when she answers the knock. Turning the knob in my hand I open the door, slowly stepping into the room.

"Savannah, dear, where's Hunter?" she asks me softly looking around me for her son, as soon as I cross the threshold.

Walking over, I kneel on the floor at her knees. "He's in surgery. He was shot."

Shock crosses her face and tears sting my eyes, seeing the pain my words caused her. "And I'm sorry Mrs Mackenney, but it's all my fault, if he dies it will be my fault."

I look up at her and the tears break through when she strokes my cheek softly. Her next words are a lot calmer than I expect, "Whatever do you mean dear?"

"He...he was shot b...by my husband," I stutter through my sobbing. I expect her to be angry but instead she shows genuine compassion for me, rubbing my hair soothingly as I sob.

"And I'm scared I'm going to lose him. I can't!" I wail, tears still streaming down my cheeks.

"Did you tell him that you love him?" She asks tugging at my heart.
I nod. "Y..yes."

"Then it's not goodbye sweetie."

"What do you mean?"

She lets out a laugh. "My son is absolutely wholeheartedly in love with you Savannah. He wouldn't leave you without making sure you got to feel how much he loves you."

I'm a little taken aback at her surprising words that leave me with a deep longing feeling.

"How do you know he loves me like that?"

"I know my son. He was already in love with you the day he brought you to meet me. He's a Mackenney man after all."

"Sorry, what?"

"Mackenney men fall hard and fast for the woman they are meant to be with. Hunter is his fathers son for sure."

"But Mrs Mackenney how do you know he loves me?"

She strokes my hair again. "Because he came in here the day he thought you were gone and he was absolutely heartbroken. I'd never seen him like that before."

"That's how I feel now, but after all of the pain I've been through with my ex-husband I don't know how to let him know how I feel."

She presses a kiss to my cheek, a sweet gesture that makes my heart swell with love for her too.

"Just like his father, he is the most patient and caring person and he loves you. You have all the time in the world because now you truly have his heart he won't let go."

A wide smile crosses my lips. I feel incredibly happy to know that even Hunter's Mum approves of us being together. She seems to be so wise and is truly sweet. It makes my ache a little thinking about my own Mum.

I stand up, readying myself to leave, to go back to the hospital to see if Hunter is out of surgery.

I press a kiss goodbye to her forehead and she says softly with a smile, "Thanks sweetheart. Are you heading back to the hospital now?"

Even though she's smiling there's a hint of pain and sadness in her voice and I know I have to ask her, "Do you want to come with me?"

She shakes her head. "The nurses wouldn't allow it."

"I'll talk them around."

"I don't know sweetie, could you push my chair all the way there?"

"Of course. You don't know my strength," I say flashing my non existent arm guns at her. She laughs deep in her chest.

"Savannah you're a sweetheart. Wheel me out!"

I grab the wheelchair handles in my hands as she opens the door for us to leave.

Just as I said I persuade the nurses to let her out to see Hunter and promise that someone will bring her back safe and sound.

Once out of the rest home doors she lets out a delightful squeal as she inhales the fresh air.

"Ahh...fresh country air. There's nothing better."

"I agree with that," I muse starting to push her wheelchair down the street towards the hospital, thanking my lucky stars it's slightly downhill.

"Are you ok?" I ask her, hoping this isn't all to much for her.

"Never better honey. There's no doubt Hunter is alive. And he will wake up from surgery surrounded by those he loves."

She's right. She will be by his bed, Quentin will surely be back as well and I will be there.

We all love him more than anything in the world.

(46) Hunter

Waking up, a touch of grogginess in my head I concentrate on focusing on my surroundings. The pain from earlier has somehow disappeared and I realised that's probably due to the fact I'm in a bed in a small hospital room and drugged up on a copious amount of painkillers, that aren't exactly helping quell the pain much at all.

I have a tendency to feel claustrophobic at times and this situation in this small room should have been one of those times, considering that the bed takes up most of the room and it's surrounded by three people.

But claustrophobia doesn't surface as the three people around the bed, are the three people I love the most in the world.

Mum, my brother and Savannah are looking down at me, smiles spreading across their faces when my eyes focus on them.

Mum is on my right and wheeling her wheelchair closer, trying to not get tangled in the IV attached to my arm, that appears to pumping blood into me, she presses a kiss to my forehead.

"My baby boy, how are you doing?" she asks, with the sweet caring tone that only comes from a mother's mouth.

"Better now my two favourite women are here," I say as she touches my hand.

I smile at her before looking at Savannah and see that tears are stinging her eyes. The emotion in the room is definitely evident and breaking the silence I look at Quentin.

He seems a little forlorn, like he has something on his mind, that he needs to get out.

"Hey little bro, I guess I have you to thank. I should have listened to you."

He shakes his head, touching my leg in comfort when he speaks, "Nah Hunter, you shouldn't thank me. I'm sorry but none of this would have happened if I'd just done my job in the first place."

I laugh a little, pain shooting through my body. His statement has truth to it, but we can't change the past.

There's definitely some things that our family wants to keep in the past, but it isn't the time to think about the past now. I have to reassure my brother that despite what he thinks, he's still a good police officer.

"Don't say that Quent. You're good at your job, whats done is done. No point dwelling on the past."

He nods. "Yeah I guess, but I still feel bad."

Mum is smiling, obviously not worried about what has happened and not mad at Quentin either for his part in what has occurred.

She's clearly also not worried seeing me in a hospital bed with an IV in my arm, and the dressings over the gun shot wounds on my lower chest and back.

I'm not sure how she's even able to be here, as the nurses never let her out of the rest home under normal circumstances.

What I do know though is that she loves us both more than anything in the world, and that's evident when she happily says, "I'm just happy to see both my boys."

She gives me a wink, before she speaks again, "Quentin darling, how about wheeling me out to give Hunter a moment with his girl?"

"Sounds like a plan Mum," Quentin replies as he crosses to the other side of the room and wheels her out, shutting the door behind them.

Savannah sits on the edge of the bed and even though there's silence between us, it isn't an uncomfortable silence. I'm just glad that I don't have to say goodbye and even more glad that Savannah is here for me, just like I've been there for her in the last few months.

Taking my hand in hers, she softly speaks, "I'm sorry Hunter, for everything."

"Don't be sorry, baby, it's ok."

"But it's not ok. You could have died, because of me."

I shake my head. "Yeah I know baby, but I couldn't lose you. I would have rather have died than lose you."

"I know," she says softly, pulling back the bed sheet and lifting up my not so stylish hospital gown.

Kissing the bandage covering the bullet wound on my chest she asks softly, "Does it hurt?"

"No, not as much as thinking I lost you."

I have to tell her again how I feel just as I'd told her lying on the road, waiting for the ambulance. I can't recall if she'd heard me or even if she said anything back because thinking back it's all a bit hazy.

I know I've lost a lot of blood, and that even just being in this hospital bed alive is a miracle. I can still feel where the bullet hit me, under my ribs.

Squeezing her hand in mine, and gazing directly into her eyes I speak softly, "I love you, Savannah."

"I love you too, Hunter," is her reply that causes my heart to pound in my chest, and the pain from my wound rises in my body. I wince and her eyes dilate, sensing the pain I'm feeling.

"Are you ok, baby?" she asks, as though she wants to take away the pain.

"Kiss me, baby," I say with a hint of cheekiness, "it will take the pain aw..."

I don't have a moment to finish the sentence as she presses her lips against mine, softly at first and then harder. The kiss is deep, and full of longing.

It seems like forever since I'd kissed her and despite the pain in my chest, I find myself melting into it. There's nothing better than kissing her.

Pulling back she asks, "I didn't hurt you baby did I?"

"No, baby."

"But you're in pain?"

"Yes, baby, I am but it's not your fault, ok?"

"Ok, but I just want to take the pain away."

"I wish you could. But I just want you to lay with me," I tell her moving over a little in the bed, again the pain rushing through me.

"Ok, but tell me if I hurt you," Savannah says softly, grabbing my arm to put it around her before lying next to me.

She presses a kiss to my cheek. "I love you Hunter, so much it hurts."

"I love you too Savannah, so much I literally nearly died for you."

(47) Savannah

I'd stayed with Hunter every night for the week he was in hospital. He had slowly started to get feeling back in his arms and legs, but the pain was still evident in his chest.

He was changed to IV painkillers the second day, after he'd gotten off the blood IV and they seemed to help more.

I'd literally not left the room, except to get myself copious amounts of coffee and to search the lost and found for some clothes to wear. Other than that I'd stayed wrapped in his arms in the small hospital bed that was like a tiny plank of wood and extremely uncomfortable.

On day six of his hospital stay, lying next to him I ask, "Hey baby, was someone going to check on Blitz?"

"Yeah Quentin was going out to the farm every couple of days until we get home."

"That's good. Are you feeling any better?"

"The painkillers are working, but it still aches a bit."

He sits up a little, grabbing me around the waist and pulling my body closer to his. He winces a little in pain. "Baby, please don't if it's going to hurt you."

"Its not Savannah. I need you."

Having him close feels beyond right and I press my lips against his in a demanding kiss. He bites down softly on my lip beckoning me to open up to him.

I let out a deep moan that I know drives him absolutely wild for me. He smiles against my lips as our tongues dance together.

"Fuck Savannah, you have no idea what you do to me, but not here yeah?"

"I know, but can I kiss you again?"

"You don't have to ask to kiss me."

I press another kiss to his lips, pulling back when Doctor Rivnay comes in to see how Hunter is.

He'd at least had the decency to knock, giving us a moment to collect ourselves before we let him in.

I know we probably both look a little disheveled from our make out session and my hair is like a birds nest, having not been able to brush it for a week. As well my lips are a little red from Hunter's kisses and the stubble of his chin that he'd not been able to shave for the past week he'd been in the hospital.

"The doctor won't be happy with us. I'm a mess," I whisper to him.

He gives me a devilish smirk that set the butterflies inside my belly a flutter.

"You look beautiful baby. And I think kissing you is just what I need to get better."

"Glad to help, sexy," I tease.

"Sexy, huh?" He says poking a finger into my belly.

"Yes, Hunter you're damn sexy," I reply licking my lips.

"Baby, don't you dare tease me now. The doctor needs to see me."

I kiss his cheek softly. "Sorry sexy," I giggle, just as Doctor Rivnay enters the room.

He gives me a look that makes me feel incredibly guilty and kind of like a naughty school girl getting caught making out in the change rooms.

He's probably Hunter's age but seems to have an old soul about him and I can't help but wonder if he's married or has a girlfriend.

He definitely needs one if he doesn't as wouldn't be a bad thing for him to lighten up a little bit.

"So Hunter, you're damn lucky really," he says slightly unprofessional in his tone.

"Yeah, what do you mean Doc?"

He glances at the notes in his hands. "Well, the bullet just missed your lungs, and the impact fractured your ribs but as the bullet wasn't lodged internally like we first thought, there was no internal bleeding."

He stops speaking for a moment to let what he's saying sink in.

"Thankfully your blood loss was minimal though, plus your girlfriend here curbed the bleeding well. But honestly you're lucky to be alive."

Hunter nods as Doctor Rivnay's words sink in.

"I had a lot to live for," he says looking at me and smiling, squeezing my hand and pressing a kiss to it.

"Yeah," Doctor Rivnay replied softly, pain in his voice.

He's definitely hiding something about his past and I wonder if the town gossip club has any ideas about the mysterious new doctor in town.

Hunter asks, "So I'm guessing I'm all good for discharge tomorrow?"

"Yeah will keep you for one more night for final observation and a nurse will be in to change your dressings in the morning before you're discharged."

"Ok, can I get out of this bed tonight?"

"Sure. Take a walk outside," he winks at us as he leaves the room, as though he knows we'd gotten a little bit naughty before he came in.

Laughing I turn my head to look back at Hunter. "So where were we sexy?" I tease.

"Hmm, I'm not sure," he teases back, "I think I was making out with my incredibly gorgeous girlfriend."

He again pokes his finger into my belly, the teasing gesture setting the fire burning in me again.I want him so much my whole body aches.

"Yeah I seem to remember making out with my incredibly handsome boyfriend."

"Handsome and sexy?"

"Mmmm," I mumble pressing a kiss to his lips. He responds, pulling me closer to his side, still wincing a little in pain before he kisses me sweetly and softly, taking his time to taste my lips. I really could get used to this. There is nowhere I want to be more than laying wrapped in Hunter's arms.

~ ~

Leaving the hospital the next day with Hunter feels like some twisted sense of déjà vu. We'd barely slept a wink, passing the time just revelling in being together like we had when I'd been holed up in the hospital and partly because we had been laying side by side, just together, kissing each other softly.

At the front desk after the nurse had been in to change the dressings on his wounds, Hunter is filling out the discharge paperwork, holding the crutches under his arms to support himself.

I stifle a yawn, and shake my head realising the nurse is talking to me, "Ms Galison? You will need to drive Mr Mackenney home."

"Hmm," I yawn, a hand over my mouth.

"Is that ok?" She asks me.

"Yes, yes that's fine," I say stifling yet another yawn.

"So how do we get home? My Ute isn't here," Hunter says to the nurse.

"Yes, it is actually. It's parked out the front. The Sergeant drove it over from the scene last week."

"Ok thanks," He says taking my hand, squeezing it softly as he laces his fingers with mine.

We walk out together, Hunter leaning into my side for support, struggling with the crutches.

Just as the nurse had said his Ute is right out the front of the hospital.I help Hunter in, clicking his seatbelt and throwing the crutches in the back of the ute before I jump in the drivers seat.

I can feel his eyes on me and I have to take a deep breath as I start the engine. I can do this. I've driven his stupid manual car before, but in trying to get my feet to cooperate I stall the engine.

Hunter lets out a laugh, "Can't you drive a stick baby?" He teases.

"I can drive a stick just fine," I reply reaching over to touch between his thighs teasingly.

"Oh really?" He taunts me, his delicious smile and dimples spreading across his face, "Well to be honest baby the key to driving a stick is to go slow."

I withdraw my hand from between his thighs and start the engine again. This time I edge the pedals out slower and we bunny hop out of the hospital car park.

Once out on the open road back towards the farm I crunch the gears when changing them. Hunter laughs again. "I'm sure you know how to drive a stick baby. I'm just teasing you."

"It's not funny," I spit back in a mocking tone.

"It is a little bit."

He laughs again, harder but cringes when the pain in his ribs surfaces.

"How about some music?" I ask flicking the radio on.

As soon as the sound from the speakers fills the car I'm the one to break into laughter, as Hunter begins singing the lyrics to *'The Fighter'* at the top of his lungs, surprisingly in tune and it's pretty damn hot.

I can't help but sing along with him. The words are exactly us, our whole relationship summed up in song. He grabs my hand and presses a kiss to it and raising his eyebrows teasingly he taunts me even more when he licks his lips.

"Stop Hunter. I'm trying to drive," I protest meekly, not able to honestly hide the fact that I don't enjoy his teasing.

"Lucky we're almost home then," He taunts again as we reach the farm gate.

Leaving the engine running I jump out to open the gate before driving in slowly so I don't have to change gears.

Stopping just by the farmhouse verandah, I cut the engine and run back to shut the gate before helping Hunter out.

He doesn't even let me grab the crutches for him, immediately pushing my body against the side of the Ute and leans closer to me for support in staying upright.

"Thanks for getting me home in one piece."

He breathes against my face. I can feel the rise and fall of his breath against my chest that's pinned against his and can see the longing in his eyes that are locked on mine.

"Are you going to show me how well you can really drive a stick now baby?" He teases, not letting me reply before pressing a hungry kiss to my lips, and running his hands over my sides.

His touch sets my insides on fire and I grab his hair between my fingers as I urge him to kiss me deeper. I want all of him, want to taste him and devour him.

I'm certain now that nothing will stop me from opening up to him again. Laughing against his lips, I pull back from from his kiss, realising that we're standing outside in the middle of the day, and I'm kissing him senseless.

Even though there isn't another person for kilometres it fees illicit and intoxicating.

"It's hot out here," I say with a teasing tone.

"You don't say. That was a fucking hot as kiss Savannah."

"I think it's time to take this inside." I wink at him.

He grabs my hand and drags me to the farmhouse, urgently, struggling to walk but desperate to be inside.

He utters a greeting to Blitz before yanking the farmhouse door open, slamming it closed and pushing me against it.

He clearly doesn't need the crutches. Demandingly he presses his lips to mine in a kiss that is fierce and urgent like he will never kiss me again. The fire in my body is moving lower and I moan against his lips, feeling desperate for his lips to return to mine when he breaks our kiss. He speaks with lust in his voice, "Oh Savannah you drive me fucking wild." His hands are running up my sides, his callous hands on my skin setting me on fire, awakening every nerve and making me feel more alive than I have in years.

"I want you Hunter."

"Mmmm," he moans clutching the hem of my t-shirt in his hands. His eyes are locked on mine, even as he lifts the t-shirt over my head, only breaking contact for the moment the fabric covers my face.

Kissing him hard I fumble with the buttons of his shirt, helping him slide it off his arms, my lips not leaving his.

Pulling back from the kiss he whispers in my ear, "Bedroom. You. Now." His tone is carnal, like Tarzan and it sends a delightful shiver through my body.

With my hand laced with his and his body leaning against my side we head to the bedroom. He falls against the bed, pulling me down with him, kissing my lips lightly before kissing my neck and down my body.

Standing up over him, I shimmy my skirt over my hips discarding it to the floor and straddle him in only my lacy underwear.

His eyes are full of longing as he runs his hands down my sides, causing the fire to burn everywhere he touches. I love the way his hands feel on me, on my skin as he assesses the curve of my hips.

"Savannah you're so fucking beautiful."

I lean over him and kiss him in response. Against my stomach I can feel his desire increasing and desperately my hands edge down fumbling with his belt. Cupping my face in his hands he deepens the kiss for a moment before he pulls away and takes my hands with his.

"Slow down baby. I don't think I'm up to it tonight."

His words hurt a little, but he's right. There is no rush. We have all the time in the world.

"Sorry baby," he apologises.

"It's ok. I got a bit carried away," I say, matching his apologetic tone.

"You know I want to be with you more than anything, yeah?"

"I know, we don't have to rush."

"Come here," he says patting the bed next to him. I crawl up the bed to lay down next to him and he wraps an arm around me, pressing a soft kiss to my forehead.

We lay in silence for a moment, just listening to each others breathing. It's perfect but a thought comes to mind and I have to break the silence.

"I was thinking I should organise to officially change my name."

He looks over at me, an almost worried look on his face.

"Yeah maybe. What would you change it to?" he asks like he honestly has no idea at what I'm suggesting.

Without a doubt I'm Savannah Galison with him, I always had been but I don't want even that to be my name anymore.

"I was thinking maybe Savannah Mackenney," I say with a hint of humour in my tone, hoping that he won't take my suggestion the wrong way.

He smiles at me. "I like the sound of that but maybe not yet baby."

My heart sinks at his response that feels like a stab to the heart.

Does he really not want me and love me as much as I think? As much as he's told me he does.

I shake my head, not really sure what to say in response, so instead I kiss him quickly before closing my eyes to go to sleep.

Despite his response, here with him is exactly where I'm supposed to be and I don't doubt that soon my name will be Savannah Mackenney. I'm absolutely sure of it.

(48) Hunter

I fucked up.

I upset her.

The moment the words left my mouth and she pressed a chaste goodnight kiss on my lips, I knew I hadn't given her the answer she wanted. I was truly taken aback that she feels that way towards me, that she wants to change her name to Mackenney. It's more than her saying '*I love you*'. It's a complete declaration of her love and my response to her was idiotic because it isn't what I feel at all.

I'm absolutely head over boots in love with her.

Fuck, I'd run towards a maniac with a gun to save her life, I love her that much, but I'm scared, overwhelmed with everything that has happened in the short time I've known her.

My fierce protector instincts kicked in from the moment I found her in the spare room that first day and guilt plagues me still for the choice I made to not go into the supermarket with her.

Now watching her sleep, holding her close I know I have to let go of that guilt, plus also the guilt of the past and focus on the future.

Guilt always got to me, and in the past it held me back, making my heart ache from the loss that always followed.

It all stemmed back to the day of my grandfather's death, his murder. I'd been too busy flirting with Addison, playing around out in the paddocks and I wasn't there to protect him.

Granted it shouldn't have been my job to protect him, but with my father out droving and my Mum in the farmhouse with him and Quentin I should have been there, as the oldest son it was my job when my father was away to protect my younger brother.

Mum can't even say the word *'killed'* now, it's an unspoken word. Quentin still has nightmares from what he saw that day, but he never speaks of them and it breaks my heart a little for him.

When I'd thought Dante had killed Savannah, that was when the true guilt hit me, like all the guilt from my past collided with my present. I have to make it right, to right all the wrong of my past, all the wrong that Addison brought into my life.

I don't hate her, I couldn't ever but she turned my world upside down in the wrong way.

I'd been so blind for years, even when we were together to how toxic our relationship really was and I can't even bear to think about my life if I'd married her. I honestly don't think she even knows the full story, yes, part of our breakup was her vindictiveness towards my choice to stay on the farm after Dad got sick, but I've never told her the whole truth.

I don't know if i'll ever to be able to tell her what her family did to mine, as I only knew part of the story myself.

Savannah grunts in her sleep. I don't want to wake her but I need some air as the thoughts of the past are becoming all consuming and I'm suddenly feeling even more guilty for not sharing my past with her, just like she'd openly shared hers with me.

Carefully grabbing her arm from over me, trying to not wake her I roll out of the bed, tiptoeing down the hallway, stumbling a little on my feet to go and sit on the verandah seat.

Blitz gives me puppy dog eyes, questioning my erratic behaviour since we'd come home earlier.

Something has definitely shifted between Savannah and I, the longing and need between us is becoming more urgent and consuming.

Being a hot blooded male I can't deny I've loved every kiss and touch we've shared but I feel like we're moving to fast.

Dante has not even been gone for forty-eight hours and she wants to change her name, it just seemed like all to much and I can't quell the feeling of being in too deep, that the desperate consuming love I'm feeling for her is to good to be true.

Running my hands through my hair I curse out loud causing Blitz to look up at me and give me a stink eye look.

"Sorry buddy, I've fucked up."

He turns his head, looking at me, searching my face for answers.

"I love her buddy, but I can't marry her, can I?"

God, whats wrong with me? I'm asking my fucking dog for advice.

I have to tell Savannah the truth about the past, the reason for my reaction. If I want to make her realise how much I love her and to be open to correcting my stupid comment, I need to open up and be open to actually making her mine completely.

I know I also have to tell Addison the truth about what I know about our families past in the hope it will take the guilt away, to make her see that no matter what she might think there is no way I can ever be with her. Even though I'd desperately loved her to the point of asking her to marry me, we were never meant to be. Our families were never meant to be united.

It's uncanny that the present always makes you realise how the secrets of your past could hold you back from opening up to your future and as though my future knows exactly that, the door creaks open.

Turning towards the door I find Savannah standing in the door jam, in her underwear, rubbing her eyes sleepily.

She looks absolutely breathtakingly beautiful and my heart skips, looking at the hurt still present in her eyes from my stupid comment.

"Hey baby, come sit with me. We need to talk."

(49) Savannah

Waking up in the dark in Hunter's bed I panic when he isn't lying beside me.

For a moment I think that the past days with him have all been some crazy dream, that it isn't real that Dante is gone.

That I'd practically thrown myself at Hunter, making out with him like a desperate school girl, a love drunk fool.

But when I pinch my arm I'm very much awake and I know it isn't a dream.

The way my body feels on fire and is aching for Hunter also tells me that the kisses we've shared are definitely not in my head. There's no way my mind could make me feel the desperate hunger and need I feel for Hunter. I do know one thing that has me scared though, that I'd stupidly told him I want to be *'Savannah Mackenney'*.

I'd practically proposed to him without actually asking the question directly and he rejected me. It didn't seem like him at all, his reaction so unloving, it gave me a sense that something is bothering him or he's hiding something from me.

Getting out of the bed I stumble through the house in the dark to find him.

He's nowhere to be seen inside and it crosses my mind that maybe he'd gone out droving without telling me, but his hat is still hanging on the hallway stand, his boots still by the door and he never leaves without those.

Still wondering, I open the door to see if Blitz is around.

It creaks when I open it and I'm shocked to find Hunter sitting on the love seat only in his jeans.

He looks up at me and his face is full of pain. My heart constricts when he speaks softly, "Hey baby, come sit with me. We need to talk."

What good ever came from those words? He's going to break up with me, he's going to rip my heart out. How could I have been so stupid? I knew this was going to happen.

I go to sit beside him, and he reaches out to put his arm around me trying to pull me closer but I shrug him off.

"Don't touch me Hunter," I spit at him angrily.

"Oh Savannah, please I'm sorry ok," he says, sadness evident in his tone.

"Just say it Hunter. You don't want me. You don't love me."

Standing up, he balls his hands into fists showing me he's angry at my words.

"How can you fucking think I don't love you? I never said that."

I bite down on my lip, not knowing what to say to him.

"You...you said that I shouldn't change my name to Mackenney," I say, feeling as though I'm about to burst into tears.

"Yes, and I meant it, but not for the reason you're thinking Savannah."

"So you do want to be with me?"

"Of course I do Savannah. I fucking love you."

"But?"

He sits back down, not meeting my eyes, his head in his hands.

"You might not want to be a Mackenney when I tell you the truth."

I lift his chin with my finger, pressing a kiss to his forehead.

"I highly doubt that Hunter."

I can see tears stinging his eyes, the obvious pain of a secret that's plaguing him.

"Hunter, please talk to me," I coerce.

He grabs me almost forcefully, pulling me against his chest, his breathing deep and almost tortuous.

"The obstetrician, Addison, you know she's my ex-girlfriend yeah?"

"Yes, but what's she got to do with this?"

"Her grandfather did a terrible thing when we were younger."

"Hunter what are you saying?"

"He killed my grandfather Savannah."

My mouth is agape, as the shock of his words hit me. I have no idea what I can do to offer him comfort, so instead I just wait a moment until he speaks again.

"I..I was out in the back paddock with Addison, fooling around...and Dad was out droving.." he pauses, his face constricting like it's painful to tell the story.

I squeeze his arm in comfort.

"And he came into the farmhouse screaming something about my Dad and his daughter."

"I don't understand."

"I...I don't know much...I just know it was him. My grandfather was at the kitchen table and he shot him fatally straight between his eyes."

Instinctively I place my hand over the bullet wound on his chest, as he draws in breath thinking about how he could have met the same fate at the hands of Dante.

"But you and Addison were still together after this?"

"She doesn't know. Her grandfather didn't mean to kill mine. He was after my Dad."

"Oh Hunter, and after this your Dad fell ill?"

"Yeah. It was all kind of swept under the rug. I don't even think my Mum knows the real reason he killed him."

The tears have started to fall down his cheeks, as all the loss of his past comes rushing back into his mind. It makes sense to me now how he felt thinking I was gone when Dante found me, and I feel a pang of guilt for causing the man I love to have to endure that pain.

He continues talking when I don't respond. "The Yorke's moved away for awhile and when they came back I became friends with Jett again and fell in love with Addison. Mum didn't tell us anything about what happened until after Dad died and Addison rejected my proposal."

I turn his face to mine, pressing a kiss to his lips.

"Why would this make me not want to be a Mackenney?"

"Because I don't know the real reason behind his death, Savannah. It's the Mackenney family secret and I'm scared."

"Scared of what exactly?"

"That the secret is a curse. That somehow history will repeat itself."

I chuckle softly. "Your family is not cursed, Hunter. The past is the past. We need to focus on the future."

"I know but you've already had too much pain in your life. I can't bear to think that I might cause you more pain."

"You won't."

He doesn't reply, instead pulls me against his chest more, smashing his lips to mine in a deep kiss.

Grabbing his hair I pull him closer, as close as possible, urging him to open his mouth to kiss me deeper. He's opened his heart to me and I want to kiss away the hurt of his past, just like he'd done the same for me.

Reaching behind my back he expertly unclasps my bra, and runs his hands over my breasts, down my body, moaning against my mouth before pulling away with his face still a whisper from mine.

"You're so fucking beautiful Savannah. I love you so fucking much."

"I love you to Hunter Mackenney," I reply, emphasising *'Mackenney'*, before I kiss him hard and passionately.

No matter the past secrets I'm still sure of one thing.

I want to be Savannah Mackenney.

(50) Hunter

Opening up to Savannah about my family's past had been difficult and I wished I could have told her more, but to this day I don't know the real reason. Quentin had seen it happen, but hadn't shared much with me because it was too painful. He was too young to understand at the time anyway and Addison didn't know anything about what happened either, too young to understand herself too, plus her parents whisked her and Jett back to the city pushing everything under the rug and making the rumours fly around town.

She knew her grandfather was in jail for a time before his death a few years later but she didn't know why. Thinking more about it, it was probably why my Mum had never really approved of my relationship with Addison, but Dad seemed to not care at all, like he had a secret that tied it all together.

The more I thought about it, even though it wasn't important now it seemed as though this secret meant that Addison and I were not meant to be, ever.

~ ~

All I want now is to be with Savannah, more than anything.

The pain of having secrets had brought us together and we'd not spent a moment apart since we'd come back from the hospital after I'd been shot.

The wound has mostly healed, but a scar remains and I kind of love the scar. It's a reminder of the love I have for her and I know in my heart there's only one way forward.

Savannah pulls me into a hug, just as I'm trying to walk out the door.

"Baby I gotta go. I'll be back in a few days."

"I know, but i'll miss you."

"I'll miss you too, but this farming conference is really important."

"I just want to go with you."

"I wish you could, but when I'd organised to attend it I was a single man," I taunt her, poking the soft flesh of her belly. She laughs at my emphasis of single.

"Will you think about me?"

"What do you think Savannah?" I ask teasing her.

"I don't know," she taunts me, "I'll be thinking about you." And with those words she kisses me, an all consuming kiss that's wild and delicious.

I lick her lips, running my tongue along the soft sweetness, tasting them before I delve into her mouth to play with her tongue, tasting her and lavishing her.

Pulling away I grunt. "Kiss me again like that and I'll never leave baby."

She licks her lips, a devilish glint in her eyes, taunting me, begging for another breathless kiss.

"Oh Savannah, I want to...I really want to...but I really have to go."

She smiles at me, lacing her fingers with mine. Placing a kiss on her forehead I pull away from her grasp, crossing the verandah to head to the Ute, fighting with myself to leave or run back to take her in my arms, and kiss her senseless.

"I love you Savannah. I'll call you tonight when I get there."

"Ok. I love you to Hunter."

I climb in the Ute and wave at her standing on the verandah as I drive away, hoping that I'll get some time in the city away from the conference.

~ ~

Flopping down on the hotel room bed I sigh deeply, my whole body aching from the trip that had been utterly exhausting.

Six hours doesn't seem that far but when driving on your own, with only your own thoughts to keep you company the time seems to drag. Savannah had barely left my mind for a second, the whole time I could still feel her hot kiss on my lips, her hands on my body.

We'd definitely gotten a lot more intimate in the last month or so since the whole Dante situation, but I'd wanted to do so much more than kiss her for months and she'd started to let her guard down, letting me touch her more.I crave the feeling being with her gives me.

It sends warmth and desire through me and even just thinking about kissing her is making my pants bulge with want.

There really is only one thing that will make her let her guard down completely and I want that to, more than anything but the pain of rejection in the past is still heavy on my heart even though I know it shouldn't be. Plus the other secrets of my family's past are heavy on my heart too.

Do I really want her to bear the Mackenney name?

Savannah couldn't be more different to Addison though. In the last month she'd fully embraced living on the farm with me, showing me she isn't afraid to get her hands dirty by helping fix the paddock fences and coming out droving with me. I can't help but smile thinking about that, laughing at how she'd gotten more confident driving the Ute, no longer bunny hopping every time. But it was the first night we'd spent together so close to taking the next step that is at the forefront of my mind.

Her touch set me on fire and even though it was utterly freezing outside the cocoon of the swag and us being completely naked, there was only warmth.

She'd run her hands all over me, awakening something deeper in me that I wanted to explore, but I couldn't take her then, having not thought about protection. Part of me also knew that despite her teasing, her hot as kisses and obvious desire for me, she wasn't ready to take that step without commitment from me.

Oh fuck, now I'm horny as.

My eyes feel heavy with sleep, so I yank my jeans off without undoing the belt which is not an easy feat when the longing is evident in the front of your pants. Pulling my shirt over my head I toss it to the floor to lay back further on the bed.
Reaching down my body, towards my crotch to alleviate the need I jump back in shock when I hear a familiar sound, a ringing followed by "Savannah calling."
In my exhaustion I'd forgotten to call her like I'd promised and I practically dive off the bed towards my bag to retrieve my phone, but still miss her call.
I'm too tired to call her back so I send a text instead.

Hunter: Sorry baby. I'm super tired. xx
Savannah: That's ok. I just wanted to say goodnight. xx
Hunter: Goodnight baby. I love you! xxx
Savannah: Do you want to see what I'm wearing to bed?
Hunter: I'm already thinking about you naked, but ok

A picture message pops up on my phone, her posing seductively on the bed in a white button shirt that is clearly mine.

Hunter: Is that my shirt baby?
Savannah: It might be ;)
Hunter: You look damn sexy in it

Savannah: Wish you were here to take it off me
Hunter: Oh baby so do I...guess I'll just have to dream about it
Savannah: Wicked dreams...goodnight sexy xxxx
Hunter: the best kind...goodnight beautiful...I love you xxxx
Savannah: I love you too handsome xxxxx

Putting my phone on the side table, I close my eyes, thinking of the picture she'd just sent me.

I really need to sleep, but like many nights before sleep isn't going to come easy when all I can think about is Savannah naked and moaning my name as I finally make her mine.

God, I love her, I really fucking love her.

~ ~

I couldn't wait to get out of the farming conference. No doubt it had been interesting hearing about ways forward in farming and opportunities like meat production and small goods, but I had a more pressing matter to attend to on my last day in the city.

I gathered up some brochures on the new opportunities and raced out the door.

I don't like being in the city much, the air thick with fumes feels like it's assaulting my nose every time I take a breath.

Walking the streets I gaze in the windows of the jewellery stores, gaping at the prices, the reality hitting me that although Savannah is worth everything I can't afford any of them.

It makes my heart sink.

I want to give her the most beautiful ring, one that would be unique and show her how much I love her. Looking in the windows, after gaping at the prices of all the rings that struck my eyes, the sudden realisation hits me that I already have the perfect ring for her.

Country Secrets

The perfect ring for my beautiful Savannah is tucked away in my drawer at the farmhouse.

A smile crosses my face remembering when my Grandmother gave it to me, after my Grandfather was murdered.

She'd told me I'd know when I found the right girl, because there would be no way she'd refuse to marry me when I presented her with the ring and that any girl that refused to marry me, well she'd have to be a damn fool. At the memory I laugh, thinking that Addison was a fool, but also that I was more than glad she was a fool that'd I not married because this time around, I'd found the right girl. I could only hope that she thought the same of me.

~ ~

When I arrive home late after the farming conference Savannah is already asleep in my bed.

I grin at how peaceful and beautiful she looks.

No doubt she'd slept in here the whole three days I'd been gone.

She murmurs softly, clutching the sheets in her hands and entangling herself in them.

All I really want to do more than anything is to crawl in beside her and hold her close, but first I need to find the ring.

Trying to not make too much noise I edge the tallboy drawer out, digging through my shirts to the bottom of the drawer.

It's still there, buried deep, the small velvet box. I brush my fingers over it, before taking it out and flipping it open.

It's even more striking than I remembered and I know it's the perfect ring for her, as the sapphires sparkle just like the hint of blue in her green eyes does.

About to put it back in the drawer, I turn startled when I hear her voice, groggy from sleep. "Baby is that you?"

"Yeah, baby it's me."

She sits up, looking at me, her eyes trying to focus on what I'm holding in my hands.

I'd slip them behind my back and she asks, "What are you hiding?"

"Nothing, baby, go back to sleep."

Snapping the box shut, I drop it into the drawer without turning around. Pushing my butt against the drawer I force it shut.

Savannah pouts at me. "Come to bed baby," she teases.

"I was planning to, but i'm not ready to go to sleep yet."

"Mmm, what did you have in mind sexy?" she says in a seductive tone.

I yank my t-shirt over my head and climb into bed next to her.

"You're still wearing my shirt?"

"Yeah, and?" she says biting her lip.

That only means one thing. She's wearing only my shirt, meaning underneath she's completely naked.

"Thats a little bit naughty Savannah," I tease, poking her belly teasingly, pulling her closer and tickling her, loving the sweet giggles that escape her lips.

"I know," she says, licking her lips, our teasing kiss me now gesture.Her invitation to kiss her doesn't go unnoticed.

Grabbing her around the waist I lean over her and begin trailing kisses down her neck, over her collarbone and across her breasts through the fabric of the shirt.

She moans when my hand slips under the hem of the shirt.

"Tell me what you want Savannah."

"You. Hunter. I. Want .You," she says drawn out and raspy.

Her words excite me, and I press a fierce kiss to her lips.

Pulling me closer, she grabs my hair in her fingers, to pull me as close to her as possible.

Her moans of pleasure are a straight shot to my pants and I feel a little relieved when breathless she pulls back, looking up at me with lust in her eyes. "Please Hunter, I...want..."

"Oh baby, I want you so bad, but if I have my way with you now, I won't last a minute."

Her pout is so damn sexy, but my words are more than true.

I want to take my time, to really show her what she does to me, to show her how it can be when you truly love someone, she deserves as much.

"Please Hunter. I just want to be with you," she begs.

"Soon baby. I promise it'll be worth the wait."

She doesn't respond, just kisses me softly and cuddles closer to me.

I never thought I'd be the one holding back from sleeping with anyone, but I want to keep the promise that being with me will be worth the wait and everything she'd never thought it could be.

~ ~

I've been planning the perfect night for weeks; the perfect night that will be the true beginning of our life together.

The plan is to take her into town, to relive the best parts of the night when I realised I'd completely fallen in love with her.

Firstly to see Mum to tell her my plan, followed by dinner, and a walk to the oval, where I'm planning to drop to my knee to present her with the ring between the goal posts.

It's all in my head, and I want it to be perfect, just like she is.

Checking myself in the mirror, I tuck my brown shirt into my jeans, before shrugging my sport jacket on. Opening the drawer, I dig out the velvet box again, and slip it into my pocket of my jacket.

Nervousness is plaguing me even though I know she loves me.

Addison had loved me , but she rejected me and I'd been so hurt by that rejection I never thought I'd love anyone again.

But I've fallen completely in love with Savannah, more so than I'd ever been with Addison and this is right. I just know it.

I'd told her to dress nice but casual in anything she liked from my mothers cupboard.

Time is ticking as we really have to get going to make it into town before visiting hours end at the rest home.

Nervousness is plaguing me even just walking down the hallway to the guest room. It isn't her room anymore, as she's always in my room, our room.

Stepping up to the door I take a deep breath, and knock.

"Are you ready baby?" I call out.

"Yeah nearly, come in," she croons.

Turning the knob I slowly open the door, taking in the sight of her in front of me.

She's wearing a semi see-through white long sleeved blouse, strategically unbuttoned to show just a hint of cleavage and has it tucked into a red mini skirt that hugs her hips, and extenuates her legs.

I'm shocked at how absolutely breathtaking she looks, but I'm also shocked that she found such attire in Mum's closet.

"Fuck Savannah, you look absolutely stunning."

"Thanks, you don't look to bad yourself," she says winking at me as she tugs some red high heels on her feet.

"Ready?" I ask, patting the pocket with the ring in and extending my hand to her to take.

Taking her hand in mine sends an electric shiver up my spine. I still can't believe I'm actually going to do this.

I lead her outside, ready to help her get in the Ute, but something seems amiss and I ask her, "Baby, have you seen Blitz?"

"No, why?"

"I think I can hear him whimpering."

We both concentrate, listening intently and Savannah speaks first, "Its coming from that way."

She's pointing towards the barn at the front of the main paddock and I know that if Blitz is down there it means only one thing, my perfect night is ruined.

Not even saying anything I run towards the barn to find the exact scene I'd expected. My heavily pregnant heifer is lying on her side, in the late stage of her labour and is clearly struggling.

Blitz is nudging her, whimpering. Ruffling the fur on his head I say, "Its ok buddy. We're going to help her."

From around the barn I grab some rope to help pull the calf out if needed and kneeling down beside the heifer I tug my jacket aside, throwing it behind me, when I hear Savannah's voice behind me. "Hey, that hurt," she screeches.

I'd thrown my jacket at her and it had hit her leg, her calf as funny as that was.

She looks around the barn at what is happening and doesn't hesitate for a moment in asking, "Can I help?"

"Yeah, I'm going to need your help to keep her calm."

"Ok, how do I that?" she asks, tugging her shoes off and rolling her sleeves up to her elbows.

"Kneel down by her side and stroke her belly. It will help calm her."
She follows my instruction, her face calm.

"Is this right?" she asks softly.

"Yeah, i'm just going to tie this rope around the calf's legs to pull it out. Keep her calm ok baby?"

She nods. "Ok."

Tying the rope with a loose knot, I pull hard and with a yelp of pain from the heifer the calf is born. Blood spatters across our chests and I can't help but smile at Savannah.

This has essentially ruined my perfectly planned night, but when she speaks excitedly I know the timing couldn't have been more perfect than any night I'd planned.

"Oh my god Hunter I just helped a cow give birth, yeah?"

"Yeah baby you did."

"It was amazing," she says excitedly making my heart swell with love for her.

Wiping my hands across my jeans, I then brush my fingers against her cheek.

"You're amazing Savannah."

She blushes a deep shade of crimson, and tries to speak but her words are frozen on her tongue.

It's now or never.

Feeling around the ground I find my jacket, the little velvet box sitting next to it in the dirt.

Picking it up I hold it up to her, flipping open the lid.

It isn't me down on one knee and her standing, it isn't out somewhere and it's far from perfect but it's the right moment.

Her eyes light up, the sparkle of blue present in them as she looks at me and then at the sapphire encrusted diamond ring I'm holding out to her.

"Savannah, I know this isn't the perfectly planned night, the amazing moment that every girl dreams of, but having you here with me, helping me and accepting my life is my idea of perfect. And the only thing that would make my life more than perfect would be having you as my wife. Will you marry me Savannah?"

Her grin says it all, spreading right across her face. "Yes, yes, Hunter, I will marry you," she says excitedly.

Taking the ring from the velvet box I toss the box aside and slip the ring onto the finger of her left hand, placing a kiss on it.

"Its beautiful," she says, holding her hand up to admire it.

"It was my grandmother's."

"Oh Hunter, I love you," she squeals happily.

I don't respond, instead pull her body close to mine to kiss her, giving her through my lips on hers all the love I feel for her.

We take a moment to settle the heifer down, to make sure the calf is able to suckle.

The night definitely hasn't started out perfect but it's sure as hell going to end perfect.

Standing up Savannah brushes the dirt off her butt, smirking at me cheekily as she does so.

"You're such a tease Savannah," I say smiling wide.

"Mmmm, but you like it?"

"Damn right. I love it. How about we head inside to get cleaned up?" I say suggestively.

A cheeky grin spreads across her face and she blushes more as she runs back towards the farmhouse. "Dibs on the shower then," she calls back to me.

Laughing I pick up her shoes and my jacket following her, with Blitz at my heels.

Everything is perfect.

(51) Savannah

Running back to the farmhouse I can't help but stare at the ring on my finger. The sapphires are most definitely real and I know that means it's worth a great deal of money.

It feels really strange to be wearing a ring on my wedding finger again, a mix of feelings, like I don't deserve the happiness of it, and a what if it all goes wrong feeling just like my wedding previously.

I can't think of that now though.

The night is too perfect to ruin with my melancholic thoughts of the past. I'll have to tell Hunter at some point, but right now I need to be with him.

Stopping at the farmhouse door, standing against it, I watch him run towards me from the barn with the biggest grin on his face, once again showing his adorable dimples. I don't move an inch, even when he steps up to me, his nose against mine.

"I thought you were having a shower first?" he taunts.

I giggle before closing the distance between us with a kiss, wrapping my arms around his neck to pull his body closer to mine.

Pulling away I breathe into his ear. "Maybe you should join me?"

He lets out a guttural moan, that sets the fire burning in my belly.

I want him now. All of him, now.

Grabbing his shirt in my grip I suggest, "It'd be a shame to waste water."

He bends down to try and kiss me in reply but I hold my finger up to my lips instead and reach behind me to open the door.

Following me, his gaze does not leave mine even as I sashay down the hallway towards the bathroom, discarding my clothes on the way.

Once I reach the bathroom, wearing only my underwear, that barely covers any skin , I stop to stand in the doorway again.

He takes one longing look at me, taking in the sight of me practically naked before he pushes me into the bathroom and against the wall.

Grabbing my arse in his grip makes my skin burn with his touch.

"A g-string Savannah?" he questions, his lip curling on one side.

"I was wearing a tight skirt," I defend cheekily.

"Yeah true, but I'd prefer if you had nothing on."

Lifting my hands above my head he kisses my neck, licking my skin in delight.

His lips continue placing kisses across my shoulder, stopping a moment to look up at me with the carnal Tarzan look in his eyes that drives me crazy for him.

I can't tear my eyes from his.

The desire to be with him is heading south and I can feel the minimal fabric of my g-string becoming soaked with my want for him.

"Kiss me, Hunter," I demand.

He licks his lips, before smashing his lips against mine in a fierce kiss that is just like our kiss before he left for the farming conference.

He licks my lips, forcing me to open my mouth and all I can do is respond, my mouth melting against his.

He's still completely dressed and with my arms still above my head I feel completely at his in control in a way I've never felt before, so alive and so cherished.

Pulling away from the delicious kiss I teasingly say, "Baby, I think you're supposed to be naked for a shower."

He lets out a deep laugh, his eyes locked on mine as he slowly strips from his clothes, discarding them to the floor.

As he pushes his boxers to the floor I gasp in shock seeing him completely naked, his dick hard showing his desire.

In his Tarzan voice he groans at me, "Touch me Savannah."

I reach towards his body, grabbing his throbbing dick in my hand, slowly running my hand up and down his length. He moans so deeply I think he's going to let go right away, but instead he grabs my hips, his fingers grazing along the edge of my g-string.

Leaning closer to me he whispers seductively, "Do you want me to touch you Savannah?"

"Yes," I say, my tone raspy and before I even have a moment to think about what he's asking my g-string is on the floor at my feet.

Pressing a kiss to my lips, at the very same moment he plunges a finger into my hot waiting body, causing me to moan into his mouth, giving into the sheer pleasure of his kiss and touch.

Panting he pulls back. "You're so fucking wet Savannah."

I bite my lips, feeling the heat rise in my cheeks.

"Don't be embarrassed baby. It's hot as!"

Those words awake something even more in me.

I want him so much it hurt, my whole body alive, my core throbbing, demanding release.

Biting my lips again I teasingly edge my bra straps down my arms, unclasping it and discarding it to the floor.

His eyes light up with longing again, his eyes gazing over my nakedness when he speaks, "You're absolutely breathtaking Savannah."

Stepping closer to me, pressing his body against mine he begins his trail of kisses again, across my collarbone, to each breast, teasing the nipples with his tongue.

The sheer pleasure has me breathless, as he continues lower, kissing down my scar, until he reaches my hips.

Looking up at me, he grabs my arse in his hands, before his kisses reach the inside of my thighs.

He lets out a strange but delicious growl, kissing my clit, licking, tasting and sucking.

Grabbing his hair in my fists, I buck my pelvis against his face.

Nothing has ever felt this amazing before, the sensation of his tongue deep within me is something I want to feel again and again.

"Oh fuck, Hunter. I'm going to come," I scream out, wanting the sweet release to overcome my body when his tongue leaves my intimate flesh and he looks up at me again, a satisfied smirk on his face.

He stands up, his face so close, a whisper from mine and he croons, "Not yet baby."

Closing the gap he kisses me so hard I can taste myself on his lips.

It's damn hot and I can feel the desire between my legs building again, not to mention his desire pressing into my belly.

Breathless he pulls away from the kiss. "How about we get clean before we get really dirty?" he says suggestively in a seductive tone that makes my stomach flip flop and my heart pound.

I know exactly what he means and I'm going to enjoy every second.

He grips my hand, dragging me across the bathroom to the shower, pushing the curtain across and turning the taps on.

The steam begins rising to the ceiling and he steps into the shower, beckoning me in with his sexy smirk on his face.

Stepping in I slip on the tiles, my body crashing into his.

"Careful baby," He coos, stroking my hair.

There's silence between us for a moment, an unspoken connection as we just look into each other's eyes with the water cascading over our bodies.

Hunter breaks the silence, "I love you Savannah and I want to make you mine completely."

His words again cause my insides to stir in want, my whole body feeling a rush of warmth with the feelings this gorgeous man invokes in me.

"I love you to Hunter. I'm yours."

He licks his lips, our little unspoken tease and I respond by licking mine and stretching up to him with my arms wrapped around his neck to lick his lips and kiss him passionately.

Shivering I pull back from him. "Cold baby?"

I shake my head. "No, hot. And you, me, bedroom now," I taunt running my hands down his body and grabbing his dick in my grasp.

"Oh I'm there baby," he teases back, shutting off the taps and following me out of the bathroom to the bedroom.

The look in his eyes is pure want but absolute love; when he stops at the bedroom door to find me sitting on the edge of the bed with my legs crossed, my hands pressing into the bed.

I've never wanted to be with someone more.

There's no doubt in mind that I'm hopelessly in love with Hunter Mackenney.

(52) Hunter

Stopping in the doorway of my bedroom, after running from our hot bathroom session I can't help but stare at her sitting on the edge of the bed in a seductive pose, like she is literally saying, *'Fuck me now'* and god do I want to.

God she looks absolutely fucking amazingly beautiful

I've literally wanted this for months, from the moment I first kissed her, and every kiss after that.
Every night she's been naked in my arms I've wanted her and just like I knew it would proposing to her with the promise of our perfect life together has awoken the desire within her.
The delicious grin on her face is causing my desire to rise for again.
Heading into the room towards her I stop just centimetres from her crossed legs, pressing a kiss to her forehead, my hands on her thighs to push her legs apart, stepping in between them. Standing over her she edges back on the bed.
"Tell me what you want Savannah," I taunt seductively, my voice husky.
"You Hunter. I want you to make love to me."
She lies back on the bed, exposed and vulnerable, naked, ready for me to make her mine.
Crawling up the bed I close the gap between us, covering her body with mine, kissing the sweet spot I'd found on her neck that makes her hips buck against me.

Again I lick along her collarbone, down across her breasts, teasing and licking her nipples, making them again rise to attention.

Her breathing has become panting, so desperate and hot that it makes the need to have her close, so desperate. I need to feel her skin against mine, need to feel what it's like to be inside her.

Licking along her scar again I speak softly, "Every inch of your body is beautiful."

She doesn't speak but instead lets out a little gasp, biting her lips.

Grabbing her hips I pull her body onto my lap and my heart swells with love at how she's like putty in my arms, knowing exactly what I want, what we need.

Her legs wrap around my arse and her arms around my back, as she look into my eyes. "I want you Hunter," she says huskily, her voice filled with desire.

I smash my lips with hers, in a desperate desire filled kiss.

Our tongues dance together and I feel completely drunk on her. She's mine and I need all of her now, need to make our bodies one.

Breathless from her kiss I pull away and whisper in her ear, "Please let me make you mine Savannah."

"Mmm," she muses softly, unwrapping her legs from around me and lying back on the bed, seductively throwing her hands behind her head.

Stretching over her and kissing her softly I push my body slowly into hers, opening her sweet folds as she takes my length deep within her. Moaning against my lips, she bucks her hips to meet mine as I thrust in and out of her, desperately but slowly, taking my time to feel the overwhelming pleasure of finally making love to her.

She cups my face in her hands pulling me closer for a desperate kiss, her hips still moving with mine. Being inside her is so amazing, her body made to be one with mine.

Her hot kiss becomes breathless, her climax building.

I can feel her body clinching, her muscles contracting around my dick, ready to release.

Brushing a stray hair from her cheek I urge her, "Come for me Savannah, come for me baby."

With a hard thrust into her, looking deep into her eyes I watch her as she lets out a deep moan. "Oh Hunter, fuck!"

Her climax is hard and strong with mine following, filling her hot body before I collapse against her chest, panting, not ready to be apart from her.

Her hands grab at my hair and she presses a kiss against my head when I look up at her.

"That was amazing," she says softly, not tearing her eyes from mine.

It was better than amazing; it was more than I could have ever dreamt of. I don't doubt that I'm meant to be with her and pulling out of her body, I lay next to her, propping myself up on my elbow and running a finger along her body.

"Amazing doesn't even begin to describe it."

"Mmm...I love you Hunter."

"I love you too Savannah, so fucking much."

Softly kissing me she looks up at me with a hint of regret in her eyes, running her finger along her engagement ring.

Caressing her cheek I ask worriedly, "Please don't tell me your having second thoughts baby?"

She sighs before she replies, "No I want to marry you but.."

The pain in her eyes has me worried.

I'd just made love to her after proposing to her and she's now going to reject me.

My heart is pounding. I want to scream at her, a thousand words tumbling in my head, but instead I try to remain calm when I ask, "But what baby? Did I hurt you?"

She shakes her head. "No...I just wish my Dad could walk me down the aisle."

"You wish?"

Tears have started to fall down her cheeks. I brush them away with my thumb.

"Please baby, tell me what's wrong."

"He can't Hunter. And my Mum can't be there either, again."

The tears are sobs now, retched sobs that tug at my heart.

"Baby what do you mean?"

"My parents are dead. They had a car accident on the day of my wedding."

"And you still went through with the wedding?"

She sits up, pulling the sheets to her chest, using them to wipe the tears away.

"It was all a big mess," she begins, trying to not to sob, "Dante didn't want the big wedding so we'd just planned to go to the registry office and we're going to meet our parents for dinner after."

"And they never came?"

Her tears are flowing again. "Yeah...I couldn't find my phone and Dante...oh god I can't..."

I pull her close, letting her cry into my shoulder as I rub her back.

"It's ok baby. You don't have to tell me."

She turns her head to look up at me and even with her tear stained face she's still absolutely beautiful, the most beautiful woman I've ever known.

I kiss her cheeks and she giggles, her guard softening again.

"So..um well...Dante wouldn't let me use his phone to call them and told me that his parents had cancelled on coming at the last minute."

"Seriously?"

"Yeah I know. I shouldn't have believed him, but I was stupid and naive."

"You're not stupid, baby. You were in love."

Shaking her head, she says, "No I was blind. You know what happened after that. If my parents were alive..."

"You can't change the past baby."

"I know but I can't help but think what if...and if he had..."

"Oh god Savannah, please don't even say that."

I kiss her forehead, trying to comfort her somehow, absolutely shocked that I'm still learning things about her past that have caused her so much pain.

"I'm sorry Hunter. I just want our wedding to be perfect."

"It will be. Because it's us. I'll take you to the city tomorrow baby if that's what you want."

"No, no, this time even though my parents can't be there I want the whole big wedding, white dress and all."

Touching her cheek softly I kiss her. "Anything for you baby and you know what?"

"What?"

"Traditions are silly anyway," I say, grabbing her around the waist, tickling her.

"I don't get you," she says through giggles.

"We don't have to follow the rules to have a perfect wedding."

"Yeah I guess you're right. Just marrying you will make it perfect."

"Yeah," I agree.

She lets out a loud laugh as a thought crosses her mind. "Maybe Blitz could walk down the aisle with me?"

At her suggestion I have to laugh because she's right, "That sounds more than perfect."

Her response is a kiss, a perfect kiss that makes my heart melt.

I'm absolutely hopelessly in love with her and I'm sure things will turn out just perfect.

(53) Savannah

It's a been about a month since Hunter had proposed and we'd spent the perfect first night together. We've barely left his bedroom since, content to lie naked in each other's arms, but a thought keeps popping up in the back of my mind; a question of how we could continually be able to have non interrupted hot sex and the thought that goes along with that is it's has not been weeks but months since I've had that monthly visitor.

Sitting now at the kitchen table clutching my coffee, a sudden urge to vomit rises in my throat.

Swallowing it down, I gag at the taste it left in my mouth.

Hunter is at the stove, cooking his mean bacon and eggs.

"Baby are you ok?"

"Yeah just choking on my coffee," I reply, not meeting his intent gaze on me. He turns back to the stove but I can feel the tension in the air, like he doesn't believe me for a second and when he places the plate of bacon and eggs on the table in front of me I can't fight it.

The sick feeling this time starts in the pit of my stomach, the moment the smell of the egg hits my nose, rising up in my chest I can feel it in my oesophagus and in my mouth.

Swallowing it this time isn't going to happen so smashing the coffee cup down on the table I clap a hand to my mouth and bolt down the hallway to the bathroom, slamming the door behind me.

Clutching the cold porcelain of the toilet bowl I feel as though I've literally puked my guts out. It isn't very ladylike to say as much but it's the truth.

I hear Hunter knocking on the door. "Baby are you sure your ok?"

"I'm fine," I screech back, not wanting him to come in and see me looking like I've been dragged through the bush backwards.

Of course being the caring protective type he doesn't listen, opening the door slowly and rushing to my side to hold my hair back as I retch again. Coffee certainly doesn't taste so nice coming back up.

Brushing my cheek with his fingers he says softly, "You're not fine baby."

Not responding I stand up, pushing him aside as I flush the toilet and proceed to wash my hands in the sink.

"Savannah please don't push me away."

I tilt my head under the tap, gulping down a stream of water, swallowing it hard to get rid of the god awful taste in my mouth.

Hunter is standing behind me when I look up at him, with his hands on his hips.

The look on his face is worry, but also like he wants to say something but doesn't know what.

"I'm fine. Probably just a bug," I say reassuringly, knowing exactly what he's thinking, because I'm thinking the exact same thing and that can't be possible.

"Baby," he starts stepping closer to me, "your not pregnant are you?"

His eyes light up at the possibility of his statement and my heart constricts when I speak, "You and me both know that's not possible Hunter."

He pulls me into a hug, rubbing his hands up and down my back in comfort.

The tears are stinging my eyes and he pulls back from the hug, kissing my forehead.

"Please don't cry Savannah."

"But Hunter you obviously want a family..and I can't give that to you," I sob.

"Yes, I'd love a family Savannah but you know there are many ways to have a family these days. All I really want is you."

"You say that now, but what if I can't..if I have another miscarriage," I plead with him, desperate for him to see it from my perspective.

He again hugs me and I bury my face against his chest, listening to the pounding of his heartbeat when he places a kiss on my hair.

"Don't give up on the possibility of trying IUI again because your scared of the worst," He says sternly.

My words are muffled, "I'm not scared to try. I'm scared that you won't love me anymore when it doesn't work or I lose the baby."

"Sorry, but that's not even possible," he promises.

He kisses my cheek then and I love the giddy feeling that always gives me. I don't deserve him.

Just as before the sick feeling is rising up in my chest and instinctively I pull away from Hunter, only just reaching the toilet bowl to vomit again. This is some crazy bug.

He has again come to stand behind me and hold my hair back.

"I'm taking you to the hospital."

I shake my head in protest. "I'm fine Hunter."

"You're not fine Savannah. I'm not going to take that for an answer."

There's no point arguing with him, as he's right that I need to see a doctor.

Helping me up he takes my hand, to lead me out to get dressed.

In the bedroom I tug my too big track pants on, touching my stomach as I catch sight of my body in the mirror. I'm getting fat, so bloated.

"Ready?" Hunter asks, a frown crossing his face when he looks at me and the expression on my face as I check my appearance in the mirror.

"Do I look fat?" I ask.

"No, you look beautiful," He says smiling.

He takes my hand and leads me outside to the Ute.

Once out on the open road into town, I wind my window down to practically suck in the fresh air to quell the nausea in my stomach. Hunter has never looked so worried and he reaches across to touch my thigh in comfort.

"Do you want me to pull over baby?"

"No, I'm ok. The fresh air is helping."

We drive the rest of the way to the hospital in silence, me clutching my stomach wondering just maybe.

~ ~

The nausea has subsided on the drive from the farm as I practically sucked in the spring air but walking into the hospital the overwhelming smell of bleach comes at me full force. I vomit into the rubbish bin by the door.

Hunter has raced up to the nurses to get me in as soon as possible.

Wiping my hand across my face I step up behind him, and he draws me to his side with his hand on the small of my back.

The nurse speaks loudly, "I understand Mr Mackenney, but you're not her emergency contact."

"But we're engaged," He protests, a hint of anger in his tone.

Patronisingly the nurse replies, "Congratulations, Mr Mackenney but the answer to can you go in with her is no."

He looks down at me plastered against his side. He's clearly pissed off with the nurse.

"I'll be ok Hunter."

"I know but I just want to make sure that's all."

He brushes his fingers across my cheek and kisses my forehead.

The nurse is furiously tapping her fingers on the keyboard and her tone when she speaks again is stern, "Take a seat Ms Galison. Doctor Yorke shouldn't be too long."

Great, just the doctor I want to see, Doctor Addison Yorke, snotty ex-girlfriend of my now fiancé
Why does she have to be fucking doctor on duty?

Hunter is sitting next to me, his elbows resting on his knees. He seems so worried and it tugs at my heart, to know how much he cares about me, how much he loves me.

Pressing a kiss to his cheek I say softly, "I'll be fine Hunter. She's a good doctor and knows my history."

"I know baby. I just don't like seeing you in pain."

I have no words to say to his response. He's so amazing, so different to Dante, who'd gotten off on seeing me in pain.

"And baby I'm sick of being in this place."

That I can agree to, "Yeah me too."

He sighs, pulling me closer to him with an arm around my shoulder.

The air in the room suddenly feels thick with tension, the click clack of high heels on the hard floor coming closer.

Doctor Yorke is standing right in front of me and she looks at Hunter first, then at me, her gaze stopping to focus on the sparkle of my engagement ring.

I swear I actually see her heart constrict in pain, probably thinking it should have been on her hand instead.

Letting out an exasperated breath, she says, "Follow me please Ms Galison."

Hunter kisses my hand as I stand up to follow Doctor Yorke to the examination bays. Pulling the curtain across she directs me to sit up on the bed and gets straight to the point.

"So Ms Galison, you're in today for severe vomiting, correct?"

"Yes."

"When was the last time you vomited?"

"About twenty minutes ago when I got here."

"Ok and any other symptoms?"

"I've been really tired and irritable."

She only says, 'hmmm' like she's thinking of her next question.

"Do you think it's some gastro bug?"

"No...I..." She says hesitating and flipping through the notes on her clipboard chart from my previous hospital stays.

"Ms Galison, have you had another period since your miscarriage?"

I gulp, swallowing hard as I try to comprehend what she's saying.

"No, I haven't."

She looks at me with pain in her eyes, a tear stinging the corners. She's obviously still in love with Hunter because her professional stance appears to be waning.

"And since your last hospital stay, I'm sorry if this is difficult..." she gulps and continues, softer in tone, "have you been sexually active?"

Her eyes lock on the engagement ring as she says the words.

I blush. "Yes, I have."

"Um...Ms Galison...is it possible you're pregnant?"

I shake my head. "I don't think so. I had to do IUI to get pregnant last time."

I can't decipher the look on her face and I'm suddenly worried that if I'm pregnant that it's Dante's, not Hunter's and that the poor child will look like Dante.

That would damn near kill me.

Doctor Yorke lets out a little chuckle. "It can be easier to get pregnant a second time, even after infertility."

"Really?" I ask intrigued.

"Yes, so I'd like you take a urine test and then if needed we will do a blood test and ultrasound."

"Um ok."

She turns behind her to the supply trolley and hands me a specimen jar. "You know where the bathroom is. Bring it back here when you're done." I ease myself off the bed and head for the bathroom.

Peeing into a tiny jar when you don't really need to go is quite a challenge but I manage to half fill the jar.

Washing my hands at the sink, I check my appearance in the mirror, trying to spread a smile across my face, ready to find out if the impossible is possible.

Back in the examination bay I sit back on the bed, too scared to watch as Doctor Yorke unscrews the specimen jar lid, filling the pipette to drop three drops of urine on the cassette pregnancy test.

Placing it down on the supply trolley the fluid runs across the window and I have to look then, as two clear pink lines become visible.

My heart practically falls out of my chest in shock.

I'm Pregnant. I'm actually PREGNANT!

"Well, Ms Galison, I guess congratulations is in order."

I'm speechless.

Literally there are no words and her saying congratulations like she actually means it is rather odd. Maybe she does actually have a heart. "So I'd like to do a blood test to see how far along you are and then we can organise an ultrasound when the blood results come back."

Her words are going in one ear and out the other. I'm absolutely giddy.

"Um..sorry..I just..can't believe it."

"Hmm...yeah," she says, a hint of pain in her voice.

"Um Addison?" I say trying to appeal to her as a friend and not my doctor

"Yeah?"

"I'm sorry."

"For what?"

I touch my ring instinctively.

"For taking Hunter away from you."

She laughs. "You didn't take him away. He fell in love with you."

"Yeah but...I know you love him."

"Yeah I do...but I can't give him what you can."

Her words show genuine pain and I don't want to push things further when she already seems so on edge, not only finding out we are engaged but that I'm also pregnant.

"Please don't tell him yet," I plead to her.

"Sorry...you don't want him to know?"

"I want to tell him please?"

She nods. "I know. So are you ok with blood tests?"

"No but I'll suck it up."

She laughs, preparing the needle and vial for the blood test. She's methodical in her work as she lifts my sleeve up my arm, rubbing a cotton ball over it with rubbing alcohol on it in preparation. I turn away as she presses the needle into my vein, verbally hissing at the pin prick sensation. It's over as quickly as it started.

"So I'll send this to the lab and we should have the result in a day or so."

"Ok..um how far along do you think I might be? And the sickness?"

She places a hand on mine.

"Without the blood results I really can't say but maybe four or five weeks. I think you may be suffering from Hyperemesis Gravidarum."

"What?" I spit confused at the medical jargon.

"Severe morning sickness. Just see how you go the next couple of days. Keep your fluids up and try to eat if you can."

"Ok but what do I tell Hunter?"

"That you're pregnant. He'll be over the moon."

She hands me another pregnancy test. "Use this at home."

"Thank you Addison."

"No worries. I'm just doing my job."

I hop off the bed and I'm about to leave when she says softly,

"Congratulations for the engagement too Savannah. You're really lucky to be marrying Hunter."

"Thanks," is all I can manage to say and maybe it's the pregnancy hormones but I feel a pang of guilt for making her so upset.

She leads me back out to the waiting room to a panic stricken Hunter.

"Are you ok?"

"Better than ok. I'll tell you later."

He looks at Addison with worry on his face.

"Addison?" He asks.

"She's fine Hunter. Just a stomach bug. Plenty of fluids and rest."

Hunter says thanks to her, not noticing the wink and nod she sends my way as I walk out of the hospital clutching Hunter's hand in mine.

I push my hand in my pocket checking to make sure the other pregnancy test is still in there.

I have the most perfect idea about how to tell Hunter the news and I can't help but smile just thinking about how he's going to react.

(54) Hunter

Savannah is a little distant on the way back to the farm, even though her nausea has subsided a little, she still has the window down to breathe in the fresh air.

Her silence is getting to me, especially as she has a ridiculously cute grin on her face and I can't help but look at her.

"Baby what are you smiling about?" I ask her, hoping to get her to talk.

"Nothing. I'm just happy to have you in my life."

"Me too baby."

Her answer doesn't exactly make me feel any better as there's definitely something she isn't telling me.

"Was Addison at least nice to you?"

"Yeah, she was actually. Too nice."

I touch her thigh, leaving my hand resting on it when I ask, "What do you mean too nice?"

"She was just really friendly, and even congratulated me on being engaged to you."

I have to laugh at that, because I thought Addison would have been a complete bitch about it. It's no secret she still loves me.

"Well, you're pretty lucky to be engaged to me, right?" I tease.

"Thats what she said."

Savannah laughs softly. "And yes I am lucky."

I smile wide at her, and she smiles back even wider, before licking her lips. Seeing her teasing gesture I've never been more glad to be back at the farm.

"Just you wait until we get inside, teasing me like that," I taunt, smirking at her.

She giggles, as I jump out to open the gate before driving in.

As soon as we stop she jumps out and races to shut the gate.

The crazy happiness that has taken her over is endearing, but she's definitely hiding something.

I don't dare think of the possibility that she really is pregnant.

After closing the gate, she comes running at me to hug me tightly. Pulling her close to my chest, I kiss her hair and whisper in her ear, "I love you Savannah, so much."

She looks up at me, still with her arms wrapped around my back.

"I love you to Hunter. And I need to tell you..."

She pulls back suddenly to run inside. I don't even have a moment to catch her hand and pull her back. I have a feeling I know what she's going to say, but the conversation we had before heading to the hospital is tumbling in my head and I don't want to think that it could really be possible.

~ ~

When I follow her inside she has disappeared, as has Blitz. I don't want to bother her as I'm feeling really confused about how to react after she seemed so unwell one minute and then insanely happy the next minute. She also isn't throwing up anymore and it doesn't make any sense.

I've started to fix myself a coffee, opening the fridge to grab the milk, dropping it on the floor when Blitz comes tearing into the kitchen with a long white item in his mouth, between his teeth.

I ruffle his head fur, speaking to him, "Hey buddy what have you got there?"

He drops it on the floor in front of me, and my heart leaps in my chest.

Picking it up I can't help but let out an excited yelp.

It's a positive pregnancy test.

"Savannah?" I call out, "Savannah, get in here!"

I'm still clutching the pregnancy test in my fist, when she saunters into the kitchen, the grin still plastered on her face when she speaks, "Yes Hunter?"

"Is this real? Did you just take this?" I say, waving the pregnancy test at her.

She nods. "Yes, I did. I'm pregnant Hunter."

I drop the test and race over to her, pulling her into a hug, honestly not knowing what to say.

I'm absolutely over the moon excited. Pulling back from her I kiss her forehead.

"I can't believe it. I'm gonna be a Dad!"

Her grin has gone, her face now showing sadness at my excitement.

"Savannah? What's wrong?"

She pulls away from me, sitting down at the table, shaking her head.

"I'm happy Hunter, but I'm scared."

"Scared of what?" Tears are stinging her cheeks.

"I'm scared it Dante's."

I kneel on the floor in front of her, grabbing her left hand in mine and kissing her engagement ring.

With a finger I lift her chin up for her to meet my eyes with hers.

"Even if it is, I'll be here for both of you and love you both no matter what."

"But what if the baby looks like him?"

"Let's not worry about that now, ok? Let's just be happy you're pregnant."

"Ok," she says, kissing me softly, smiling against my lips before she pulls away.

"I'm pregnant Hunter. I'm pregnant," she says excitedly.

"Yeah I know. We're having a baby!" I say matching her excited tone.

Lifting her t-shirt up I kiss her belly and she giggles at the sensation of my lips on her skin. Standing up I bend down and kiss her hair.

"How about we head to the bedroom and celebrate?" I say, winking at her and licking my lips.

She stands up, giggling and presses a hungry kiss to my lips.

"That sounds like a good plan, I'm so fucking horny."

"I think I can help with that," I tease with a laugh. I'm happy to have my gorgeous teasing fiancee back.

I grab her around the waist, pulling her body closer and kissing her hard. Things lately have definitely been a whirlwind, but I've never been happier.

(55) *Addison*

As soon as Savannah came into the hospital and I'd looked at the symptoms she was presenting I knew she was pregnant.

It broke my heart.

It took all my strength to not cry when I congratulated her, looking at how excited she was and the glistening of the engagement ring on her finger.

She had everything I wanted.

She had Hunter, and she was pregnant most likely with his baby.

I sensed her hesitation that it was her ex-husbands child but getting her blood test results proved otherwise.

I needed to question her more as her answers the day she came in didn't make sense.

Calling her would be the hardest call I'd ever have to make in my career.

She is pregnant to the man I'm desperately in love with.

~ ~

I dial her number, partly hoping she won't answer.

"Hello," she says so sweetly I feel like bursting into tears.

"Hello Savannah. It's Doctor Yorke."

I hate being so formal but there's no way I'm going to get through this phone call without trying to maintain a professional tone.

"I'm calling to inform you of your blood results."

"Yes. Are they good? Can you tell how many weeks I am?"

"Yes, your numbers are great. Your blood HCG level is 105 which puts you around four weeks or so."

"Oh my gosh, really?" she asks excitedly, driving the pain further into my heart.

"Yes, Savannah I don't mean to pry but can I ask you something?"

"Um I guess."

"Were you worried about how far along you'd be because of the situation with your ex-husband?"

I can't bring myself to say rape. It's too callous and too painful.

"Yes, because I hadn't gotten a proper period."

"Did you have any bleeding around that time?"

"Yes, but I thought it was from what happened."

It's clear to me that her bleeding then was a period and that means the baby is Hunter's.

I can feel tears in my eyes and audibly sniff them back.

"Well, Savannah I believe that may have actually been your period returning. Our bodies can get a bit mixed up after a miscarriage."

"I didn't know that, but thank you. So when do I come in for an ultrasound?"

"We like to see you around six weeks to confirm the dates so in approximately two weeks. A nurse will call you to schedule a time."

"Thank you. And Addison are you ok?"

"Yes, I'm fine. Congratulations again. Bye."

I hastily end the call before she can respond or hear the tears that are streaming down my cheeks. She's having Hunter's baby. She's able to give him everything and he loves her.

He'd always wanted a family and when he proposed to me my rejection wasn't as vindictive as he thought.

I did it for him, because I couldn't give him what he wanted, but being away from him I missed him and just wanted him back in my life.

I'd hoped that just me and my love would be enough, but it wasn't.

My stomach clinches and I pound my fist against the desk.

It isn't fair.

I'm startled by a knock on my office door.

Zane opens it and a worried look crosses his face when he looks at me. "Addison, are you ok? You look like someone died?"

"Yeah me."

"Sorry what?" he asks crossing the office and standing at the side of my desk with a hand on his hip. He isn't wearing his scrubs, but a white button down shirt open a little too far, and black slacks with a black belt that sits low on his hips, hugging his legs.

I've never seen him look so dapper and it sends heat rising in my cheeks at how gorgeous he looks.

"I...um...feel like a part of me died today."

"How so?"

"Savannah is pregnant."

"And what's that got to do with you?" He asks in a tone that makes my blood boil at how insolent he sounds.

"It's clearly Hunter's."

He leans closer to me, so close I can feel his breath on my cheeks.

"He doesn't love you Addison. Move on," He whispers, causing goosebumps to rise over my skin.

I have no time to reply before his hands find my cheeks, grabbing them between his palms.

His lips are suddenly on mine in a hungry kiss and I find myself melting into his mouth, his fierce desire filled kiss.

I let out a little moan when his lips part from mine and a panty dropping smirk crosses his lips before he licks them.

"Have a good night Addison. I'll see you tomorrow."

Winking at me seductively he walks out of my office. I touch my lips, still feeling his kiss against them.

Fuck, that was some kiss. And since when has he been so damn gorgeous.

Caz May

Grabbing my handbag I sling it over my shoulder. It's time to go home, to have a long hot bath and have a good hard think about my life.

(56) *Savannah*

Getting off the phone with Addison after she told me the baby is Hunter's has me both excited and confused.

She'd hung up on me, clearly upset, but when Hunter walks through the door moments later I run up to him, wrapping my arms around him.

I lift my head to meet his eyes. "Guess what sexy?"

"I don't know, what?"

"You're going to be a Dad!"

He looks down at me confused, like he's giving me an I already know this look.

"Addison called me and said I'm about four weeks or so along from my blood test results."

His adorable smile appears on his face, his dimples clearly showing and my heart melts with how much love I have for him.

"So you're telling me that we're having an engagement celebration baby?"

"Seems so," I say stretching up to kiss him, moving my hands from his back to his neck, pulling his mouth closer to mine.

I seriously love kissing him, it's like a damn drug that I can't get enough of and being pregnant makes me want him so much more. The heat and desire runs through my body whenever he's near me and all I want is for his body to be pressed against mine, showing me how much he loves me.

Pulling away breathless from the crazy kiss, he muses, "I love you Savannah."

"I love you too baby daddy."

Laughing he says, "Cute, I like the sound of that."

He pulls away to go make a coffee.

I'm pondering asking him about Addison's reaction but don't want to upset him, but at the same time I want to know what would make her so upset other than the obvious, plus I don't like there being any secrets between us.

"Hey baby daddy, can I ask you something?"

"Anything," He muses, a slight smile cornering his mouth.

I grab him from behind, whilst he's waiting for the kettle to boil.

"Would there be any reason, other than the obvious one, that would make Addison deeply upset that I'm having your baby?"

He turns in my arms, cupping my cheeks between his palms and kissing my nose.

"Um...maybe but what does it matter?"

"It doesn't really. But she just seemed really upset."

"Yeah I don't know, baby."

He shakes his head and I get the sense he doesn't want to tell me something about their relationship.

"Hunter you're not telling me something."

He kisses my forehead. "You're right baby, but it's not my place to tell you."

"Huh?"

"Forget it. It's not important," he snaps, seeming upset that I'd asked.

I want to push it further but don't want him angry at me. Still I blurt out my next sentence without thinking, "If it's not important then why do I get the feeling me asking you has made you upset."

He slams his coffee cup on the counter.

Fuck, I've struck a nerve.

"I don't want to talk about it ok?"

"Um..ok...sorry," I say my chest hitching at him raising his voice at me. It's out of character for him, and it's a little scary.

I feel hurt too that he's shutting me out and I need to make it better.

"Sorry baby. Come here," he says apoplectically.

He holds his arms out towards me and I close the gap between hugging him.

"I just want to focus on the future please," he states not really as a question.

Taking a step back from him I reply, "Me too. And our future is growing inside me."

He laughs, lifting up my shirt and kissing my belly.

His eyes then focus on mine and he kisses me hungrily, his fingers finding the hem of my t-shirt.

Breaking the kiss he pulls my t-shirt over my head, before kissing my belly again; his kisses edging higher to kiss my breasts over the lace of my bra.

Murmuring with a hint of cheekiness in his tone he says, "I'm looking forward to these getting bigger."

He practically moans as he takes a nipple in his mouth through the lace.

His lips on my skin set it on fire and I moan as the pleasure rushes through me. His kisses reach my neck, his tongue licking my neck, sucking and tasting my skin.

My moans continue, increasing when I feel his erection against my belly. "Hunter, please...take me now."

He responds to my plea, kissing me fiercely, running his tongue along my lips, urging me to open up to him.

Melting against him, I let out a moan, letting the pleasure overtake me. "Oh Savannah, you drive me wild," he murmurs against my lips.

Breaking away from our kiss, he grabs me around the waist, to turn me around and lift me up onto the kitchen counter.

Pressing another fierce kiss to my lips, he reaches down to touch my throbbing body through the lace of my knickers.

"Savannah, you're so fucking wet."

My cheeks flush when he lets out a moan.

"Its hot as, baby."

"Mmm..." I muse, softly fumbling with his belt to undo it.

He whispers into my ear, "Let me help you with that."

I giggle, watching as he slides his fly down and discards his jeans and boxers at once. His erection is full and ready.

"Please Hunter. I need you," I say raspy, locking my eyes on his.

His fingers graze the edge of my knickers before he plunges them down the floor to my ankles.

His dick is now at my entrance, the tip teasing me.

My hands ran up and down his chest under his t-shirt, towards his hips.

"What do you want Savannah?" he teases, his eyes locked on mine still, the love and desire evident in his dark blue irises.

"You. Inside. Me," I say breathless.

With a passionate kiss, he thrusts into my body and I grab his butt, pushing him deeper inside me. Maybe it's just being pregnant, but it feels like every thrust is taking me to new heights of pleasure.

His hands grab my hips, to steady me as I meet his thrusts.

"Oh Savannah, fuck," he screams out.

"Hunter, I'm gonna come...Oh fuck...I'm gonna come so hard."

He kisses me again, hard and passionately, thrusting harder as my orgasm overtakes me.

Breathless I pull back and collapse against his chest, feeling his dick throb in me as his climax fills me.

Stepping back, he grabs his pants from around his ankles, pulling them up before he kisses me softly.

"That was hot Savannah."

"Mmm...we should fight more often." I laugh jumping off the counter and pulling my knickers up.

He's just looking at me, the silence between us electric.

"I love you," he muses, pulling me into his embrace again.

Still embracing me he kisses my hair, whispering, "I can't wait to have this baby with you."

"Me too. But I guess we will have to postpone the wedding now? I don't want to be a pregnant bride."

"You'd be beautiful no matter what, but we can wait."

I'm still a little confused about why he'd shut down when I'd asked about Addison being upset, but really I'm overwhelming happy and for the first time in ages I feel like I deserve to be happy.

"Hunter?"

"Yeah, baby?"

"We should go and see Mum to tell her our two pieces of news."

"Yeah most definitely," he says happily.

Stepping back I touch my belly, looking directly at him.

"Maybe when we go to my ultrasound in a couple of weeks."

He puts his hand over mine on my belly and my heart pounds, feeling the love and amazing connection between us that has created the baby growing inside me.

"That sounds wonderful," he says smiling wide and making my insides melt.

I love him so fucking much.

~ ~

Hunter is like a kid in a candy shop, walking into the hospital with me clutching my hand. The last two weeks since finding out I'm pregnant he's been so sweet, showering me with affection, not letting me lift a finger to do anything. The nausea is still plaguing me though, but it isn't anywhere near as bad as the first few weeks, so thankfully I hadn't needed to return to the hospital other than walking in now for the first ultrasound.

At the desk, Hunter pulls me to his side, greeting the nurse rudely, "Marg, we're here for Savannah's ultrasound and I don't give a fuck what you say I'm going in with her."

Marg looks at him with a scowl. "There's no need to swear Hunter Mackenney. You are the father of the child yes?"

He smiles, full dimpled, showing his elation when he replies, "Yes Marg I am the father."

He squeezes my waist when he says father and it makes me feel like melting.

"Then you're welcome to be in the room with Ms Galison."

He sighs and whispers in my ear, "Mrs Mackenney sounds better."

I touch my hand to my heart, kissing his cheek and I say, "In my heart I am, but not officially."

Marg breaks our moment. "Doctor Yorke will be out soon. Take a seat."

Great! Doctor Yorke again. Why does she have to be the local obstetrician?

Sitting on the hard waiting room chairs, Hunter puts his arm around my shoulder.

"Scared baby?" he asks.

"A little, but i'm sure everything will be fine."

"Yeah I hope so."

He kisses my cheek softly, just as the tension in the room shifts when Addison enters the waiting area.

"Ms Galison, follow me."

She doesn't even address Hunter and he looks a little upset, but still he stands up, taking my hand in his. His grip is possessive, which excites me a little as it shows I'm his.

We follow Addison towards a private room, the whole time she's giving him an evil looking scowl. She holds the door open for me to enter and I pull Hunter in with me quickly as it looks like she was going to shut the door in his face.

I feel anger rising in my chest at her behaviour towards Hunter. I know she's upset, but he's my fiancé, the father of my child and I want him here.

As though she knows what I'm thinking she asks, "Do you want Mr Mackenney here for this?"

I laugh at her not calling him *'Hunter'*.

"Yes, of course I want him here."

"Ok, just hop up on the bed then and we can get started."

She doesn't even look at Hunter, turning the ultrasound machine on and wheeling it closer to the bed. Hunter is standing on the left side of the bed, holding my hand tightly in his.

The ultrasound machine makes a beeping sound, and she starts to prepare the wand to begin.

Her actions are so methodical, her face not showing any emotion.

"Can you just lift up your top first?" she asks monotone and emotionless.

"Um..ok," I reply feeling a little angry at her.

Putting the icy gel on my belly she speaks again with no emotion, "I'm not sure if we'll see anything and this might be cold."

Damn right it's cold, it sends a shiver through me and not of the good kind.

She begins waving the wand over the skin of my belly and it seems like nothing is on the screen.

I have no idea what to look for though. I've had so many ultrasounds before and my insides all just look like big blobs of black and white to me. She stops suddenly. "Um...I...will have to do a vaginal ultrasound instead..."

The room feels claustrophobic all of sudden. She looks up, her eyes meeting Hunter's. There's something unspoken between them. He's practically seething and her eyes are full of tears that have started dripping down her cheeks.

"Sorry...I can't do this...give me a minute."

She practically bolts out the door, the tears breaking free the moment she turns away from us.

I look at Hunter, not sure what to feel. He shakes his head at me, as if to say don't ask. It takes a lot of willpower to keep my lips sealed.

A minute or so later, she reappears with Doctor Rivnay, standing at the door she speaks to him softly.

Her cheeks are stained with tears and touching the small of her back he draws her close to his side and presses a kiss on her tear stained cheek before he walks into the room, shutting the door.

The tension in the room seems to shift then and he speaks professionally but casually, "Sorry about that. Doctor Yorke isn't feeling the best, so asked me to step in to complete your ultrasound. Is that ok Ms Galison?"

I nod.

"Ok, are you ok with a vaginal ultrasound Ms Galison?"

"Yes."

"You'll need to step behind the divider there to take off your underwear and put the gown on."

He hands me a scratchy hospital gown as I slide off the exam table.

Hunter winks at me as I go to change behind the divider.

When I come out to climb back up, my naughty fiancé takes a look at my bare arse at the back of the gown, tapping it sneakily. I can't help but smile, at his cheeky side coming out again.

"Ok, so just relax Ms Galison. This might hurt a little, but I'll try to be as gentle as possible."

Doctor Rivnay lifts the gown up a little, careful to not expose me too much. He slowly inserts the wand into my body and wiggles it around a bit.

It's a little uncomfortable and I try not to wince from the weird pain but pleasure sensation it gives me.

A different image of my insides pops up on the ultrasound screen and his words are music to my ears, "Well Ms Galison, you're definitely pregnant. And as Doctor Yorke has told you appear to be about six weeks."

"And all is good?" Hunter asks, squeezing my hand.

"Yes, this here is the baby and you can see here it's heartbeat," he says pointing at the screen.

My heart skips a beat, watching our baby's heart beating on the screen.

"Can we hear it?" Hunter asks excitedly.

"Unfortunately not yet, but from all measurements everything appears to be on track. Congratulations!"

"Doctor Rivnay, is there any chance of getting a picture?"

"Sure, i'll print some out for you," he says sweetly, as he pulls the wand out from my body.

"Thanks," I reply, looking at Hunter. He's smiling so wide, full dimples on display, so obviously in love with our baby already and it melts my heart.

"You go ahead and get dressed again. I'll be back with the pictures in a moment."

He leaves the room, and I jump off the bed, ripping off the scratchy gown. Hunter grabs me by the waist, pressing a passionate to my lips, reaching down to tease me with his fingers.

"Hunter, stop." I giggle.

"I could see you trying not to squirm."

"Hunter, please. Doctor Rivnay will be back in a minute."

He licks his lips and I almost beg him to touch me, but know it's incredibly naughty.

But I seriously want it, so pushing him behind the room divider, I kiss him fiercely, my hands in his hair as he devours my mouth.

In his ear I whisper, "Touch me Hunter."

He doesn't respond, instead plunges his finger inside me, teasing my clit slowly. He again kisses me, his fingers still teasing me slowly.

It feels like mere seconds, when I feel myself twitching, and releasing over his hand.

Withdrawing his finger, he puts it against my lips and drags it down my chin, before putting it between his own lips and licking it clean.

It's so damn hot, I swear I nearly climax again.

"Fuck, Hunter. You're so damn hot."

A knock at the door startles us back to reality.

"All good in here?" Doctor Rivnay calls out.

"Yeah, just a sec," I say a little to raspy, still coming down from my intensely quick climax.

I yank my knickers and pants back on, grabbing Hunter's hand to pull him back near the bed.

Doctor Rivnay opens the door and takes one look at us before letting out a little chuckle.

"Here's your pictures," he says, handing me a kraft envelope.

"Thank you," I say, trying not to laugh.

"So Ms Galison, we will see you in another couple of weeks to make sure all is going well."

"Ok, sounds good. Thanks again Doctor Rivnay. Will we see you next time?"

"Yes, I'll be taking over from Doctor Yorke for the remainder of your pregnancy."

He turns to leave then and gives us a little wink on the way out.

"You guys are sweet together. Have a good afternoon. I'll see you in two weeks."

Hunter laughs. "I think we got busted."

I poke him in the stomach playfully. "You don't say."

"So time to see Mum and share our news. You ready?"

"Yep," I say taking his hand to follow him out.

We pass Addison on the way out. She looks distraught and I really want to know what had gotten her so upset.

Doctor Rivnay's comforting kiss on her cheek didn't seem exactly professional either and I wonder if there's something going on between them behind closed doors.

~ ~

A sense of de déjà vu rushes through me as I follow Hunter into the rest home.

He nods to the nurse on the desk and they buzz us in straight away.

He knocks softly on the door of room five.

"Come in," his Mum calls out.

When we enter, a smile lights up her face immediately and Hunter wastes no time in greeting her, stepping up to her to kiss her cheek.

"Hi, Mum."

"Hi darlings," she says, looking at him and then me, the smile still plastered on her face.

"Mum, we have some news to tell you," he says, urging me forward with a hand on the small of my back.

I hold out my hand to show her the ring on my finger.

"We're engaged Mum."

"Oh Hunter, oh Savannah, thats wonderful," she says struggling to stand up, falling against Hunter.

He wraps his arms around her, and kisses her hair, whispering into her ear, "And thats not all Mum."

She pulls back, sitting back down in her wheelchair and looks across at me, instinctively looking towards my stomach.

"Are you pregnant Savannah?"

"Yes, i'm pregnant," I say, opening the kraft envelope to take out the ultrasound photo for her.

"Thats wonderful. I'm so happy for you both."

"Thanks Mum. We're beyond excited."

He pulls me to his side, kissing my cheek. His Mum squeaks in delight.

"Anyway Mum, we should get going, but we wanted to share our news with you."

"I'm glad you did, sweetie. Have you told Quentin yet?"

"No, but I will. We'll come see you in a couple of weeks when we have the next ultrasound ok?"

"Sounds wonderful sweetie. Take care of her," She says winking at me, and placing a hand over my belly, "And this one too."

"I will Mum," Hunter replies, kissing her cheek again before we turn to leave.

We walk out of the rest home, holding hands.

"Can we go for a walk before we head home?" I ask Hunter.

"Sure baby."

We walk towards the oval. I take a deep breath, the memories flooding me from the night I saw Dante at the fundraiser, and the pain that followed in the days after.

All it is now though is distant memories, a painful past that I no longer have to endure, because I now have the love of Hunter Mackenney, the amazing man who's clutching my hand in his.

I'm ready for whatever the future holds for us, our baby, our marriage and our whole future.

It's no country secret that I love Hunter Mackenney with all my heart.

(Epilogue)

Hunter

A year and a half later

I can't believe this day is finally here.

My emotions are all over the place.

I'm nervous, yes, but so happy. It feels as though my heart is going to burst.

Standing out in the garden of the farmhouse, underneath an arch of ruby red roses, my heart is pounding in my chest. Quentin pats a hand against my back.

"You nervous, big brother?"

I turn to look at my younger brother standing behind me, my best man.

"Just a little. I've been waiting my whole life for this day."

"I know Hunt. It'll be perfect."

"I hope so," I say adjusting my black bow tie.

"I know so, and Savannah will look stunning. I'm sure of it."

I gulp as the music started.

This is it.

The guests turn towards the aisle.

My heart starts pounding harder, as firstly Addison walks down the aisle.

Her blonde hair is cascading over her shoulders, the ruby red strapless dress draping down her body.

If she looks so amazing, I know Savannah is going to be absolutely breathtaking.

Addison stops at the arch, standing opposite me. She forces a smile, not meeting my eyes.

It means a lot she was willing to stand up as maid of honour after our past together.

The music continues and I can't help but grin wide when River stops at the start of the aisle with the cutest grin on his face, holding a sign in his tiny hands, '*Wait til you see my Mum*'.

He starts tottering up the aisle with Blitz by his side. His unsteady steps are so endearing. Tears of absolute joy sting my eyes.

Quentin taps my shoulder and I turn to look at him.

"My nephew is god damn cute."

I nod, turning back to look at my gorgeous son still tottering towards me. There's no doubt he's mine, with his dark chestnut hair and deep blue eyes. He's a mini me.

He stumbles forward at my feet when he reaches the front of the aisle. Blitz nudges him, grabbing the buckle on the back of his little tuxedo and pulling him up. It's damn cute and our guests laugh at the sweetness.

It's then that my heart stops, before pounding wildly in my chest, seeing Savannah standing at the end of the aisle.

Her deep brown hair down over her shoulders, in loose ringleted curls.

A tiara atop her head.

Her dress has lace straps that lead to a low sweetheart neckline at the front, her breasts just visible at the top.

It hugs her body, tight at her hips to a flare bottom and a train that follows her as she walks slowly towards me.

Quentin was right. She looks absolutely stunning. Breathtakingly beautiful.

I'm without a doubt absolutely wholeheartedly in love with her.

The music ends and she's standing in front of me. I take her hand in mine as she steps closer towards me

Smiling at her I scoop River up, holding him against my hip between us.

"Ready to be my wife?" I whisper in her ear.

She looks into my eyes.

"I was ready the moment I laid eyes on you Hunter."

I smile wide, kissing her cheek softly, as well as the soft cheek of my son.

I lean closer to her, softly whispering into her ear, "It's no country secret that here with you is right where I'm supposed to be."

River kisses her cheek and a wide smile of absolute pure loved crosses her face.

Nothing could have be more perfect.

Savannah

Being a bride for the second time was beyond surreal, and so different from the first time.

Walking down the aisle to marry Hunter Mackenney, seeing him and our son River waiting for me under the arch of ruby red roses in our farmhouse garden made my breath hitch in my chest and I felt beyond happy.

Saying I do, declaring how much I love him, beyond words for saving me and giving me the happiness I deserve made me feel complete.

Even though my parents are no longer with us, Grace had become more than my mother in law, she is my 'Mum'.

After at the reception as we are about to leave, she pulls me close to her in a hug. "I love you Savannah. You and Hunter are meant to be dear and now you have the heart of a Mackenney man he will never let it go."

"Thank you Mum. I love you too," I reply kissing her cheek and smiling at Hunter who has sauntered up to us to stand by my side.

"What are you telling my wife, Mum?" he teases.

"Only good things, dear."

"I hope so." He laughs, kissing her cheek too.

Taking my hand, we take deep breaths in, and he whispers in my ear, "You ready baby?"

"Ready, husband."

Bending down we rush through the arm bridge our family and friends have created right to the door. Awaiting us outside is a stretch limo, the door open ready for us to slide in.

Hunter holds out his hand for me to help me in and slides in after closing the door.

The driver starts the engine, and we start to move away from the curb.

Picking up the champagne on ice he holds it up, pouring a glass and handing it to me, before pouring his own and clinking his glass with mine.

"To us, forever," he toasts.

Sipping my champagne, I revel in how it tastes sweet and tickles my tongue.

Hunter is looking at me as I swallow.

"Why are you looking at me like that Hunter?"

"I bet you'd taste sweeter than this champagne, my beautiful wife."

Giggling I down the rest of my champagne, my gaze locked on Hunter's as he downs his as well.

"You're so fucking beautiful, my wife," he muses, brushing a stray hair from my cheek and pressing a kiss against it. His eyes focus on mine lustfully. He then tosses my hair aside kissing my neck, licking and biting the sweet spot that he knows drives me crazy.

I let out a moan, as his lips move lower across my collarbone and his tongue grazes my neck. "Mmm, wife, you're delicious," he says, his licking reaching my chin before running across my lips.

I bite his lip, to pull his lips to mine in a zealous kiss. A kiss that sends desire rushing through me, straight to my core, heating every cell in my body.

A momentary thought comes into my mind about my previous wedding night, and how callous Dante had been. I'd never even thought about having sex with anyone else after how vile being with him had been, but I'd never counted on meeting Hunter.

He's kissing me fervently, but lovingly and whenever we have sex his love for me is evident in how he takes his time to know I'm enjoying it just as much as him.

I know this wedding night is going to be beyond amazing, one to remember in a good way, not a bad way like last time.

Breathless I pull away from Hunter's sweet loving kiss, as we pull up to the motel.

"Ready to celebrate, husband?" I tease.

"Am I ever, wife, he teases back, kissing my forehead as the driver opens the limo door for us to step out together.

Hunter

Reaching the motel room door, I put Savannah down for a moment to open the door.

It swings open and we both scan the decorated surroundings. Red and white rose petals are scattered across the floor from the door to the edge of the four poster bed, which has a heart of rose petals on the white doona cover.

Between the posts of the bed hang white lace curtains, that are draped to one side, ready to slide across. Candles are on the bedside tables, and what appears to be an electric oil burner is already switched on filling the room with the intoxicating smell of jasmine.

Savannah smiles and inhales the jasmine scent. "Wow, it's amazing!"

"Mmmm...you're amazing wife," I muse kissing her forehead, before scooping her back into my arms and stepping across the threshold.

Kicking the door shut behind me, I continue carrying her across the rose petals on the floor and place her gently onto the bed.

Her hands grab my cheeks and she pulls me down to her lips for a kiss so heated my body jumps to attention, straining against my black dress pants.

She starts moaning, wanting more but I want to take this first night together as husband and wife slow and sweet.

Breaking away from the kiss I take her hips in my hands and pull her body against mine as I stand up.

"I think it's time I take this stunning dress off to see what delight awaits me underneath," I tease her, running a finger along her lips that she licks with her tongue.

Without saying a word, she turns around and leans over the bed, pressing her arse against my thighs. Running my hands down her sides I feel her body rise up at the sensation.

"Please Hunter, take if off," she begs huskily.

At her neck, I brush her hair aside and press a kiss to the nape of her neck and down her back, closer to the zip of the dress.

Her hips arch higher, her arse sweetly torturing the want in my pants.

Taking hold of the zip in my thumb I begin sliding it down her back, following it with kisses as more of her glorious milky skin is exposed.

Stretching back over her I lick from the nape of her neck, down her spine to the top of her arse.

Sweet moans escape her lips and my groin is aching painfully but still I want to savour her.

Pressing my body against hers, leaning over I take her ear between my teeth, before whispering, "Roll over baby."

Sensually she turns over, inching back on the bed a little, throwing her arms behind her head.

Beneath the lace of her bra I can see her hard nipples, begging to be caressed but firstly I need to get her dress off.

It's caught on her hips, so teasingly I lick across her skin underneath her belly button and her skin instantly heats as her hips buck at the sensation. "Oh Hunter don't do..." The words catch in her throat as I plunge her dress to the floor.

Now her sexy lace underwear, complete with nude stay up stockings is all that's on her body.

Grazing the edge of the stocking on her thigh I slide it down her leg, repeating the process with the other one. Pressing a kiss to her ankle, I slowly kiss and lick up her calf to her thigh, and towards the lace knickers she's wearing.

Kissing her core through the fabric again she moans. "Oh Hunter, please."

Laughing I yank them down, kissing her core again and licking her bud lightly.

"Do you want to come wife?" I taunt.

"Mmm...But husband?" She muses propping herself up on her elbows.

"Yes, wife?"

"You have too many clothes on."

She stands up, pressing her body against mine, grinding against me as her hands brush my Adam's apple, before slowly undoing my bow tie, a seductive smile on her lips.

Her fingers move lower, undoing each button of my shirt and slipping into my pants as I shake my jacket and shirt off.

I fumble with my belt desperately wanting to discard my pants and underwear to be fully naked to make love to her.

Hooking my fingers in the sides of both I plunge them down my legs, stepping out of them when they reach the floor.

Savannah grabs my hardness in her grip and I gasp at the contact.

"Mmm, you take my breath away husband," she teases.

"So do you wife," I tease back in response reaching around her back to unhook her bra.

She lets it fall to the floor.

"So fucking beautiful."

There's silence between us, our eyes searching each others, looking at each other's nakedness like it's the first time we've seen each other bare. Cupping her cheeks in my palms I crush my lips to hers in a zealous kiss, licking her lips and moaning into her mouth as she gives me entrance to lace my tongue with hers. It's the most desperate consuming kiss we've shared and panting I pull away overwhelmed at the sparkle in her eyes when she temptingly says, "Make love to me Hunter."

She sits back on the side of the bed, edging back on it and beckoning me to her with a finger, biting her lip hard.

I dive at her, as she pulls back the bed covers, sliding into the crimson red satin sheets and giggling. Slipping under the sheets beside her I pull her body to mine and kiss her hard, our bodies entangling themselves together until I'm on top of her, my dick pressing into her stomach. Breaking the kiss, she asks desperately, her tone raspy, breathless, "Please Hunter make love to me."

"Ohhhh...Savannah," I murmur, gliding myself into her waiting body, not wanting to be apart from her for another second.

As I enter her, she moans. "Hunter. Oh...Hunter."

She's bucking her hips up to meet mine as I slowly thrust in and out of her. Her core is deliciously wet and her moans are guttural and drive me wild with longing for her.

Pushing harder into her I stretch over her chest taking her mouth in a consuming kiss, burying myself inside her and slowing my thrusts as I devour her mouth with mine.

Wrapping her legs around my arse she pushes me further in, as far as possible, truly making us one before breaking away from the kiss.

"Make me come Hunter," she says illicitly.

"Oh Savannah, I want to make you come so bad baby," I muse, almost pulling all the way out before thrusting back into her hard, making her gasp in pleasure.

Continuing the slow in and out pleasure of making love to her I watch the way her body responds, her hips meeting mine, her chest rising and falling and I revel in the sweet moans she's making.

Her breathing turns to panting and I can feel her beginning to twitch around me.

Clutching the sheets in fists she screams out, "Hunter I'm coming, oh Hunter, fuck, I'm coming."

Her whole core clenches around me, her squirting hot climax over my hardness still buried inside her. It drives me to explode into her, in ecstasy and I scream out, "Oh fuck Savannah, I love you."

Sliding out of her I pull her close to my side, kissing her sweetly.

"That was incredible my beautiful wife."

"Better then incredible, it was phenomenal my handsome husband."

"Oh yes it was...and you know what?" I tease her tickling the sensitive skin of her stomach.

"No what?" She giggles.

"I think you squirted, baby," I tease huskily whispering in her ear.

"Oh Hunter, shit really?" She says embarrassed, her cheeks flushing as crimson as the sheets.

"Oh yes, Savannah and it was so damn hot I'm planning on making you do it again and again."

"Sounds like..oh," She gasps as I've already slid under the sheets pressing a kiss to her entrance, ready to make her come again.

Our wedding night has only just begun and I plan on making her come over and over again, not just this night but every night I damn well can for the rest of our lives.

Savannah makes my life complete, she's now my wife and I love her with all my heart. That will never be a country secret.

The End (For Now)

Playlist

Below is the playlist of songs for this story and the associated chapter if applicable. They are not in order. The Spotify playlist link is at the bottom.

1. You Are The Reason-Calum Scott (Ch 34)
2. My Songs Know What You Did In The Dark- Fall Out Boy (Ch 33)
3. Between The Raindrops- Lifehouse (Ch 38)
4. Body Like A Back Road- Sam Hunt (Ch 2)
5. The Fighter- Keith Urban ft Carrie Underwood (Ch 49)
6. Hurts Like Hell- Fleurie (Ch 45)
7. Falling In-Lifehouse (Ch 47)
8. I Want You Anyway-Jon McLaughlin (Ch 48)
9. My Escape-Ravenscode (Ch 52)
10. Never Letting Go-Tim McMorris (Epilogue)
11. Forever in Time-Tim McMorris (Theme)
11. Somebody to Die For-Hurts (Theme)
12. Wanna be that song-Brett Eldredge (Theme)

Spotify Playlist

https://open.spotify.com/playlist/3eblo2801bD3SO0R4JbrYB?si=StO6NT8VTD61b7nCU6LB-g

About the Author

Caz May is a librarian/teacher by trade, but was always destined to be an author from a young age. In her spare time, she can be found devouring books or writing her own stories with characters that may not be the typical romance heroes but are loveable just as much.

Caz is married to her own real-life bearded hero and has two fur babies.

She lives for Iced coffee, especially from Gloria Jeans or a Farmers Union but pretty much just loves food in general.

When she's not writing, or reading a book most likely she can probably be found asleep or binge-watching shows on Netflix.

Check out her Instagram or other socials to get in touch.

Instagram- @cazmay25

BookBub-Caz May https://www.bookbub.com/profile/caz-may

Goodreads-https://www.goodreads.com/cazmay

Facebook- @CazMayAuthor https://www.facebook.com/CazMayAuthor/

Spotify- cazcat25 https://open.spotify.com/user/cazcat25?si=mXsD2VW7R86CN7Qc7_r7Nw

Website- https://cazcat25.wixsite.com/cazmay-author

Acknowledgments

Well, here we are! Acknowledgements for the first book in this series!

I honestly don't have many acknowledgements for this book, but I definitely need to give a big shoutout to my first readers of this book on Wattpad.

Most importantly Felicity Vaughan who with her best friend has published her amazing paranormal romance novel 'Edge of the Veil'. She was one of the first people I connected with on Wattpad, who first read this book and gave me encouragement with my writing from the very beginning. Go check out her book on Amazon and her Wattpad page for other books. You won't be disappointed.

I also need to give a big shoutout to my amazing Nanna, to whom this book is dedicated. I spent many hours as a child at her farm, where my Mum grew up. Hunter's farm is based on my grandparents farm and Ridgehope although a fictional town is based on Pinnaroo in outback South Australia. I have such fond memories of the time I spent there and have included lots of that in this story.

Also, I've found some amazing new readers through Instagram, who are eager to read every book I write. Ang, Nicole and Karen, thank you for your support and reviews that make my heart happy.

And lastly, as usual I need to thank my rock, my amazing, super supportive hero Cam. He is the perfect husband, and no book boyfriend could ever measure up to him.

Anyway, that's all from me! For now!

Caz May

xx

Look out for Book Two of
The Mackenney Family Saga
(Addison's story)

Coming Soon

See below for a teaser

(Prologue) Addison

Seeing Hunter at the end of the aisle, a stupid grin on his face makes my heart constrict.

I should have been walking towards him, in a big white dress, not the ruby red strapless one I have on.

But I'm not the one marrying him.

I'm the Maid of Honour for his wedding to someone else.

And it's truly painful.

It wasn't as though I could have refused when he'd asked for me to a part of his special day.

Savannah, his soon to be any minute wife didn't really have any friends in town since leaving her past behind in the city and stumbling into Hunter's farmhouse nearly two years ago.

Plus it isn't that I hate her. I can't. She's just too sweet.

And I'm around them a lot more than I want to be at times, as I'm godmother to their gorgeous son River.

I swear I've never seen a kid that looks so much like his father.

The kid is gorgeous, just like his Dad Hunter is.

Get a grip Addison. Seriously, you're not the one marrying him.

Taking a deep breathe I start to tentatively walk down the aisle, scanning the crowd for my older brother Jett. He hadn't really wanted to attend his ex-best friends wedding, but I called him to come along, desperate for the moral support.

It also doesn't help that I'm also stuck being partnered up for the wedding with Hunter's annoying, but somewhat attractive younger brother Quentin.

We'd slept together a year or so ago, and it was pretty damn hot, but he'd had to make it complicated by confessing he was in love with me.

Part of me knew I should have gone along with his advances and given him a chance.

Or even taken a chance with someone else.

But I can't let go of his older brother, even now as he's about to marry someone else.

I sigh, realising I'd reached the front of the aisle.

I step to the side, feeling Hunter's gaze on me.

I plaster a fake smile on face, mentally telling myself to suck it up.

He is marrying someone else.

I need to move on.

(1) Zane

Getting posted to Ridgehope Hospital, six hours from the city was just what I needed.

There was too much pain everywhere I turned in Adelaide, and always that hope that Amy would walk back in the door, like she'd never left.

It wasn't that I blamed her for leaving me, but still it hurt like a bitch.

It was though our wedding vows meant nothing to her. In sickness and in health she'd promised, but she apparently only promised health, not sickness.

I couldn't think about her leaving me know though.

I was in Ridgehope for a new start and the country air was welcoming the minute I drove up to the rundown house on the outskirts of the quaint one main street town. It needed some TLC but it was roof over my head and I was unlikely to be spending much time there anyway.

That was another reason Amy had left me. Apparently I was married to my job. I was hoping that moving a small town like Ridgehope might make that less likely to happen. Not that it really mattered now when I was single and heartbroken from her walking out on me three months earlier.

I was after a fresh start, although I was hesitant about getting to know the people of such a small town. No one, except my close family and friends knew me in Adelaide, but here it seemed everyone would know my name.

I wasn't sure if I was ready for that.

Come on Zane, put your big boy pants on.

I have to suck it up, and get out of the car.

My brand new black V8 Ford Mustang seems a little out of place in this town, but I love her and I'm hoping the cops aren't anal about speeding, as I plan to take her out for a speedy drive down the back roads and really run the engine in.

Ok, Zane, big boy pants, get out of the car.

I open the door slowly, stepping out, scanning my surroundings, taking in everything I can. I press the button for the boot and it springs open, revealing my two suitcases.

I'd not brought much with me, just some basic everyday clothes, underwear and a few black slacks and white shirts. The hospital would have brand new scrubs to wear and I often didn't wear them when not in surgery anyway.

Wheeling my two suitcases towards the house is quite a feat in the soft red dirt. It's wispy and feels like it's getting everywhere, under my clothes, through my hair and in my fucking eyes. It stings like pins stabbing me, but I blink hard, desperate to get inside the house.

Thankfully I'd not needed to worry about furniture as the house is fully furnished and quite pleasantly too. Dropping the suitcases inside the door I race straight to find the bathroom to flush the dirt from my eyes.

Looking at my eyes in the mirror, they are bloodshot, my face sporting a serious five o'clock shadow and bags under my eyes so dark you could mistake them for two lovely black eyes.

I've not slept for days, worried about the move, but also feeling some pains in my legs that have me worried too.

It's only mid afternoon, but I need sleep.

Stumbling down the hallway, only just able to see out of my dirt irritated eyes I search for the bedroom, falling against the bed the minute I see it.

I drift to sleep, thinking about what the hospital might be like when I start there tomorrow.

Caz May